BASH

—

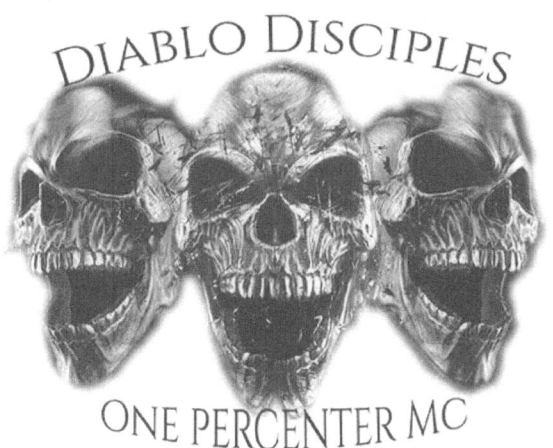

By V. THEIA

BASH

This is a work of fiction. Names, characters, places, and events are the products of the author's imagination or are used fictitiously. Any resemblance to persons, living or dead, is coincidental.

Names and characters are the property of the author and may not be duplicated. The use of any real company and/or product names is for literary effect only. All other trademarks and copyrights are the property of their respective owners.

Bash

Cover photo: Depositphotos.com

Cover Design: V. Theia. ©2024

Published by V. Theia 2024

All Rights Reserved

If you've ever fantasized about being pursued by a dirty-talking biker without realizing you're actually dating that dirty-talking biker, this one is for you!

Charlotte

Charlotte 'Lottie, to everyone' Martin never expected to be blackmailed by a Diablo Disciples biker one time, let alone multiple times this year.

Especially blackmailed by a smiling biker who carried unassuming charisma like an accessory.

A biker she liked, if not for the, you know, *blackmail* part.

It would be the last time she did a good deed for someone.

That's what happened when her stupid soft spot engaged. Now look at her. Sneaking around the hospital, stealing things for the biker.

You'd imagine that being in her late twenties, she would have more sense than falling for the old blackmail scam.

"You know, you can buy all this stuff, right? You walk into CVS, and it's on the shelves. Try Amazon. They'll bring it right to your door."

Her heart was beating too fast, afraid that this would be the time she got caught giving medical supplies to the local biker gang. Lottie tossed another box of antiseptic wipes onto the pallet that was half full of similar wound items and stepped back against the ceiling-high shelving with a sigh.

"But it wouldn't be free." Denver smiled, looking relaxed. "Casey wants you to come to dinner this week."

"Tell your wife thank you for the invitation, but no."

He'd extended the same invite several times, and the answer was the same.

"You ever gonna say yes?"

Fiddling with the end of the braid over her shoulder, Lottie gave the biker a skeptical look. Was he serious? He thought she'd sit at his dinner table.

"Are you serious?" she asked aloud. "Let me remind you, Denver, you came into the ER with a stab wound not so long ago. I was the nurse who treated you. And then you and your biker gang turned my life upside down, and you expect me to come to a friendly dinner?"

He had the audacity to chuckle as he grabbed another sizeable box from the shelf to add to the pallet. All things they could easily buy in bulk.

But no, they had to make her risk losing the only thing she valued, the thing she'd worked her butt off to achieve.

"You like my Casey."

That wasn't a lie. But it had been a mistake since she was now in a situation out of her control. The night Denver was brought in with a stab wound, she'd been the nurse to make sure the wife remained calm while they triaged her husband, before he was taken up to surgery. The waiting room was filled with biker after biker for the next few hours, until it was wall-to-wall leather, denim, and thunderous scowls.

Everyone else on shift had feared the club-affiliated people.

But not Lottie, because, months previously, she'd been working in the ICU when one of their other biker brothers had been involved in an explosion and was in a coma for months. She'd gotten to know them all by face, their road name, and what level of behaving they stuck to. So she'd been the one who was sent out to make sure they kept the noise down, told them they couldn't smoke, and was the on-staff presence when they had questions. Once he'd been out of danger, she'd taken Casey to see her husband. Her unique mix of strength and charm made it impossible not to like her.

It was probably that which had made her do something she never did. She befriended a relative of a patient. And because of that slip, she answered a call for help from Casey several days after Denver had been sent home. One of the younger bikers, she later found out, had accidentally shot himself in the leg, and could she come to their compound to help? Usually, Denver was their in-house medic, and he was incapacitated. She'd told Casey to call 911, but they insisted it wasn't serious. Okay then, take the guy to the ER. Not possible, Casey had explained calmly, because it was done with an unregistered gun.

During those few days when the biker men and women had filled Denver's private room and spilled out into the hallway, she'd seen what a family meant. They were there for each other. Sure, they'd been loud, and her colleagues looked to Lottie to wrangle them. She'd done her best, but it never stopped them from being noisy or flirtatious with her. One was incredibly flirty. He always followed her with his smoldering eyes and called her little darling. He even brought her coffee several times a day, but she'd put a closed sign in his face each time he asked her out.

At first, she'd thought it might be a particular biker who'd been hurt, and panic set in. But it wasn't Bash. He'd been waiting outside in an SUV to take Lottie to the MC territory.

It wasn't the last time she'd seen Bash. But enough thought about him, the better.

She'd told no one how she'd slowly become infatuated with a man who lived by danger and breaking the law. Bash was unaware of her crush. She dismissed it as silly and expected it to fade soon.

For as much as he'd chased her, she'd run in the opposite direction.

The attraction and spending her free time cyber-stalking a hot guy was one thing, but dating a criminal, after avoiding those types of people for years, was a lot of baggage she didn't want to deal with.

Even if he had the dreamiest eyes and smile.

He filled out a pair of denim jeans to perfection.

And his voice was rusty and seductive.

Every sighting of him was savored like a fine wine and sometimes taken in with unhealthy gulps.

Lottie was content being single and had no desire to mingle. Her focus was on her career, not her relationship status.

"Yes, I do like your wife, Denver," Lottie addressed his statement. "Look what you're doing. You threatened to report me to the hospital board. And you hacked into the camera to lift the footage of me taking stuff from the supply room. So I could help *your* biker buddy! You've used that over my head ever since, so you can help yourself with all this stuff. And I'm supposed to be friends with you guys?"

"Yes." He said with a calm smile. "It's nothing personal."

"It feels a lot personal when you're threatening my career. I wish I hadn't been on shift to help any of you that day. And I should have left that idiot with the bullet in his leg."

Denver chuckled. "Mouse never shuts up about how heroic he was by having a bullet dug out of him." And then the man in the leather jacket, wearing mirrored shades over his eyes, smiled again. "How much did those cancer care machines cost for the children's wing? A few million, I reckon?"

Lottie frowned at the redirection of the conversation. "I don't know, why?"

"And the donations to the same unit that come several times a year, that's a sizeable chunk of change, isn't it?"

"It's a lot, yeah." Those donations meant it was the best children's ward in the state.

"The Diablos do that, Lottie. We hold a yearly bike rally and gather donations for the cancer kids. Our old ladies organize local cookouts and bake sales for the town, and we give whatever's raised to this hospital for the kids. Last year, it was nearly four million. I don't think they'll mind if we take a few Band-Aids." He smirked.

Lottie scoffed and rolled her eyes. She hadn't realized the children's oncology unit, which had expanded last year, was down to the Diablos donations.

"I'm sure you claim it on your taxes."

Denver chuckled. "Don't know, that ain't my domain. So stop worrying, yeah? It all balances out."

Lottie looked at the pile of things he was taking with him this time, and her brow furrowed. "How often are bikers injured if you need all this?"

"We're accident-prone." He lied with a straight face. And then. "You ever gonna be nice to my boy?"

"Who's your boy?" she already knew and dreaded hearing his name.

"The one who sniffs you out like a bloodhound, the one you reject when he asks you out."

Lottie turned red. She felt it coloring her skin and heating her from the inside. She moved then, walking through the basement storeroom.

Once she was out of there, she didn't care if Denver got caught red-handed. Though, deep down, she did. Besides the blackmail and the theft, he seemed to be a decent guy with a lovely family. However, if Casey knew about the blackmail, how nice would that make his wife?

"I know a lot of men. That could be anyone." She snapped and heard Denver chuckling.

"Shit. Don't let my buddy hear you saying that, or it'll be more than bullets you dig out of a leg when he goes on a jealous rampage."

Lottie shivered from the top of her skull to her toes, which curled in her comfortable work Crocs. The idea she could induce that kind of reaction from anyone, least of all from the man she thought was the sexiest thing created since apple pie à la mode, caused her a momentary lapse of logical thought.

"See you next time, Lottie," Denver called out gently, like they were old friends who hadn't seen each other in a while.

Not if she could help it, she thought.

She didn't want to see him or any other swaggering biker again.

Bash

A ll Bash ever wanted was to be a biker, nothing else.

Without even understanding what it meant.

When he first saved enough cash from yard work at seventeen to buy a used Honda Rebel, Bash knew it would become a part of him. He would prioritize being able to ride bikes and live without constraints, no matter the job he got.

Nowadays, he was forty, and he'd scaled up from that Honda to a Harley Night Train. Being a ranked officer in a well-established MC earned him a lot of money. It was the best life he could have envisioned for his younger self.

Bash switched off the engine and swung his leg over the seat, keeping the half helmet in his hand. He was a biker from the tip of his black hair down to the scuff of his leather boots, crunching the asphalt underfoot as he walked toward the prison entrance. He'd been coming here for four years since Primo got locked up, so he was an old hat going through the security process. Before long, he was shown through to the visiting room.

While he waited as a guard led in the prisoners, Bash felt a prickling on the back of his neck. With a quick scan around the rectangle room, he found the culprit. A young blond thing was waiting at her table, eyeballing him like a side of prime beef. She smiled when she got caught, but Bash didn't smile back and only glanced briefly before looking away.

He wasn't interested in the woman; even if he was, she was way younger. He was already into another woman the same age, go figure, and *she* wanted nothing to do with him. He thought of her brown wavy hair and average height, and the image in his mind of her smiling instead of scowling made his heart race. Once he added her hazel eyes to the image, things got so intense that he had to stop his thoughts. Or he'd embarrass himself big time before his club brother arrived.

Just then, Primo appeared. He had on the same puke-colored uniform he'd worn for four years. He got up, and they shook hands, then went in for a quick bro-hug.

Way back, when Bash was in his early twenties, he spent about two months in jail. It was way too long, and even though he pushed the boundaries of the law most days and often crossed that line with their club's activities, Bash knew he couldn't handle prison again.

Primo, though, seemed to be doing great as he grinned and plopped his butt on the other plastic chair. "Good to see you, Bash."

Whatever the circumstances at the clubhouse, they'd attended the twice-weekly visitations throughout his entire prison stay. Primo's mom and sister occasionally came along if they were in town. That a patched brother went to jail didn't imply they were abandoned in the wild. The club had their back. By visiting in person, calling, and keeping his commissary account funded, life inside was a little more comfortable than others. Primo was not only patched, but also one of Axel's trusted advisors as their IT guy.

"You're looking good, you handsome prick. Have you stacked on more muscle since I last saw you?"

Primo grabbed the coffee that Bash had ready for him. He used his other hand to go over his shaved head and beard.

Most prisoners let themselves go once behind bars, but Primo had kept himself in shape. The IT specialist had a massive brain and knew how to use it. Axel recently greased a lot of palms to get Primo a computer. They hooked him up with a cell phone in the early days. The brothers would've gotten him a hooker if Primo had wanted one, but he never asked.

"This place will drive a man mad if he's not kept busy. The gym here is pretty decent. Enough about me," he said, "tell me everything I'm missing at the club."

He knew most of it because Splice was the last to visit and that chatty Lothario loved gossiping. If any man were to infiltrate the mob of old ladies, it would be Splice. Though the ladies seemed to gravitate toward Ruin, no one could figure out why.

The entire visit was dedicated to sharing the news with Primo that Tomb and Nina were back on track and happier than before. Reno's step-kid was always at the club, following everyone around and asking many questions. He spilled all the tea to Primo about how Ruin's old lady was putting together a charity concert. This would be her first time back in the spotlight. Primo hasn't met Aurora Kidd, but he's heard about the popstar connected to their resident lunatic. Last, he talked about how Axel tries to handle the club's First Lady and how hilarious it is to see their tough president crumble when she gives him a pout. They constantly exchanged insults, like it was some weird sex game. Bash didn't get it, but he didn't have to. Axel seemed happy with his old lady.

They didn't discuss any club matters. They didn't risk it, knowing the visitation room probably had cameras on them. The law was always out to catch them doing something illegal.

"Splice said you've caught feelings for a nurse at the local hospital."

Fucking Splice was going to be sporting a fat lip when Bash saw him later.

"Splice has a thing going with every-fucking-woman in Utah and the neighboring states."

Primo laughed and finished the coffee. "He's always talked with his dick. So, about this nurse. What's her name?"

"He didn't fill in the details?" snarked Bash. Splice was a notorious button pusher.

Primo smirked. "He did, but I'd rather hear it from you, brother. I'm bored as fuck in here. I've read everything the library offers."

"I'll see about getting you some more books."

"Appreciate it. So?"

"She's called Charlotte. And for some unknown reason, she hates bikers."

Another laugh from Primo. "Fuck, Bash. You know there's easier pussy out in the world that won't make you give up shit, right?"

Bash didn't have a response because he wasn't that close to Charlotte, even considering they had an uncertain friendship. What he'd be willing to give up for The One in the future was a moot point.

"Why does she hate bikers? Did you slurp soup using a fork?"

Part of his tension fell from Bash's shoulders, and he half shrugged. "Splice overstepped. I asked a woman out, and she said no. That's the beginning and end of it, Primo."

"She doesn't hate you then?" the Einstein was bored if he was mining Bash for gossip.

"After turning me down again, I was leaving, and I heard one of her colleagues asking if she was crazy because I was so hot. Charlotte told her she'd never date someone in a gang."

Primo whistled and gave Bash a look of sympathy, which sucked.

"Splice mentioned that a bunch of new sweet bottoms are showing up. Take your pick, dude, and forget about the nurse. No point crying over untapped pussy."

"You've turned to philosophy since you've been wearing prison clothes. And Splice has already tried out all the new sweet bottoms more than once."

"He's gonna get dick rot one of these days."

Bash agreed, but that was for Splice to deal with one day.

They only had 40 minutes for each visit. It was never enough, and Bash felt bad seeing Primo being led to the cells. Luckily, if he stayed out of trouble, he'd be out in a few months.

He'd only clipped on the helmet when his phone buzzed. Primo was using his prohibited phone.

Primo: Forget what I said about getting over the nurse. If you want her, do whatever you need to. It worked for Chains.

Bash laughed and stored his phone without replying.

He wasn't about to force Charlotte into a marriage of convenience, primarily because she didn't have a father who would sell her like Chains' father-in-law had done.

However, he was not ready to give up on Charlotte just yet.

While her mouth said she wasn't interested in dating someone like him, her greedy eyes, lapping him up when she thought he wasn't looking, told a different story.

And Bash liked that story.

Very. Fucking. Much.

It was a book he could read every night while the sweet nurse and her fiery temper writhed on top of his lap.

Charlotte

Some shifts in the ER department were better than others.

But it only took her friend, Porter, to utter those cursed words. "It's quiet today." And from there, the day had gone to hell and back several times over, with people streaming through the doors needing help with one affliction after another. From the flu to a half-severed leg.

Lottie was exhausted, and it showed as her coffee went untouched, too tired to drag it forward to take sips. Yawning until her jaw cracked, she slumped her head in her hand, letting her eyes drift closed for a second.

"I could kick you in the balls." Lottie's other friend told Porter. Toni was the loudest and most honest of the three of their work friends' group, brutally so. With the way Porter and she bickered, anyone would assume they were hot for each other, but Porter was gay and very taken. And Toni's preference for men was usually unavailable pricks.

"I said I was sorry. What more do you want from me?" He sighed tiredly.

"A pound of flesh," announced Toni. "And for people not to stick objects up their buttholes and blame it on an oopsie." All three dissolved into laughter. "You can get me a muffin, and I might lessen your sentence."

"You're all heart," Porter got up from the table and turned his eyes on Lottie. "What do you want, babe?"

"Nothing for me. I'm too tired to eat." He strode off to the cafeteria display counter.

Working the late shift always messed with her body. It was only six p.m., their 'lunchtime,' and she still had hours before home time. Lottie would give anything to leave early and curl up on the couch after the longest hot shower. Ice cream would feature heavily in those plans.

"Hey, I was thinking." Started Toni, who sounded more awake than Lottie felt. That never boded well if Toni was having ideas and Lottie braced for the inevitable shenanigans. The last time she had a thought, they ended up in New Mexico for the weekend, and Lottie got sick from food poisoning. Good times.

"This weekend." The weekend couldn't come soon enough for Lottie, who planned to catch up on neglected housework and get some much-needed rest. "We should put on our sexiest underwear, go dancing, and scoop up a few men."

Lottie groaned. "After the week from hell, my ass isn't fit to go dancing."

"Come on, Lottie! We need to let loose before we're old bitches and have tits down to our kneecaps. Go dancing with me, it'll be fun. Maybe that'll be when you meet someone to rock your headboard." Toni, who worked in the same department, wiggled her eyebrows.

Lottie resisted the urge to sigh. She'd heard it all before. She had no idea why Toni was so obsessed with getting Lottie some action, but her nagging was getting old.

"You get laid."

"I will. But you need it more."

Lottie wasn't interested in being the focal point of any conversation that centered on her sex life, non-existent as it was. It was private.

At that, Porter returned, bringing an apple muffin for Toni. "What are we talking about?"

"I'm trying to get Lottie into meeting men this weekend. She's being boring again by refusing."

It was hard not to take offense and feel hurt coursing through her breastbone at that character assassination. She was plenty fun when she wanted to be. Considering how busy she was with work and how expensive it was to step outside the house these days, she didn't prioritize being social as much as Toni did.

"Stop harassing her." Scolded Porter, and she smiled her gratitude. Porter was such a good guy. "If you girls want a quieter weekend, you can join game night."

"With all the gays?"

"It's four couples." He answered Toni. Porter and his adorable barista boyfriend were game night masters.

"Thanks, but I'll pass. You boring stiffs can keep the yawn-fest games while I live for the three of us," Toni announced.

"You can be a real bitch, you know that?" said Porter with a smile. He hardly ever got mad at Toni's remarks, but he always made sure she took responsibility for what she said.

"Someone has to balance out you two old maids."

Lottie felt relieved when her break ended, allowing her to escape Toni's scrutiny. She had so few close friendships. Acquaintances and work colleagues, sure, but very few she wanted to hang out with.

After using the restroom and washing her hands, she returned to the floor in the ER. Lottie couldn't help but think about what Toni had said.

Was she boring? Probably, but she liked who she was and what she'd built around her. Who said hooking up with strangers every weekend was the benchmark for fun, anyway? Given the choice, she would opt for a good adult coloring book and a new pack of crayons.

Approaching the gateway to hell, aka the ER department, Lottie swiped her security card and heard the noise as she pulled open the door.

Toni might not be correct, yet Lottie wished she could be more like her friend and speak her mind. Especially when people thought it was cool to step all over her feelings or give unwanted advice about her life. It was only ever after the fact she could think of the perfect comeback, but by then, it was too late.

For someone so self-assured in her career, you'd assume she'd be more outspoken elsewhere, but conflict brought Lottie out in hives. Her neurodivergent brain didn't work that way, and she'd avoid conflict at all costs. Unless faced with burly bikers who got rowdy, she'd been quick to put them in their place. Whenever wasted people ended up in the ER, Lottie was the go-to person.

Work Lottie was a force to be reckoned with.

It was all the other versions of Lottie that needed work.

And according to her closest friend, *that* Lottie was boring and needed a few dicks to make her interesting.

She sighed and brushed it off as she powered through the rest of her shift, dealing with sickness, two traffic accidents, and an overcrowded department.

When she drove home, she greeted the aloof cat, who only stared at her from behind the couch. One day, Prince would love her. She was determined to earn that cat's devotion if it was the last thing she did.

Tiredness won, and after a shower and a few crackers, she crawled into her queen-sized bed with the blue flowery bedspread and let the soft mattress envelop her sore muscles. Working the late shift was worse than a vigorous spin class.

As she found a comfortable spot in bed, she used the remote to switch on the wall-mounted TV, then lowered the volume. She hardly paid attention to it at night, but she needed the background noise, or her brain wouldn't let her sleep. If the apocalypse occurred or she ended up on a deserted island, her genuine concern was how she would sleep without white noise.

When she was a kid, people called her weird so much that she believed it for a while. Nowadays, they call it neurodivergent, which meant Lottie's brain worked differently, but she's still totally normal.

She hyper-fixated on things or she was indifferent.

While she loathed being overwhelmed by noise or tasks, she relied on continuous stimulation to manage her racing thoughts. It was a nonstop struggle to adjust the levels correctly.

As the TV din played a crime investigative show, she slowed her breathing and snuggled half her face into the soft pillow.

It was maladaptive dreaming time. For a grown-up, she shouldn't enjoy daydreaming as much as she did. If Toni knew she enjoyed imagining scenarios before falling asleep, she would think she was odd. Things became chaotic, and she had to reset everything. As the narrator, you'd think they'd go wherever she wanted, but nope.

Tonight, however, Lottie softly hummed and remembered where she left off in her imaginary world yesterday, placing her hand under her chin.

Until about a year ago, she would daydream about random people or celebs. She used them as props to tell stories about living it up, globetrotting, and being loaded.

Then *he* entered her world and blew her mind with made-up adventures and new daydreams, all about emotions. It wasn't even that Lottie would weave a romantic plotline for herself. It just never came up. In her dreams, she was successful, popular, wealthy, and confident. But never the love interest.

She should hate him for controlling this part of her, but that would mean he knew all about it. This was Lottie's secret indulgence.

Lottie was steadfast about what she wanted to achieve from a young age.

First, it was to leave home at eighteen, almost to the day of her birthday. After her mom died from a long illness, ten-year-old Lottie and her younger sister were left with a loafer father, bouncing from job to job, who couldn't get his shit together. Lottie had to become an adult too early.

She'd worked her butt off to get through college and nursing school. She found pride in her job despite its demanding nature. Her achievements included owning a house, having savings, and a small group of close friends.

But nowhere on that goals list had she ever prioritized a relationship.

While other teens were figuring out who they were into and crushing on people, Lottie wasn't interested. She never developed feelings for actors or pop stars. She'd never masturbated over a school crush or felt belly flutters if a boy held her hand.

She dated because she felt she had to fit in and not be seen as weird.

But those feelings were never there.

It hadn't been a worry. She never saw herself as odd or messed up. She didn't ask therapists for answers.

Despite taking a psychology class, Lottie couldn't comprehend her lack of sex drive, given the absence of depression or anxiety. She had no history of sexual trauma and wasn't afraid of close relationships, if it ever happened.

The need for one never came up, so it wasn't something she strived for.

The last date Lottie went on—again, because she was trying to appease being peer-pressured by Toni's insistence she needed to date—turned out to be a big fat waste of her time.

Even self-pleasure wasn't much of a curiosity to her, so it saved a bunch on the sex toys' budget, mainly because she didn't even own one toy.

But then something happened, and since then, her maladaptive daydreams have centered on only one man. For a woman who put little stock in sexual desire, she sure was a fast learner, at least in her head.

Behind her flickering eyelids, as Lottie felt her muscles relax one after the other and her breathing shallow, she imagined a pair of the bluest eyes staring back at her. A smile was playing on soft lips, surrounded by a clipped goatee. There was temptation in that smile.

And his voice. It curled her toes beneath the sheets when she brought it to mind. If chocolate could talk, it would sound just like that. His voice was so smooth and captivating that every woman wanted to hear him speak a little longer.

There was no need to make up fake conversations when she'd had many with him already, so all Lottie had to do was press replay.

Whenever he saw her in a rush at work, he would bring her a coffee and muffins to make her smile. When she was half-asleep, she kept thinking about all the times he asked her out - first casually, then more seriously. She remembered how his voice got deeper, more rugged, and how determined he looked when he held her gaze.

But there was no need to talk about dating. Not when *this* imaginative Bash helped her onto the back seat of his rumbling motorcycle. The beast of a machine felt like a purring tiger as Lottie latched onto his trim waist. His physique was solid and lean, and he stood at a satisfying height of six foot three.

Every inch of Bash, the established Diablo Disciples biker, was attractive. If she found anyone's body perfect, it would be his. It was obvious he took care of himself without being conceited. Even though he was thirteen years older, he was the hottest person she had ever seen. And within the safety of her mind, Lottie could indulge in something new pulsing through her veins, goose-bumping her skin and making her breath pause each time those eyes turned her way. Anything with him was possible in her dreams, but she repeatedly went back to this scene when she was free, riding his motorcycle. It always ended the same way, with her caught in a biker's arms, and a mouth made purely from sin and bad intentions, pressed to the dip in her neck as he told her how he'd keep her forever.

Of course, it was a *fantasy*, not something Lottie would indulge in.

She wouldn't.

Nope.

She wouldn't know how to date a man like him.

Gangs were notorious, and she'd brushed up against a terrible gang in the past and had no desire to repeat it. If nothing disrupted her monotonous world, she would be as happy as a chunky tortoise feasting on arugula.

Fantasy was safe and sensible.

Going out with a man who had dangerous connections would be the most foolish choice she could make.

It would be like jumping from the toaster right into the air fryer. Or, however, that saying went. And Lottie wasn't bacon.

Her sister was knee-deep in a gang, and Lottie couldn't think of a worse life to lead.

Bash hadn't given her bad vibes, but she knew when to listen to her instincts.

She was also the world's oldest virgin. Maybe that fact had a *little* to do with her caution.

People talked about how bikers were bed hoppers. Once he knew that uninteresting fact, there was no way Bash would still pursue her.

A virgin — who was in no rush to change that status — and a wild biker did not mix.

She was not ready for a Kama Sutra show-and-tell just yet.

And she figured if that ever changed, she'd need someone just as average. Bash's sexual allure would burn her down to the bones.

However, that didn't stop her from fantasizing about kissing the too-hot-to-handle biker.

Charlotte

"Prince. Come and get your second breakfast." She rattled the treat box and heard the thud of her beastly cat jumping down from his throne.

Her silver Maine Coon padded into the kitchen with a haughty glance as he gave her a pity rub against her leg so she'd dole out the treats.

Lottie was such a spoiling cat mom and grinned at him, then fed Prince one of his favorite kitty chews. He nibbled it between his teeth and sauntered off. Lottie was ignored once more. He loved her, really. She was twenty-six percent sure he wouldn't feast on her innards if she ever dropped dead in the hallway.

Though indifferent to his owner, Prince followed Lottie into the lounge room, his fluffy silver fur shifting in the air. Probably following only in hopes of more treats. When none appeared, he sprawled out on the entire length of the light gray couch.

"It's my last late shift for a while, Prince, yay. I bet you're excited to have mommy home at regular hours again," she said. She was not insane talking to her cat. She'd read it was good stimulation for them. But Prince looked uninterested, his large, pointed ears twitching.

Such a cutie-pie was her evil Prince.

And she was only eighty-five percent sure he was a descendent of Beelzebub.

"Now, what do you want to watch today? Are you in the mood for some Disney? No? Okay, fine. We've discussed how you don't like the sweet stuff, but it wouldn't hurt to give UP a second chance. I know you hate dogs, but it's a good plot, and you like balloons. Ah, here we go. I found a bird-watching channel. Try not to lunge at the TV."

With his water fountain filled with fresh water and his electronic feeder set to disperse his food at a specific time, Lottie grabbed her lunch bag and purse, told the cat she'd see him later, and walked through the hallway, remembering to set the alarm. She loved her house. It was demurely decorated. She didn't collect many knick-knacks, and the only photo frames she had were of Prince, but every piece of furniture was bought by her, in her choice of colors, and coming back each day felt like peace she knew she'd more than earned.

Whatever good mood Lottie felt as she started toward the hospital fragmented into adrenaline-fueled focus when she encountered a traffic accident. It was going toward an on-ramp before the freeway, a few miles from the hospital. Slowing immediately, she took in the scene. It looked like a car and bicycle collision. The driver was a stressed-out woman on the phone, and a kid was lying on the ground.

Lottie put her hazard lights on to alert oncoming traffic.

It might not be the safe environment she was used to. Still, Lottie's triage instincts kicked in, and she took a visual of the boy, who was breathing and awake. However, he must have been thrown far because half of his clothes were torn.

The woman was freaking out on whoever she was talking to. "I'm trying to tell you I didn't see him! He came out of nowhere, Frank!" She howled, tears pouring down her cheekbones.

"Ma'am, are you talking with 911?" Lottie had to repeat it several times before the woman looked over.

"No. My husband." *Un-fucking-believable.* "He's mad about the car."

"You need to call 911 right now." She snapped and went down to her knees in front of the kid. He looked to be around sixteen or seventeen. "Hey, I'm Lottie. I'm a nurse, and you're going to be okay. Can you tell me your name?"

"Samuel." The kid tried to move, and she placed gentle hands on either side of his neck to stabilize him. "Try not to move, Samuel. Help is coming." From the ugly position of his knee, his leg was undoubtedly broken.

"How does my bike look?" he groaned. His forehead was bleeding, and his left arm was bleeding even worse.

"Your bike is toast. Can you tell me where it hurts?"

"Every...where. Fuck, is it wrecked? My dad will kill me. I only just got it. *Shit.*" He started coughing and groaning, and Lottie touched his shoulder to keep him calm. She turned her head to yell a reminder at the woman. "Call 911 now."

"I'm on with my husband," she snapped. "He needs to call the insurance company."

The top of Lottie's head nearly exploded, hearing the selfish woman.

"I don't give a shit. Call the fucking paramedics right now *and* the police."

The mention of police made the woman's head snap up. Perhaps now she was understanding the severity of her situation.

Lottie removed her cotton jacket and attempted to stop the bleeding on the boy's forearm, but he soon lost consciousness.

This was not good. She relied on her training and searched for a pulse, but couldn't find one. Thankfully, she heard the woman speaking to the emergency services and promptly started CPR.

The woman tearfully described Lottie's actions to the 911 operator, insisting it wasn't her fault. Lottie needed her help. If he bled out, it'd be pointless trying to save him, but the woman was no help at all.

And then she heard the sweetest sound as the noise of a rumbling motorcycle engine loomed from around the bend. *Please, god, let them stop.* She only hoped the person saw her hazard lights before she had a second collision on her hands.

But a higher being was on her side as she continued to push on the boy's chest, mentally reciting the song *Staying Alive* because it has the number of beats needed for CPR. She couldn't turn around to look, but she caught the bike stopping.

And then. "Fucking hell, *Charlotte*?"

Lottie's heart leaped in her chest.

There was no time to register her shock at seeing Bash striding fast, and then he crouched down right next to her, so close she caught drifts of his masculine cologne.

"Are you hurt, baby?"

"No, it's not me. The boy was knocked off his bike," she panted, winded from exertion. Her arms ached already, but she'd done CPR for much longer many times and could handle it. She kept repeating the same rhythm and then yelled to the lady. "How long are they going to be?"

"They're four minutes out."

"What do you need me to do, darling?" Bash asked, and she could have cried with relief at his steadiness as their gazes locked. She relayed how to staunch the bleeding arm with her makeshift tourniquet and then to elevate it. He did as instructed without bumbling.

Throughout the longest minutes of her life, Lottie worked on Samuel and willed him to breathe while a burly biker spoke encouraging words to her. Afterward, she wouldn't recall the exact words Bash spoke, but she would recollect how he focused her with his kind voice.

Everything went by in a blur, and then there was the blessed relief of hearing the approaching sirens. The cops turned up first, followed by the paramedics, who took over before Lottie's arms fell off. She sat back on her haunches, winded.

"Let's get you over here, little hero," Bash said. Helping her up from the floor. They were both stained with blood, and she cringed, seeing it on the front of Bash's t-shirt. At least it would wipe off his leather jacket.

There was a pleased exhale when the boy made signs of breathing. It was only minutes before they had him stable with fluids and oxygen, then placed him in the back of the rig.

There were two cops. One spoke with the angry woman; the other, she noted, aimed the stink eye at Bash as he swaggered over.

"You cause this?" he asked, and Lottie's eyes widened.

"No, I didn't. As you can see, my bike is parked on the side of the road." He answered calmly, like he'd expected to be blamed.

"It wasn't him. He stopped to help me. It was the Escalade, which you can see tangled around the destroyed bicycle." She snapped at the cop, and Bash covered his chuckle with a cough.

"Just trying to get the facts, ma'am."

"The facts are I came upon the accident and stopped to help."

He eyed her up and down, noting her bloody scrubs and hospital name tag. "You're a nurse?"

"Yes." She named the hospital. "And then Bash stopped to help. That woman was no help at all." She informed, "She was more worried about her damn insurance."

She felt a hand on the base of her back, and turned her head to clash gazes with Bash. He was smiling when he murmured. "Take it down a notch, little hero."

The cop looked suspiciously at them. "You two know each other?"

"Yes," she answered, angry that the cop was directing his skepticism toward Bash.

"Mind your fucking business," Bash said at the same time, "and do your job where it's needed. We've given you what we know, so we're leaving now." And then, just like that, he used that hand on the base of her spine to walk her away. She wasn't entirely sure they wouldn't be arrested for leaving the scene, before giving a detailed statement, but as she looked over her shoulder, the cop remained there with his hand on his belt, staring at Bash.

"Do you have some grudge going with the police officer?"

"Nah, darling. He hates us, though."

"*Us*? What did I do?" she gaped.

He chuckled then, "Not me and you. The Diablos. He'd like to put me in cuffs right now and haul my ass to jail."

Lottie couldn't believe what she was hearing. Cops weren't vindictive, were they? "Are you kidding?"

Bash flashed a half-grin, and the sight of it tumbled butterflies around her stomach. It was just the adrenaline, that's all. "Wish I was. It's fine, nothing to worry about. You did well back there. I've never seen someone so in charge of a critical situation before."

"You did your part, too." She reassured.

"Do you think he'll make it?"

"He has a better chance now. That woman was useless. She was more worried about the dent in her fucking car. I ought to slash her tires." Scowled Lottie, glaring at the woman still talking with the police officers. It was a natural reaction to freeze during a crisis, but actively being a selfish twat was not.

That woman deserved to stand on all the Lego.

Beside her, Bash chuckled. "How did I miss you being a little vengeful demon?"

"Oh, shush. I'm not." She blushed, smiling. "She was probably texting and driving, the careless jerk."

"Babe," groaned Bash, his head lowering. "You need to quit the menacing talk before it kills me. It's so fucking hot."

She might be covered in someone else's blood, but hers surged through her veins, and Lottie's breath ceased on an inhale.

Her anger was not hot. Was it?

And as though it had just occurred to her how close she was to Bash, her skin became overheated, and her brain turned to mush.

"I, erm…" The words weren't wording at all.

Bash was surprisingly normal, not like a lame-brained imbecile who'd scented lust for the first time. Bash stepped back to pull open her car door.

"Were you on the way to work?"

"Yeah. *Crap*, I'm so late."

"They'll understand. Maybe you should go home." His brows fell over his eyes, a look of concern in them, and a surprised Lottie shot her left eyebrow high.

"I deal with this all day long. Not in this setting, but the same."

If anything, her answer made him look even more concerned. "Your stress levels must be fucking high."

Oh, my god, that was cute, and she couldn't stop the smile or the slight touch she placed on his arm. She knew it was a mistake as soon as she did it when Bash grunted and glanced at her hand. She quickly took it back.

Undisguised, unfiltered, and raw desire looked back at Lottie.

He'd never been shy about wanting to date her. During all that time spent at the hospital with his two MC friends, he tracked Lottie like a missile every time she was on shift. He'd never been overly pushy, but she knew he had his eye on her. One day, he'd even growled for one of the other bikers to *shut his fucking mouth* when that man had tried to chat with her. Everyone quickly realized that he had claimed her, regardless of her consent.

But Lottie had never touched him before, and now her fingertips tingled. She quickly shoved that hand into her scrubs pants pocket.

"I should get going. And erm…Thanks for stopping to help. Few people would have."

"People are self-centered shitfucks, Charlotte."

Her name rolled off his tongue, and she had to force herself not to tremble. He never used the shortened version. Always Charlotte.

"You sure you're okay to drive? I can drop you off."

On the bike? Her eyebrows jumped higher. She would *love* that. But Lottie shook her head. "I'm good. Thank you for the offer, though."

He remained in the middle of the road while she slid behind the wheel, and when she looked in the mirror, he was still there with his face oh-so-pensive.

Once at the hospital, her bloody clothes were excuse enough why she was late. She explained, quickly washed up, and changed into a spare set of scrubs.

And then the regular chaotic day started.

It wasn't until much later, as she finished triaging a toddler with abdominal pains, that she came to a halt. A pair of hot blue eyes and long legs encased in denim jeans was sprawled in a plastic bucket seat.

Without thinking, Lottie rushed over to Bash. "Are you hurt?" her heart rattled in her chest, assessing him with a fast sweep over his body, searching for injuries. Like her, he'd changed out of the bloodied clothes. He wore a gray t-shirt beneath the leather vest, announcing him as a Diablo Disciples biker. It was pretty cool to look at. It made him more masculine, if that were possible. The scary three skulls and then the rockers on either end, saying their name and location. Beneath that, one patch said he was the secretary. Huh, she wouldn't have expected that. Now, she wondered what a secretary did within the MC.

"No, darling, all's good." He rose to his height, and she nearly gulped as he grew nearer. "I was dropping this off for you." It caught her attention that he had a white paper bag and a takeout cup in his hands.

Oh, wow, he'd brought her coffee.

She might swoon in her comfortable shoes.

All she could do was stare up at the man. Words wouldn't form.

"You've had a rough day so far."

And he'd brought her coffee and a snack. Talk about romancing her.

Flirting hadn't gotten through her defenses all those months back, but the coffee held in his hand almost brought Lottie to her knees with a burst of affection for this man.

Around them, the waiting area continued to bulge, and she knew she couldn't stare like an idiot at the blue-eyed biker.

He smirked, which snapped Lottie out of her ogling as she reached for the coffee. Their fingers brushed, and the jolt was like electricity had been fired from a Taser.

"You didn't have to do that. But I will take it, thank you." She smiled with gratitude. Ahhh, thankfully, it was still hot. She couldn't stand lukewarm coffee. It had to be molten lava for her to enjoy it.

"Can you take a break?"

The question came out of the blue, and it flustered Lottie, and that was quite extraordinary for someone who didn't get rattled by much. She realized she'd taken a minute to analyze how that felt as Bash stared at her. *Oops.* She glanced at her watch and realized she'd gone way over her time and not taken a break in hours.

"Yeah, I can for a few minutes. Meet me outside? There's a bench just near the doors."

She quickly went to tell her team she'd be taking fifteen minutes, and she went to sit outside with a biker. It was probably a massive mistake because her reasons for not getting involved with him still mattered.

But the coffee gift softened her.

The way he smiled when he saw her coming out of the electronic doors did more than soften Lottie; she knew she was in the biggest trouble of her life.

But her legs never stalled from carrying her forward toward that smiling man.

Bash

She was fucking spectacular.

If he needed more proof, watching Charlotte working tirelessly to bring a boy back to life would have done it.

He'd nearly died seeing her on the ground, covered in blood. He'd flown into a protective mode he didn't know existed. But then, watching her so in charge, he'd been in awe. In a meeting with Axel, all he could think about was Charlotte, until his feet led him out of the clubhouse, to grab her something to eat. Only now, as he watched her sitting inches away from him, was Bash able to relax.

Craving a woman who didn't want him back made him ten times the idiot. He stuck around because he wanted more than just her body. He craved her presence because she made him feel alive, like she was wired into his frequency.

Down to the second he first saw her, he remembered how his heart had lurched and she'd snatched the soul out of his body.

No woman scolded him as much as Charlotte had in the past year.

Nearly every day, she had tutted her tongue at him when she saw a pack of smokes in his hand. Or she'd single him out to be quiet if things got too rowdy in the waiting area. She put Splice in his place for hitting on all the nurses. No doubt about it, Charlotte Martin was the sweetest ball buster.

Maybe the most perfect woman he'd ever known.

And the kicker was that she didn't want him in the same way. Or so she'd told him many times.

Yet he was doing the most golden retriever bullshit act because he couldn't stay away from her. Like she had an invisible line around his neck, and she'd tugged him to come closer. He didn't understand it, but when a guy got a gift, he didn't reject it.

She was here. She was smiling.

If Bash only wanted something physical, he would've bounced and left the guarded nurse alone. He wasn't a stranger to getting rejected by the opposite sex. He'd probably rejected more than his fair share, so it evened out. His pursuit extended beyond the pleasure they could create as a couple. The desire for Charlotte's taste went beyond mere curiosity. He could take a leaf out of Splice's book and fuck anything that moved. Satisfy a need and forget about the hazel eyes and saucy little mouth that haunted him when he fell asleep.

But only the best would do, not just any warm body.

And though he'd never tasted her, something deep in his gut told Bash Charlotte would be the best. The woman who would ruin him.

She brought dark thoughts out of him. Ones that involved restraints held firm around her wrists and ankles, and her fevered screams vibrating against his palm. But he had to keep that to himself. Otherwise, she'd bolt. And for now, he needed to establish a cautious friendship with the nervous woman.

If she wanted to pretend that platonic was all they were, he'd play that for a while, but she'd know eventually that Bash had much more in store for his little darling once her walls came crashing down.

Though he considered the club's old ladies' friends—it was a given with Casey because she was his best buddy's old lady. They were a package deal; he'd protect her and their kids with his life. He'd already given Denver an oath to care for his family if anything happened to him. And with the other old ladies around the clubhouse, he had no choice but to like them. They assembled in a pack and colluded heavily, mainly against the men. His brothers had chosen good women who could provide a strong spine and a loyal ear.

It was too early to know if Charlotte was that, but Bash knew to listen to the signs from his gut, and they flashed all the red alert lights that first day. Pursuing her hadn't worked. She'd backed off like a skittish rabbit and scowled whenever he tried to get closer. But something was between them; he felt it pulsing and snapping an invisible line. Her jealousy had shown the day he'd innocently spoken with one of her female colleagues. Her eyes had fired so much possessiveness his cock nearly broke in half with arousal. However, she returned to her guarded walls.

That didn't matter, not when she was sitting so close as she sipped coffee. He'd already decided he'd take it if all he could get Charlotte to agree to was drinking coffee side-by-side on a bench.

"This is a lifesaver," she sighed, smiling with her lips at the takeout cup.

"Wonder what you'd have said if I'd brought chocolate."

Her eyes flared, and Bash had to swallow a groan because all he could picture was how her eyes would burn with lust as he plied her with sweet pleasure.

"Dude, don't joke about chocolate."

Fucking *dude*. He was not her gal-pal.

Only, for now, he had to be.

If chocolate was his way into her life, he'd buy a whole candy store and give her free rein.

He pulled himself together, took a pack of smokes from his pocket, and lit one up.

Stealth dating a nurse who wasn't into him was complicated as fuck.

Charlotte

A plume of smoke drifted from Bash's lips as he asked. "How is the young kid? Did he live?"

"Oh, Samuel. Yes, he's on the fourth floor recovering. I called earlier to check how he was doing and all his vitals were improving."

"He was lucky you drove by." She blushed when he complimented her.

"You helped me, too."

"I only followed orders. Denver would have had his shit handled. You know he's a medic?"

Lottie scowled before she could mask the emotion. "Yes, his wife told me he had a medical background." The less said about Denver, the better. As far as she knew, the whole Diablos bikers risked her job, including the man beside her. Denver was the one who demanded medical equipment, so he was more responsible than the others.

As she pushed a crumb of the custard pastry into her mouth and savored the sweetness on her tongue, she watched as Bash's eyebrow winged up high. Damn, he was staring at her with curiosity, like he noticed how she cringed when his buddy was brought up.

Sure enough, he asked. "What's with the face, darling? Do you have something against Denver?"

"Should I?"

He half smiled. "I don't know. That's why I'm asking. Was he a shitty patient?"

Weren't all men big babies when they were sick or hurt?

"Casey kept him in line for the duration he was with us." She quickly changed the subject. "What is it you do for your MC, Bash? I assume you work there full-time?"

People assumed an MC was for men to play with motorcycles and hook up with many women. Probably, the latter was all true, but from what she gleaned from overheard conversations during their hospital pilgrimage, it sounded like they had a lot of fingers in different business pies.

"Technically, I run the secretarial side of the club."

"You take notes and sit on the boss's lap?" she stuck her tongue into the side of her cheek as Bash chuckled, and toked on his cigarette.

"You're not the first to think so."

"Sorry, I couldn't resist. So what does the club secretary do? If I'm allowed to ask."

"You can ask me anything, Charlotte." Her name rolled off his tongue and put hectic butterflies through her stomach lining. To stifle their clog dancing, she swallowed the last bite of pastry before she'd properly chewed it.

"I primarily keep records of everything. Transactions, administration. If anyone wants a meeting with Axel, they go through me first. I keep a database of all members, past and present. Think of me as an unofficial government within the club walls. Everything there is to know about a member, I know it."

"So, if I sent a letter, you'd be the one opening it?"

"Yes." He half smiled. "I also work closely with the other club officers, ensuring they have everything they need to make their jobs run smoothly."

"Wow," she said, impressed.

"And in my downtime, I throw my hand in at the mechanical shop."

"You're a jack of all trades, hm?"

"I don't save lives. Don't tell anyone, but the sight of blood isn't my favorite thing."

Lottie gasped, searching for any sign that he might be lying, but Bash seemed completely honest. "This morning must have been torture for you then. Samuel's artery bled a lot."

"I mostly focused on your face," He admitted, and Lottie's chest tightened weirdly. She'd seen people fainting all the time because of their aversion to seeing blood, so she felt a prickle of gratitude for how Bash had held it together, so they could help the boy.

"Tell me more about your job." She asked as the daytime sun beat down on the top of her head. She usually grabbed a fast lunch in the cafeteria if she hadn't brought a boxed lunch. But sitting outside was nicer.

"Well," he started, a glint in his eye as he smoked the last of his cigarette and then stomped it out underneath his leather-soled boot. To Lottie's surprise, Bash picked up the cigarette butt and tossed it into the nearby trash can. "Besides sitting on Axel's lap."

She burst into laughter. "It was a fair assumption. That's what happens in all Wall Street movies."

Bash winked and went on. "I keep abreast of all the data for our businesses. If he might need it, I'm also Axel's advisor."

"Do all the bikers have roles or work outside the MC?"

"Yeah, darling. Most of us have jobs and roles within the MC, especially those on the council, or the place would fall apart."

"Even the mean-looking one?"

It was Bash's turn to laugh. Though there was at least an entire space between them, his manspreading made her feel like their bodies were almost touching, as he turned his head to look at her.

"How do I know you're talking about Ruin? Even he has a club title. He didn't make a good patient, huh? If he's left a lasting impression as the mean-looking one."

"To be fair to Ruin, he was in a coma for a long time, so he made the ideal patient. No complaining about the food or calling on us to change the TV channel at all hours."

"Now it's my turn to ask a question."

"Go for it. I hope it's not my favorite color."

He smirked, and from the glint under his half-mast eyelids, Lottie braced for him to confront the elephant in the room, and ask why she'd turned him down for a date.

"What time is your lunch break tomorrow?"

Oh. That was not what she was expecting. Her brain quickly caught up and told him. That's when Bash stood, took the empty container from her hands, and tossed it into the trash can.

"Meet me here again, Charlotte."

Look, she was not expert in these things — the emotional mechanics between men and women — but that sounded more like a command than a request and it shivered her timbers right down to her curling toes. Lottie was left dry-mouthed before she dashed the tip of her tongue over her lips to give them some lubrication.

The way he stared in a concentrated way put a hole straight through her heart, because she knew that look wasn't platonic. Not in the least.

One part of her brain was up for it, willing to follow wherever that deep voice told her to go. Bash felt safe and warm, what she could imagine a decent boyfriend would be like. But the logical side wouldn't let her form any friendship with this man, because if she got in deep, all kinds of trouble would ensue. And she just wasn't about that life.

If she wanted adrenaline junkie pursuits and gangbangers at her door, she would have joined her sister with the Riot Brothers. They'd tried often enough over the years to get her to be friendly. Especially that creep her sister was dating.

"I…"

"Charlotte, it's only a bite of lunch and exchanging a conversation. Don't look so worried, darling."

When he put it like that.

And then it occurred to her that maybe Bash had a girlfriend now. Perhaps he was heavily dating and didn't look at her that way anymore. A sudden onset of turmoil mixed with trepidation made her swallow and tilt her head back to look at him looming over her, so tall and imposing. The guy was built like a high-rise building, all lean inches encased in his biker wear. And now she wondered if he wanted to have lunch with her again because he'd formed a trauma bond with her, because of today's events. That sounded more plausible, and her shoulders relaxed.

"Okay, but if you can't make it, don't worry about it."

Bash only smiled and walked her toward the electronic doors, though she insisted he didn't have to. She remained there dumbfounded while watching him stride to his parked bike, wondering what had happened for the past few minutes.

And the amazing thing was, he showed up the following day. Even when Lottie stewed over what it might mean, or if she should even turn up. But with her lunch bag in her hand, she made her way outside to that same bench, and the air locked in her throat, seeing Bash standing like a centurion near the double doors.

He smiled in greeting, his eyes darkened around the edges, and Lottie felt a flutter in her stomach. No doubt it was hunger. It couldn't be connected to emotions. That wasn't how she worked. Lottie was analytical and not powered by feelings, yet seeing that large biker waiting for her with a smile in his hooded eyes made her react solely to feelings.

"Hey, you made it." she forced out and joined him in step.

"It wasn't me who was in danger of not showing, Charlotte." He teased. "I thought I might have to track you down."

"Would you have done that?" she asked, wide-eyed, as she plopped down on the bench and took the coffee cup Bash held out to her.

"Yes." Unrepentant.

"Here, fill your unfiltered mouth with this." She said, opening the lunch bag; she brought out a wrapped sandwich she'd made for Bash. He seemed surprised, but took a thick beef and mustard triangle. She wasn't hungry suddenly as she watched his straight white teeth sink into the thick-cut white bread, so she passed him the second when he finished his sandwich.

"You're not eating?" he frowned while she sipped the coffee, savoring the perfect taste of caffeine.

"I had two protein bars on my break earlier. Go ahead, eat it. It'll only get tossed out if you don't. You don't want to hurt my culinary talents, do you?"

Then, they fell into an easy conversation. The lunch break went by in a flash. Once again, Bash walked her to the door and told her he'd see her tomorrow. Before she could protest, he'd strode off.

She sighed, watching his broad back.

Did bikers ever listen?

But she knew he did because he asked questions about her life, seemingly genuinely interested.

She couldn't work the guy out.

Why would he want to sit in a hospital entryway eating lunch with her, if he knew she wouldn't date him?

Sure, Lottie felt some chemistry toward the man, but it wouldn't last, so there was no point in losing her head over it.

Maybe they *could* be friends after all.

For the next five days, she sat outside in the blistering heat and had eclectic conversations with Bash while they each brought the other food and drinks to share. He won yesterday by bringing shortbread. She aced it today when he grinned at the sight of the buttered English cheese scones they'd discussed. So what if she stayed up late reading recipes and burning two batches before nailing the third one.

It was a *friendly* thing to do.

When she learned why he was called Bash, she giggled for a full minute, slapping her knee to calm down.

"Does anyone ever call you Ben?" his government name was Ben Laurent, totally hot. But she kept that tidbit to herself.

"Not in a long time," he gruffed, licking a scone crumb from the corner of his lip, and Lottie nearly moaned.

Whoa, what the hell was that? She was not turned on while watching the guy eating!

On a base level, she could understand an attraction (regular women were attracted to him; they stared at him often enough as they walked by) His commanding voice and work-roughened hands checked the bad boy persona.

She was enjoying Bash's company.

She didn't think he was like Nora's boyfriend, but ignorance was bliss for now, while only two friends were meeting for innocent lunchtime chats.

On the seventh day, they planned nothing, but Lottie still waited outside. But Bash never showed up.

In only a short week, Lottie had gotten used to seeing Bash, listening to his stories or his laughter when she told him hilarious tales about her cat. God, she'd talked about Prince like he was her child. It's no surprise he became bored. Any man would.

Swallowing her disappointment, she returned to work. She could handle those problems easily, no sweat.

Unlike dealing with a man and her squirrely, newly formed sexual feelings for him.

Bash

The place Bash enjoyed the most was sitting at the church table, while each chair filled up with the club council.

Bora Bora would be a close second, but the way the Utah summer sun was baking everyone alive, he didn't need to go anyplace but outside to feel like he was somewhere tropical. He'd long since ditched his leather jacket as soon as he stepped off the Harley this morning. Thank fuck for the air con blasting over him from above and cooling his bare arms.

Hearing wolf whistles, he raised his head and caught sight of hairy knees coming through the door. Bash joined the laughter, seeing Splice wearing an armless muscle tee, basketball shorts and a bandana around his forehead. He flopped on a chair next to Reno.

"Are you entering an ugly knees contest?" Asked Reno. "I think you've got a good chance at the trophy."

"Fuck off, I'm too hot for clothes. If I were at home, I'd be naked."

"Thank fuck, you've got some sense." Added Denver. "No one wants to see those swinging balls."

Then Chains walked through the door and stopped next to Splice. He eyed the SAA critically, and Bash knew some shit was about to be said. He waited with his silver-ringed fingers crossed on the table.

"Did this room turn into a beauty parlor, and no fucker told me?"

"VP." Groaned Splice, like he was in pain or about to be.

"This is church, Splice, where Axel's council meet. You come into this room without wearing your cut, which shows disrespect. It means I'll break those fucking knees. You get me?"

Amused, everyone started tapping on the table.

"It's too hot to wear leather. I'm sweatier than under a witch's tit, Chains."

"No cut, no knees. Your choice."

Splice pushed to his feet and scowled. "You're a cruel asshole, Chains. I hope Monroe's sisters come to stay for a month, and you don't get laid." He nearly collided with Ruin on his way out.

"Did he lose another girlfriend?" asked their enforcer. Ruin spoke more these days than he ever did, but it still wasn't the regular amount, and when he used his voice, it usually caught everyone's attention.

As Axel entered the room and closed the door, Splice returned to his chair, wearing gym gear and his cut.

In their line of work, regrets came in waves.

The club was in a feud with the Mexicans a few years back. A deal gone wrong when Axel discovered the cartel kingpin, Julio Ruiz, was into human trafficking, selling women and girls as young as twelve years old. He'd pushed for Axel to get in on it, too. The Diablos may be despicable, but they wouldn't go as far as using women. If Axel and Chains had agreed to that deal, Bash would have thrown his cut back and had his tattoo removed. Ruiz retaliated by fire-bombing Axel's house. It was a crappy time, but they got rid of all his generals and underlings, so the Renegade Souls enforcer could take him out, for a different reason. But the end games lined up for the two MCs.

There were no regrets in Bash's mind about what they'd done back then to secure their club and the safety of their families. Murder was no joke. Bash had blood on his hands. But if not, he and his club brothers would have been slain, eventually.

It wasn't an everyday thing. But enemies happened.

And that's what they'd gathered early to discuss.

For months now, even longer because this enemy went back years, but they'd resurfaced in recent months when Denver had been stabbed. That was personal. They knew it was his prick of a brother-in-law, who Casey had run away from years ago. Albie was unhinged. The organization known as the Riot Brothers had expanded. When they formed, they were just a stupid little gang selling weed and pills, trying to be big boys. But over the years, they'd grown under the leadership of Harvey and his brother, Kurtis. They'd even secured foreign investment until the Diablos intervened.

Bash wasn't the strategic part of the MC. That came down to Axel and Chains, though he piped up if he had input. As secretary, his role was to remember shit and all the details attached to that shit. Names, places, numbers, what was said, when, and by who. Each church gathering was special, and he felt a rush of anticipation each time as he took his seat and listened to the discussions.

Usually, it was about building their corporation, making profits, and developing throughout Utah.

The presence of the Riot Brothers gang made today's church meeting unusual, and Axel was determined to intervene before things escalated.

"Whatever happens next, that little cunt Albie is mine to finish." Grated Denver. He was recovered fine from his stab wound, but the anger went deeper than any laceration. That guy had an unhinged attachment to his step-sister, Denver's old lady. Even a decade later, the threat of him loomed. It was only recently that Denver moved his family back home after having them on lockdown for months.

"You can handle that?" A shrewd Axel threw along the table. Handle killing a man in cold blood, he meant. Bash could tell what Denver was going to say before he nodded. Denver would do anything to protect his family. Albie made the mistake of coming back and freaking out Casey and their twin girls.

"Ruin, be on 24-7 call for Denver if he needs you," Axel advised.

The enforcer could kill a man and then be tucked up in bed with his popstar old lady an hour later like nothing ever happened.

Not much touched Ruin.

Everyone thought he was made of steel and pure spite. But he'd changed in recent months. Still a fucking lunatic weapon, but Rory brought out an unseen side to Ruin. Down the table, the enforcer smirked like he relished being tagged in for a bit of execution.

"They're gutter rats, Axel." Chimed in Diamond, head of their security section.

Officially, Diamond was Axel's bodyguard. After his house was blown to pieces, the brotherhood took a vote and decided Axel needed someone with him. He'd fought against it, as was Axel's way, but he couldn't argue with an official vote. Gotta fucking love democracy. But for his job, Diamond was protection for hire. It brought a sizeable chunk of change to the club.

"What's stopping us from sitting down with Harvey and his rats and taking them all out?"

"Our police informant has told me they have eyes on the Riot Brothers, or I would consider it. I *have* fucking considered it many times. But no matter how we look at it, we get caught, and we'll all join Primo in his cell."

The laughter wasn't as strong this time, and Bash knew why. This shit had been plaguing the MC for months. First, it had been an inconvenience, an unknown buyer snapping up properties the Diablos wanted, or undercutting deals. The night Denver was stabbed triggered a series of unfortunate events that weren't just mere bad luck, but a deliberate act of sabotage.

One of their car washes was torched.

Bricks were put through each of their High Street stores, setting off the alarms in the middle of the night.

One of their bookies was robbed; fucking twice.

Citations were sent to the city about several permits to hold them up with their contractors.

The club had zero tolerance for anyone interfering with them or their businesses, even if it was trivial. The action of a single rat could cause an infestation of them.

Proposals were tabled and voted on to neutralize Harvey and Co.

Someone softly knocked on the door, and Axel told them to come in. Bash saw the president's face go from fierce to a softer expression when he realized it was his old lady. She bumped the door open with a hip and entered carrying a tray.

"I didn't think you'd want coffee right now. This heat is too much. I made icy lemonade." She strolled in wearing white shorts and a red t-shirt to match her hair. The club queen was so optimistic and happy all the time. It was hard not to get caught up in her sunshine attitude, even as they'd been discussing killing a lot of men only moments ago.

"Thank fuck for you, Scar." Hailed Splice. Grabbing a glass, he downed it in one and licked his lips. "Ruin, you don't want yours, right? I'm dehydrated, my brother." The enforcer only arched his eyebrow but took a glass and went to drink from it as Splice groaned, watching, but then Ruin slid it across the table for Splice to grab.

"Wait up, wildcat. You forgetting something?" Axel called out when Scarlett was near the door. She turned with a sly smile playing on her lips.

"Umm… I don't think so. I just brought these in like Alice asked me to."

"Get over here and kiss me."

She blushed. Even though every man there had heard those two going at it many times behind Axel's office door. "You're working."

"Don't care, move it, woman."

It felt like an intrusion to watch them lock lips, so Bash looked away, but not before he caught Axel grabbing a handful of his old lady's ass.

It was nothing new to them now. Before Axel got together with Scarlett, he'd taken the homeless woman hostage right here in the clubhouse and spoiled her rotten. While they bickered with enough verbal foreplay, the surrounding air was constantly saturated with lust. Thank fuck they gave in and screwed each other, or they would have had to put Axel down because that woman drove him crazy.

She also grounded him. If there was proof that a woman made a man into a better person, then Scarlett was it. She'd put extra energy throughout the clubhouse by involving herself in organizing the place better. Some of her ideas had sprouted businesses. She then hired the sweet bottoms. Some of those chicks came to the MC now and didn't fuck anyone, which didn't please some members. Not Bash. He'd long since got bored with random hook-ups. Not that he advertised his love life or lack thereof.

"Don't be late home, Mark." They heard Scarlett whisper, and Axel swatted her ass before she squealed and rushed to the door.

"You're asking for it," growled the Prez, eyeing his woman like a slab of cake.

"Now I need another glass of lemonade after that porn show." Complained Splice, wiping his brow.

Axel raised his eyebrow before asking. "Okay, where were we?"

"I think you were squeezing Scar's ass, Prez." offered a helpful Splice. The guy was asking to be shot between the eyes today.

When the meeting was winding down, and men were leaving their seats to get back to their regular duties, Axel called his name. "I need to see the contract for the construction over on Blythe. Did you get it? And what about the permits?"

Their most recent project, conceived by Scarlett, focused on renovating an apartment block to provide sweet bottoms with rooms to rent off the headquarters land, reducing their overnight stays at the clubhouse. Bash thought those old ladies were at it again, trying to keep their men from temptation. The sweet bottoms had no filters and offered their goodies to everyone, even the married members.

"I'll grab it now."

"How are you getting on with finding us a new lawyer?"

Their retained lawyer recently retired to Florida. Bad timing all around while they were in the depths of this new shitshow. It was convenient to have a guy on speed dial who could bail them out or grease a judge's palm to get charges dropped.

"Working on it, Prez. Who'd have thought it was so difficult to find a crooked lawyer? Time was, you could spit and hit the bullseye ten times out of ten."

Axel cracked a smirk. "Make it happen, yeah? We get Primo back by the end of the year and he can lighten the load."

"Speaking of. I ordered all the updated computer shit he'll need. It'll be here in a few days, but don't ask me to set it up. Tech isn't my specialty. He's gonna cream his panties when he sees the office Scar has ready for him. It's some advanced-tech geeky shit."

Now Axel's grin was one of pride. Bash knew he loved how integrated his wife was with the club. Thinking of an old lady put Charlotte at the forefront of his mind. He'd missed having lunch with her yesterday and probably couldn't make it today, not with his workload.

In his mind, he saw his hand wrapping around her long ponytail and using it like a leash, so her head tipped back to kiss him.

She'd be sweet and eager, standing on her tiptoes to reach his mouth, needing it more than her next breath. If she begged... *fuck*.

A restlessness worked its way through his system. Something he wasn't used to feeling. This thing inside pushed him to be wherever Charlotte was, even just for a minute, for that little fix of seeing her face. Even if she scowled and scolded, it was enough.

That's how he knew it wasn't a fast fuck he was looking for. He could get that anywhere.

He wanted the slow and the begging. The out of control and the nasty.

And no one else would do but the sweet, darling nurse.

Bash had to banish those thoughts; there were a lot of steps to go through before he even got a kiss. *If* he got a kiss, it was still pending.

Lots of time afterward for sweet, addictive begging.

If it were up to Bash, he'd have her naked already sitting on his kitchen counter and his head buried between her thighs, while she ripped his hair out.

Blowing out a hot puff of air, Bash strode through the church doorway and got to work.

Bash

Bash's gut rumbled. Not because he was hungry.

He carried two coffees in one of those cardboard carriers. Held by the other hand, he'd already slipped off the heavy leather jacket because it was hell hot today. Mirrored shades covered Bash's eyes, and he took the familiar direction through the ER department to find a pretty girl with fire in her eyes.

He'd felt the same anticipation in his torso for days while viewing for sale warehouses with Axel. Was this anything like how his brothers felt about their old ladies? Then no fucking wonder they acted insane most of the time.

Not having her phone number bothered him. And though he could have found it easy, he wanted Charlotte to give it to him. His previous attempts to ask for it didn't go smoothly. Chasing a woman who didn't want him wasn't his norm. It was even worse when she failed to notice his attempts to pursue her. With a laugh at himself, he made a left turn and entered a waiting area where sick people were seated in rows.

It was like a game he played with himself on what color scrubs Charlotte would wear today. He'd never gotten it right yet and didn't today. He'd guessed green, but as she came out of a room holding a stack of folders, he saw she was dressed all in purple. There was nothing sexy about the scrubs. They were functional for her job, but the way her ass and full hips filled out the thin fabric made his cock jerk, and he had to grind his teeth to calm down before he popped a boner right there in the emergency room.

As he willed it, her head whipped around, and their eyes locked.

Bash knew in that intense moment when Charlotte looked at him, she would be his girl. There was no other outcome. As he neared her, the air felt heavy, and he noticed her cheeks were a shade of pink. The color he wanted to taste on his tongue.

"Are you sick?" she exclaimed, and Bash grinned slowly.

She was fucking delicious.

"You gonna ask me that every time I turn up, darling? I'm in good working order." She'd find out soon just how good.

"*Darling?*" he heard another feminine voice joining them, and Bash anchored his head to see a nurse coming from around the desk. The woman looked vaguely familiar, but no one else registered with Bash when he was near Charlotte, so he only raised his eyebrow at her question. "Who's this, Lottie?"

Charlotte shot her friend/colleague an embarrassed glance, and Bash chewed the inside of his cheek to keep his amusement in check.

Yeah, little darling, who am I?

If she dared say a friend, he was going to go nuclear.

Bash's self-control was stretched to its limit. One by one, the threads holding it together snapped, leaving it hanging with a whisper of control as the grip on the coffee carrier tightened in his palm. He deserved an award for this. But he'd take a kiss from Charlotte as his prize for waiting for so. Fucking. Long.

When she shot her gaze his way, he gave Charlotte a warning stare. Daring her to let those disgusting two words come out of her mouth. *My friend.*

"He's no one you know." She answered, and then the sweet girl grabbed his arm and body-checked him out of there with fast steps.

Bash chuckled and went along with her. It was his plan, after all, to be alone with her, so this worked out perfectly.

"Who was the chick?" he asked when she had pushed him far enough out of the electronic doors.

"No one that you know."

Again, a spurt of laughter escaped Bash's lips, and he dipped his head low to look her in the eyes. "You know a lot of no one's, Charlotte. Do I have to worry you're losing your memory?"

"Funny." She huffed, smiling a little. "Toni is a nosy friend. I won't hear the last of this now. Why are you here? Give me that." She said, taking a coffee and drinking half with a happy sigh once finished. "Is this one for me, too?" She took it but returned it, making a face after tasting it. "Yuck. It's black."

"If I'd known you would steal it, I would have creamed and sugared both."

"Well, you'll know for next time, won't you?"

"Hm. I will," Bash rumbled and placed a hand on the base of Charlotte's back, directing them to their bench.

"I can't stay, Bash. My shift isn't over for another hour."

"I know, darling, just a coffee drop off. I'm heading out of town."

"Oh." She frowned, and he loved seeing her disappointed. It gave him hope. "Going anywhere nice?"

"Just a quick run to Colorado and back. What do you want for lunch tomorrow?"

Her eyes flashed, and her sweet, tempting lips became lax. Bash's gaze dropped, and he wanted to suck hard on that full lower lip until it turned a deep red.

Before she could refuse, he walked away. "Catch you tomorrow, darling. Get home safe."

"Bash. Wait! I never said…" she called out. But he carried on walking. He'd be here tomorrow, even if she refused. "Fine, I'll have a deli chicken sandwich, please. No chunky chicken, Bash. Bash! Are you even listening to me?" she huffed, and that's when he turned to look back at her. The stretch of the parking lot separating them was about twenty feet, but he mapped every inch of her while watching him.

He was an observant man.

Right now, he was a liar, acting like he was only Charlotte's friend when he wanted so much more from her and knew he would get it. If only she'd let down her walls. Nothing in her passionate eyes said she was indifferent to him. So many times, he caught her checking him out, streaking her greedy eyes over his tattooed hands. He'd let her see the rest of his ink if she asked. *Nicely.*

"I always listen, Charlotte. Tomorrow." He winked and strode to where he'd parked his bike. He was already looking forward to getting this fast trip out of the way so he could sit on a bench with a beautiful girl.

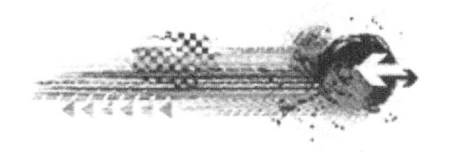

Charlotte

"You did not!" she went into a fresh round of uncontrollable laughter, unconsciously holding Bash's arm to balance herself. Once under control, she wiped away laughter tears and saw how intensely Bash was watching her. He wasn't laughing like she was, and her heart fluttered. She quickly took back her hand and placed it in her lap.

"I can't believe you walked a baby piglet. I need to see pictures."

"Ruin brought him to the clubhouse, and then was called away, so it was down to me to take it out to have a piss. I never knew pigs were so curious; he had me walking the entire length of the compound and back again."

"A pig on a leash." She chuckled again at the image. "I think that might be the cutest thing I've ever heard. And he wears outfits, you say?"

"Ridiculous ones for all seasons, bells and bow ties included. I don't know how Ruin isn't embarrassed to be seen with Lenny." She could see by his smile that Bash was teasing. He probably thought the tiny pig was adorable.

"Will you send me some pictures the next time you see him?"

"Now I have your number. I can send you all the pictures you want."

"Not dick pics." She exclaimed, immediately regretting her words and wishing she could take them back. She let out a groan and hid her face. When she dared to drop her hand, Bash was smoldering. There was no other word for it. It was bad enough she'd folded like a wet napkin when he asked (more like demanded) for her phone number. In case of emergencies, he'd argued.

"I'm forty, darling. I don't do immature boyish tricks."

Bash was far from a boy.

She didn't just mean his age. He was every inch a *man*. All hard lines and determined eyes. He was the take charge and deal with a chaotic situation kind of man. The longer she spent with him, the more she realized how intelligent he was, not just with for work but with current events in pop culture, politics, and she discovered they had a shared love for foreign food. The guy could pack the food away like a bridge troll coming off a hunger strike. She wondered how he kept so trim. She only had to look at a bag of Skittles to gain twelve pounds.

Four days had passed since Bash's Colorado trip. She didn't really resist meeting him that following day, and even though she sensed he had ulterior motives, she was having a great time with him, sharing food and laughing at his funny stories.

She expected him every day now, watching the doorway like some besotted fool. Every night, she dreamed about him.

Back in the day, before she ditched her sister's drama and realized those guys she was hanging out with were bad news, she spent some time with them. Thorn and his buddies were super creepy, definitely not friend material. They were the kind of people who believed sexual harassment was their manly privilege. Those who belittled and mistreated women, doing drugs and getting into fights. Real stand up guys.

It was difficult to distance herself from Nora initially, but she needed to prioritize a stable life. She couldn't resist the pull towards Bash and enjoyed their time together, but she knew he wanted a deeper connection. She was inexperienced, not dead. The low-lidded way he looked at her or dropped his gaze to her mouth told her he still had dating on his mind.

She would have dated him in a hot second if only he wasn't in his gang… or club.

She was judging him based on others' behavior, which she hated. It was wrong, especially because so far, Bash hadn't given her a reason to mistrust his motives, though Denver blackmailing her hadn't helped his friend's cause. But she wanted peace, not always worrying about what would happen next. If only half the rumors about the Diablos were true, then Bash was into some heavy stuff. His magnificent smile and effortless way of making her feel comfortable didn't alter that.

It was unfortunate because whenever she sat with Bash, she couldn't help but fantasize about feeling the softness of his goatee against her cheeks.

Thank god Bash couldn't read minds, or hers would make him laugh.

The biker's eyes, which were shining brightly, abruptly shifted toward her lips as she spoke, causing her already confused mind to lose focus. Lottie wondered if he'd kiss as passionately as they did in the movies. She wondered if he could sense her growing crush, making her mind empty of everything but him when he was around.

From day one, she'd been overwhelmed by Bash. Almost like his gravitational pull gave her no choice but to go where he was, to bask in that face and his deep, addictive laugh.

His age did nothing to quell just how wildly he set her hormones to a high level. If anything, his maturity was even hotter. He was too handsome for his own good. A total force of nature who owned whatever space he was in. And for someone who'd never been in a long, short or intimate relationship before, choosing a man like that, a total storm of a man, would not be the best decision.

Not only that, but she could only imagine the women he was used to, and she was guaranteed not to live up to his expectations.

Yesterday, he had growled while inquiring about a doctor who'd been on her back a few months ago. Bash confronted Doctor Harris after seeing him yell at Lottie. She felt a mixture of gratitude and anger towards him. But you know what? Doctor Harris's unpleasant attitude had given Lottie a wide berth ever since.

The fact he'd intervened in a situation still gave Lottie goosebumps.

Bash called Doctor Harris Doctor Dick. It always made her chuckle.

"You tell me if he bothers you, Charlotte." He'd growled. Literally growled with his teeth bared, and her brain glitched for a full minute while she tried to rally her hormones like unruly toddlers.

Today, she rushed out of the hospital to find him leaning against a wall. His boots crossed at the ankle. He was without a jacket because of the atrocious weather, and his Diablo Disciples insignia t-shirt was sleeveless. A pair of shades covered his eyes, but his mouth twitched with a grin, as if he'd been waiting for her.

"Sorry! I can't stop for lunch, Bash, because I have to go home. I checked my home cameras, and Prince has gone ballistic and tipped over his feeder. He'll tear down the curtains if he waits all day to eat."

She didn't want to miss their lunch, but Prince was a total diva and would pee in her bed if he didn't get his snacks.

"I'll take you." He hooked up her hand, and she was so stunned that she was standing by his motorcycle before she realized what he'd said.

"I have my car, Bash."

"I can weave through traffic and get you home to the cat quicker."

"Are you just trying to find out where I live?" she narrowed her eyes, shielding them from the sun.

"I know your address, darling."

"How?"

"We're wasting time. Hop on." He straddled the powerful machine and held out a hand to Lottie.

Oh, god, this was her fantasy coming true.

All those nights in bed dreaming of this exact scenario. Only now, her heart beat triple time as she stared at his outstretched hand.

How could she say no when she felt all giddy and terrified inside?

"Okay. Just for Prince." She said, and he smiled slowly.

"Of course." He told her how to climb on and where to hold.

He wanted her to wrap her arms around his waist. *Sweet lord*. If she fell off his bike and died, it would be because she was holding onto his waist and smelling his amazing cologne. No girl could want anything else.

Bash was right. The journey was faster on his bike as she leaned with him in and out of the traffic. Lottie loved every terrifying second of it and couldn't hold back her beaming smile when he stopped outside her suburban neighborhood, with only six houses on the block.

"How was that? I got you home in one piece."

"It was incredible. I can't wait to do it again." She grinned and realized that meant she was inviting herself onto his motorcycle again. "You're a great driver."

"Thank you. Now invite me in to meet this cat of yours."

Because Lottie was a neat freak, her house was always guest-ready. She unlocked the door, fully aware of the looming biker behind her, as she turned off the alarm.

"Don't mind Prince. He's a grump with everyone, especially strangers. If he hisses, hiss back at him," she advised, hoping her baby boy was on his best behavior today. Knowing his feeding machine had been knocked over wasn't a positive sign for a good mood.

Lottie crossed the living room into the kitchen, where the cat feeder was on its side. She crouched down to fix it, and that's when she heard.

"Fuck me. Charlotte, there's a tiger on your couch."

Laughing, she turned to see Bash staring at her regalness Prince, blinking slowly, watching the new person in the room. Once the feeder was put right and the timer reset, she walked over to the couch to stroke a hand over her cat's head. As always, he was aloof to her presence. She was the only person who spoiled him rotten, and he couldn't give her a token hello meow.

"Bash, this is my baby boy, Prince Scratchy Mittens, Viscount of Meowington. Prince, this is Bash; he has a cool motorcycle, so be nice."

"That's some name for the gigantic beast. Where did you find him? In the depths of the Amazon jungle?"

"Isn't he gorgeous? He's a Maine Coon and was only this big when I got him." She held her hands out a foot apart. "He's not the friendliest kitty, but he calls the shots." After another ear scratch, she said. "Let me make you a sandwich before I head back to work."

"You don't need to do that, darling."

"I want to." She blushed to high heaven, hating that her skin colored every time she looked at Bash. "And it's a thank you for bringing me home."

He grunted, obviously wanting to refuse, but he said nothing when she went to the kitchen to first wash her hands.

It wasn't a fancy sandwich, but she packed it with sliced deli meats and pickles, which she knew Bash favored. But the wrapped sandwich nearly fell out of her hand when she entered the living room again and saw the biker sitting on the couch with Prince sprawled across his lap, being petted. Petted! And he wasn't clawing or biting Bash's hands.

"*Oh, my god.* What's going on here?"

"I'm trapped under a tiger. I sat down, and he jumped on top of me." Bash smirked, scratching behind Prince's ears. That traitor's eyes were all glazed with ecstasy, purring like he was a docile kitty cat!

Lottie scowled and pointed a finger at her furry roommate. "You little heathen! I clean your litter tray and give you all the treats, and this is how you repay me by slutting it up with a strange man? I can't even look at you right now, Prince. You don't even know Bash! He could have cooties, and you hopped onto his lap, anyway, begging for pets."

"Thanks, little darling," the man smirked at her motherly outrage. "If you wanna get on my lap, I promise I'm cooties free."

Well, didn't that make her flame up?

She huffed. "We need to go." When Bash freed himself from underneath Prince, she glared at the cat again as he curled up to watch his bird show. "You better think long and hard about what you've done, Prince. We'll be having a family meeting later. *Unbelievable.*" She huffed under her breath as she reached the door, after shoving the sandwich into Bash's hands. The hand on the bottom of her back almost caused her steps to falter.

"I'm sure he loves you, Charlotte."

"That rotten monster would eat my decaying corpse." She said, then wanted to kick rocks. She was so jealous that her big baby boy liked someone better than her.

It was Bash, so she couldn't blame Prince too much, since she'd fantasized often about sliding onto his lap and begging for his touch.

On another bike ride, he went slower, and she loved it even more and wished they could ride longer. But soon, they were back at the hospital entrance. She reluctantly let go of Bash and got off the bike.

"I'll be here tomorrow," Bash told her, and before she could insist he didn't have to or that he must have something better to do than sit and eat lunch with her, he placed a gloved finger on her lips. Rendering Lottie frazzled from the touch.

"I'll be here, no talking back."

"Yes, sir." She joked, but saw a flash of heat going through his eyes. Not realizing what she'd said, Lottie walked into work dry-mouthed, looking back only once to see Bash straddled over his motorcycle. Watching her.

He turned up the next day and for the following week.

But she didn't take him home.

Not until her cat loved *her* the best.

And that looked like it would take until the end of time.

Bash

B ash couldn't help but notice Charlotte's repeated eye roll as a woman walked by them.

The little jealous hisses she was trying to hide were making his cock so fucking hard. She had no idea what she was gifting him.

He was aware of his appearance and women often glanced at him. Sure, he hadn't fallen out of the ugly tree, but it was also about the biker cut he wore. Women flocked to bikers like they thought they were handing out dick shaped candy. He barely noticed the attention, especially when sitting beside the woman who drove him crazy.

But it seemed his little darling didn't like the women checking him out, and she'd unconsciously scooted closer. Now their thighs were touching. Letting those women know she was claiming him? he fucking wished.

Because she was nearer, he cupped a hand around her thigh, and her eyes snapped to his face.

"Are you being my protector, darling?" he smirked, watching her catch his meaning with a cute pink blush.

"Hardly." She huffed. "I might have wide hips and some ass, but I'm lacking in muscles if anyone wanted to run off with you. I'd have to sit by and watch, maybe giving you a little wave."

Oh shit. He went into territory Bash tried not to think about when he was around her, because hiding his boner was no joke. In the shower, he'd frequently imagine grabbing those amazing hips while stroking himself.

"Also, it's not cool to stare."

For fuck's sake, how cute was she? Fucking delicious. Bash's tongue got wet just thinking about licking her up and down.

Bash squeezed her thigh, letting her know he wasn't following random women anywhere. Not unless Charlotte was the woman, and she wanted to shove him into a tiny closet and beg him to make her feel good.

"You're a good girl for trying to protect me," he stated and meant it, but he said it just to watch her eyes turn opaque at his praise.

Whether Charlotte realized it, she liked *his* praise.

And for Bash, that was a red rag to a horny bull.

It was his catnip, and he was dying to see how far she'd go for it.

Just as he was about to see how possessive Charlotte was, her phone rang and she looked annoyed.

"Probably a telemarketer," she answered with a sweet "hello." But then she had a total mood swing and jumped up, clutching the phone to her chest. "I need to take this," she excused, walking a few feet away. Her side of the conversation was clear. She wasn't thrilled to be talking to that person.

Bash's protective instincts kicked in, making him want to grab the phone and find out who the hell was upsetting Charlotte.

"I told you no. Don't call again," she said, then she returned, sitting at his side. "Sorry about that."

"Who upset you?" he demanded to know, his hand on her knee again. Charlotte would be a shit poker player because all her emotions were right there on her face. He wanted to fix whatever upset her.

"My sister." She said. Some of his inner anger receded, knowing it wasn't a man on the other end of that call. "I went no contact with her over a year ago. Now she dares to call to ask for money. It's unfortunately the same old same old. Nora never changes, and I grew tired of feeling responsible for fixing her messes."

"I'm sorry to hear that. But you did the right thing for you."

"You're lucky you're an only child." She said, "But your biker friends are like brothers, aren't they? That's how it works in an MC?"

"It can be, yeah. Not all of us get along."

"So, what happens if one of them does stupid stuff?"

"Normally, we just smack him in the head to straighten him out."

"I'll do that next time. How do I do a fist again?" she showed him with her thumb on the outside. Fuck him, she was too cute. He took a minute to teach her the right way to throw a punch. He'd be the slaying dragon in all her battles one day soon.

"Have you never been close to her?"

Charlotte shared some of their home life with Bash, explaining how she always had to look out for Nora.

"She met a guy and got in with the wrong crowd. I didn't know that at first. When I saw some things they were up to, I tried to warn Nora, and she chose them over me. It's been that way ever since. She says they're her family. But they're not good people, Bash. Her loser boyfriend, Thorn, probably made her hit me up for cash."

"Do you want me to kill him?"

"Yes." She laughed, assuming he was joking. Bash was not the har-har type, not about this. He would kill anyone who messed with Charlotte's feelings. Upsetting her was not forgivable in his eyes.

"Umm, Bash, I want to confess something. And also apologize to you."

Bash's eyebrow winged up, curious at the change of tone. Now, his little darling was looking embarrassed and bashful. Fuck. He *wished* she was full of Bash.

And now he was thinking about himself in the third person. He had to get a hold of his burning feelings.

"When I first met all you guys, the Diablos people, I was so curt with you."

"You were ice cold, darling," he chuckled, remembering those early days fondly. It had only made her more desirable in his eyes. He was still touching her knee. He saw it as a positive thing. "But I liked it. You took care of two of my brothers, so you could have told me to fuck off, and I still wouldn't have minded."

She blushed. "Yeah, well. I didn't know we were going to become friends."

Friends. That word cut him like a fucking blade to the torso.

And he wasn't having any part of it.

But she went on before he could let his sweet nurse know that. "Anyway, there was a reason behind my attitude. I saw you all in your gang, wearing your matching outfits. "

"Charlotte..." Bash snickered.

"I know, I know, they're not a uniform. Casey already educated me on that long ago. I thought..." she whittled her teeth on her lip, and Bash swore he wanted to bring her into his lap and lick that lip to make it all better. He noticed everything about her, so he saw the pulse in her neck quicken.

"I made the wrong judgment that you were all like the guys my sister is with. And that's why I was so mean—to you, especially. But we're friends now, and I needed to tell you I was sorry for judging you and the others so harshly. Axel and his wife even brought boxes of cakes and cookies to thank the staff." She brushed a wisp of escaped hair from her ponytail away from her cheek.

If she mentioned them being friends once more, Bash would rip their bench apart using only his hands.

By making her comfortable being around him, she'd gotten *too* comfortable and jammed his ass into the friendzone. And no fucking man with a working dick wanted in that zone. Now he knew he had to take this to the next phase before she offered him a friendship bracelet and sleepovers to watch Patrick Swayze movies.

Once again, Bash wondered if it was worth it to chase a woman who threw up emotional roadblocks at every turn, but as soon as that thought formed, another raced after it, reminding him he'd never felt this strongly before.

And it wasn't the cliché of wanting what he couldn't have.

Getting his dick wet every night no longer interested him. He wanted everything else that came with a relationship.

For instance, if she were his woman, he'd pull her onto his lap and cuddle her close to let her know her worries were unnecessary. Lots of folks had a negative opinion of the Diablos.

They were far from saintly, and that was the ugly truth. They'd done awful shit and would do more in the future if it came up.

It was a tough world out there, and Bash had joined the Diablos to make things better, following their rules.

Charlotte's opinion was warranted.

He wasn't sure if her sister's friends were better or worse than the Diablos. But one thing was for sure - he'd protect her no matter what.

He wanted to be the wall at her back, the protection at her front. And once he got past all her shields, he would corrupt his little darling nurse.

"Will you accept my apology, Ben?"

Shit. Real naming him did a number on Bash's dick. He wanted to hear her screaming it or sighing it into his mouth after fucking ten orgasms out of her.

"I will. On one condition…"

Charlotte frowned, and Bash smirked at her trepidation.

He bet her innocent mind was producing all kinds of dirty conditions.

Not today. But he would one day.

"What's that?"

"Come to the club cookout next week."

Phase two was going to be slowly introducing Charlotte into his world.

Before she could refuse, he interjected. "It's the only way I can accept your apology, darling. You judged me and my boys, didn't you? My feelings are hurt. This will wipe the slate clean." Bash was so full of shit he had to bite his cheek to stop from grinning.

"Fine. But don't think I don't know what you just did, Ben Laurent." She knocked his thigh with hers.

A burning started in Bash's lower abdomen. Lust so strong, he nearly groaned aloud.

He remembered when the club started making money, and all members got a fat check. The satisfaction of having Charlotte agree to attend the club event outweighed the payout.

Phase two, he thought, as he watched her take a slow sip from a bottle of orange juice, was in motion. And he couldn't wait to get her to that place where they were together.

Bash

When Friday rolled around, Bash spent the entire day with his head in spreadsheets and on calls with the Irish Murphys, who were in town for their usual monthly drug drop.

Typically, Bash wasn't part of the welcome committee at the docks. Tomb managed that side of the business when the Irish transported cheap prescription drugs from Canada.

It had been rinse and repeat with little hassles for a while. Until tonight, when Tomb called the clubhouse, saying that Harvey's boys had been spotted by the docks, Bash had grabbed his jacket and followed Axel, Chains, Diamond, and Splice out the door.

"I'm just in the mood to punch a clown. I hope they start some shit." Splice warned as he swung a leg down from his bike.

"What's got you all riled up?" asked Chains before Bash could. Splice wasn't usually the first to a fight, even if he could handle his own. "Flavor of the day didn't put out last night?" he joked, but Splice didn't grin back.

"Not everything is about my dick."

"It usually is." Added Diamond, the ring through his eyebrow glinted under the moon. They got no more out of Splice because he walked off toward Tomb and the three Murphys, who were already talking with Axel.

Bash wasn't there to keep the minutes or to make a record. This meeting wasn't legally happening, and if anyone ever got caught, the Murphys didn't know the Diablos and vice versa. When he joined the others, he only half listened, ready to pitch in if it was needed. For a long time now, the docks and ports around Utah were monitored by Diablo sources. Paid and used well for import and export deals.

Axel talked to their cargo inspector on the payroll and got information about the Riot Brothers.

"He said they've been coming by every few days to talk with a guy called Hal. He handles the paperwork in the office. Bash, you and Diamond see what you can find out from Hal."

"Got it," he agreed.

It was about half a mile to the dock's front office, not even a few steps, and his phone vibrated in his inside pocket.

Bash hummed, seeing Charlotte's message.

She'd started texting him a few days ago. Silly, nothing things, and it was fast becoming the highlight of his day.

Charlotte: My neighbor took in a package for me. Did you send Prince lots of treats???

Charlotte: He's in heaven, Bash!

She included a picture of the cat on top of the pet hamper he asked Scarlett to find online for him. Going to her for help was a mistake - the old ladies' gang swarmed him, firing nosy questions like bullets.

Charlotte: You've spoiled him, Bash. Thank you. and Meow-Meow from Prince.

"Yikes, what is that thing?" probed Diamond, spying on Bash's phone screen.

"It's Charlotte's cat."

"Cat? Look at the size of its head! Are you sure it didn't escape from the zoo? That monster is gigantic. I'd hate to see its litter tray."

Bash: I'm glad he approves.

Charlotte: You're the best. This honestly is so cute of you.

Now she thought he was cute. Bash's teeth hurt as he ground the back molars to interrupt his groaning frustration. He was one step away from being her forever friend.

Approaching the office, he thumbed out a fast reply text.

Bash: Bikers are never cute, darling. I'll show you why the next time I see you. Gotta go.

"How's it going with the little nursey?" asked Diamond. "Haven't seen her around the clubhouse..." he left it hanging like a veiled accusation.

"She'll be at the cookout next week." Even if he had to carry her over his shoulder, no more nice guy act. It was getting him nowhere other than cementing his role as her maid of fucking honor at her wedding to some schmuck one day.

That would happen over his rotting corpse. If a day ever came that Charlotte started dating elsewhere, he'd turn into a sabotaging mastermind. Killing men before they could reach her front door.

For all the time he spent with Charlotte, he wanted so much more. He wanted to knit her fucking soul to his, carry her around so he could look at her when he needed to.

"I wish you luck, my friend," Diamond declared, clapping him on the shoulder with an amused glint. "Women are complicated as fuck. Not all chicks are made to be with bikers."

Bash's jaw ticked.

He knew that all too well. Many women who entered their world over the years quickly left after realizing the unconventional biker culture wasn't for them. And because Bash knew the club bylaws back and front, he knew there was a law that stated if the patched brothers did not accept an old lady—for many reasons—but usually if she couldn't fit in or was causing too much trouble between the brotherhood, they could veto that woman. She couldn't come to any clubhouse gathering ever again.

The brothers hadn't used that bylaw in a long time, but he'd heard talk about how Axel's ex was vetoed after his daughter was born. He wasn't around for that first spread of toxicity by the president's ex, but he'd witnessed Selena's malice many times when she rolled through the doors, hoping to cause chaos before she left again.

Charlotte was nothing like that.

She'd fit in.

He just had to get her to that comfortable place between them first.

At the office, Bash and Diamond stepped through the doorway and saw a middle-aged man raise his head from behind the desk.

"Something I can help you guys with?" he asked, a cigarette in his mouth.

"You sure can. Hal, isn't it?"

"Yeah." He replied wearily.

"I need some information, Hal. There's been some people coming by the docks recently, talking to you, and we want to know what they wanted."

Hal squinted and puffed on the cigarette. "Customer details are private. You guys should know that."

"So you know who we are." Smiled a friendly Bash, as he leaned a hip against Hal's desk and picked up a framed picture, showing Hal's eight kids. Damn, Hal got busy. "Nice family, Hal." He remarked and put the frame back, but now the manager was spooked as the color dripped out of his face.

It wasn't as if Bash had threatened his family. But people read into words in the way they wanted to. If Hal thought Bash was threatening his family, who was he to tell him he wouldn't do that?

"So, about this information, Hal."

The pair left the office with the info they needed not long later, and they rejoined the others.

"They've been trying to get a freighter in from Mexico, but they're pissed because the officials won't bypass the paperwork. Hal was helpful. Do we pay him?"

Chains chuckled. "We do."

"Twitchy fella." Remarked Diamond. "Might want to give him a little bonus for a job well done for stopping the Riot Brothers in their nasty little tracks."

"I'll get on that right after I buy Ruin a brand new dolly." Chains rolled his eyes.

Bash lit up a cigarette and toked slowly, inviting the nicotine down into his lungs. Once Axel finished with the Murphys, they climbed into their Hummer and left the docks. The prez then turned to them. "So, the Mexicans part two? I can't get those motherfuckers off my ass."

"Didn't Veronica Ruiz take over when old Julio earned his concrete boots?"

"Yeah. And there was a provisional agreement she wouldn't bring her shit to these shores again. We don't know if it's her they're dealing with yet. Let's head back to the clubhouse. I've gotta make some calls to the fucking Mexicans!" Griped Axel.

It was nights like this Bash was grateful he wasn't the decision maker. He could work a spreadsheet like no one's business and memorize all the crucial details in case they had to shred their paper trail one day. But he'd loathe being the one who had to wear the headaches like Axel did.

As a group, they headed for their bikes.

As always, when Bash had moments when he wasn't knee deep in club fires, his thoughts turned to a stubborn nurse, all sweet and ripe for the plucking.

And as his actions showed, he went from being nice to being a total creep when he rode by her house and saw all the lights were off. She was most likely snuggled up in bed. Alone. Which was a pity. He'd like to test her bed out, see how strong it was, and see if it could cope with the vigorous games he had in store for them.

Hungry and tired, Bash rode home.

And he slept in his bed alone.

Bash

Leaving the Diablos grounds for a night out was rare for the boys.

They did most of their drinking in the clubhouse, where they could play the music as loud as they wanted, and any fighting that might spring up wasn't with someone who would pull a switchblade. Some civilians with only half a brain saw the club cuts and took it as a red flag to cause issues. The last Diablos night out was a wild business meet-up with the Apollo Kingsmen. Drinks were flowing, handshakes were happening, and then some drunk hick swung a chair at Diamond.

Of all the bikers to challenge, the fool chose the biggest.

Bash got a split eyebrow and busted knuckles that night, because you never abandon your friends in a fight.

They were at Chains' Den. The strip joint he'd revamped into a money-making machine. It's not just for creeps anymore. His wife was an accountant, and one of her sisters was a party planner. When those two began relentlessly discussing the revenue Chains was losing, the establishment shifted to hosting exclusive women-only parties every other Saturday, generating more profit in that single weekend than the entire month combined.

Bash was uninterested in watching a woman shake her goodies, so he didn't bother looking at the stage.

Now, if *his* woman was up there.

Nah, scratch that. If Charlotte was partially dressed and other men were checking her out with the same inappropriate thoughts he had, he would go ballistic.

He'd start wars. And break necks.

Fortunately, she was a good girl nurse.

One day she'd do a striptease, but only for his nasty eyes to feast on.

There wasn't much else to do but drink his beer and think about a woman he wanted more than his next breath. He listened to the conversation while Axel said something that made Amos from the Kingsmen laugh.

Little did Bash know, his good girl nurse was very near.

Charlotte

"No more!" she protested.

As sweet and fruity as the cocktails tasted, she wasn't an alcohol lover.

After a long, exhausting shift dealing with one disaster after another, caused by the staff incompetence, Charlotte's defenses were low when she said yes to going out for drinks with Toni. She had second thoughts about her choice, but didn't want to seem cowardly. She'd prefer to be at home watching her little murder shows and wearing moisturizing socks.

Her wide-legged vintage jeans were the perfect excuse for her to go out. She looked at the washed denim with a smile. The lower portion was decorated in floral colors. They were her style, and she felt attractive with the heeled boots and low-cut blouse tucked into the front of the jeans. It wasn't often she got fancy. No one was giving her beauty prizes for the scrubs she wore every day.

She had even taken the effort to apply makeup. Who was she? Miss USA?

Snorting to herself, she looked around the bar and caught a pair of brown eyes looking their way. The man smirked and raised his glass.

"Aren't you going to smile back at him?" Asked Toni, who'd noticed the exchange. Lottie shook her head. The stranger wasn't the man she wanted to give smiles to. It had been days since she'd seen Bash. He'd explained work at his club had kept him busy.

The better she knew Bash, the stronger her curiosity became. Against her own volition and rationality. Because most nights, when she wasn't texting stupid things to him, she was scouring the internet. It was unbelievable what she found.

Not necessarily about the Diablos.

Yet, significant information was available on various biker clubs, their functioning, and the position of women in those clubs. She delved into countless blog posts from former old ladies or the ex-partners of bikers. They revealed so much of the biker culture and hierarchy.

It was organized like politics, and women didn't have many rights back in the day, especially not in that ultra-masculine environment. Lottie wondered if it was the same today with the Diablos. She thought about Casey, Denver's wife. She appeared as someone who wouldn't give up her rights in a male-dominated society. That woman possessed a superior, outspoken, get-shit-done attitude.

If Lottie was in Bash's world, how would he and the others treat her?

Some of those blog posts were far from complimentary to MCs, which scared her. But everything she'd read didn't match up to the man she knew.

As was typical, she'd been in her thoughts for too long, and when she blinked back into focus, Toni was talking to two men at the nearest table.

Please don't invite them over. That was the last thing Lottie needed by pretending she was interested in someone else's boring conversation.

"Not tonight, babe. But give me your number, and I'll call you sometime." Toni said, grabbing her phone; she put in the guy's number and then turned back to Lottie. If only Lottie had her confidence. With her job, she was all over it, and she could handle catastrophes in her sleep. But anything remotely personal, and she felt like the new kid in school, unable to find the homeroom.

"You don't have to stick with me if you want to sit with those guys," she offered, hoping Toni would jump at the chance so she could go home to the cat.

"Hell no, this is girl's night. We need shots!"

Lottie groaned. "Please, no. Anything but that. What about a soda?"

"C'mon, Lottie. When you said you wanted to go out, I thought you'd loosen up. Don't be a bore all your life. I promise to have you home before your glass slipper dissolves." Toni laughed at her joke.

But it wasn't funny.

And as always, the mocking was at Lottie's expense.

Alcohol had reduced her inclination to maintain peace. But a realization hit her square in the chest. Was Toni a genuine friend? Lottie certainly wouldn't pick at someone constantly for what they didn't do.

"Don't *you* be a *bitch* all your life." She snapped. Hurt and anger tangled up inside of her. That Lottie couldn't be herself with one of the few people she trusted hurt a lot. Why did she always have to meet someone else's expectations or be seen as inferior?

It was extremely exhausting, and Lottie had reached her tolerant limits.

She stared at Toni, whose shaped eyebrows had shot up into her hairline. It was shocking, since Lottie hardly ever snapped. She wasn't a pushover. But she realized she'd been dumb for not telling people off when they tried to boss her around for how to live.

"Hey, I didn't mean…"

"You always mean it, but you think adding har-har you can get away with being cruel. It's not like it's the first time you've called me boring. Just because I don't want to bounce on a thousand dicks and get drunk every night. Since when did dicks become the benchmark of a perfect life? I must have missed that breaking news story."

Now she was fired up and couldn't keep her mouth shut. Lottie stared at Toni and then looked at the eight shooter glasses of blue Aftershock on the table. Suddenly, Lottie snatched two tiny shot glasses and gulped them down. And then she almost died when the citrus and mint liquid hit her stomach.

"Does this make me a better friend, huh? How about this?" Two more shots went down.

"Oh, my god, Lottie. What are you doing?" Gaped Toni, bubbling with stunned amusement. And for once, Lottie enjoyed shocking her friend. She chugged two more drinks, hating the taste, but still swallowed the last two without making a face. She knew her stomach would pay the price for chugging eight shots in defiance.

"Isn't this how we have fun? Am I less boring now? Do I live up to your fucking standards, Toni? Maybe I need a few one-night stands before I'm less dull and more on your level."

Lottie could sense the rapid effects of the liquor as her blood heated and her skin warmed. Her thoughts turned fearless and uncensored.

Uncaring if she hurt someone else's feelings. Why should she care when no one ever gave that consideration to hers?

"You're being crazy, Lottie. You know I always joke with you. I mean nothing by it. But..." Of course, there was a but. There was always a but. *You're a nice girl, Lottie, but. But if you only changed this. But if you only did that, you'd be a better person.*

"But yeah, I want you to be happy and out of your comfort zone sometimes."

"It's called a comfort zone for a reason. Partying and anonymous dicks are happiness to you, right? That's fine for you, Toni." She pointed a finger, "but it's not for me. I don't judge you, but it's a free-for-all judgment for what I do, right?"

She detested the excuse people made, claiming they said hurtful things for the sake of others. Lottie saw it as passive aggression disguised with honey.

"Babe, you're taking something simple too seriously. It's not that big of a deal. Let's relax. I'd suggest a drink, but you had them all." She tittered, and Lottie answered with a scowl.

"So, what I'm hearing is, try harder, Lottie? Hmm. What Would Toni Do?" Lottie reached over the table and seized Toni's small clutch purse, finding what she was looking for. Paying no attention to Toni's astonishment, she unsealed the small silicone container and began consuming the red gummies.

"What are you doing?"

She swallowed before answering. "You offered me an edible earlier and called me a chicken when I said no. Now we're twins, Toni." She snapped, sitting with her back against the booth seating.

"Lottie, for fuck's sake. You ate them all? There were four in there! I would have only given you half a gummy."

"Screw it. I'm wild now. I'm you, but with smaller boobs." She scowled. But internally, she was thinking, *oh shit*. She scarfed down four edibles when she'd never had one before. And the eight shots. Her brain panicked. An analytical overthinker did not make an excellent recreational drug taker, because now her mind was conjuring up every terrible scenario of what could happen. Every week, she treated drug use and overdoses in the ER. She saw what people did for fun and how it affected them.

She was a woman of science, not emotions, but she'd reacted emotionally with her stupid outburst. She just had to be calm and keep it together. Then something wonderful... or crazy happened, and Lottie let all that worry drift away on an exhale.

What would be would be. Wasn't that the famous saying?

It was time to act like the wild woman she professed to be. So she grabbed her purse and jumped to her feet.

"This bar is boring. I want to go somewhere they have dancing."

Toni cursed, but then followed suit. Her friend appeared to still be in a state of disbelief. "I created a monster."

"Nope." pointed out Lottie, a little lightheaded, but super calm and floaty. "I created myself. Let's hit the road."

"Wait outside for me. I need the bathroom. I know just the place we can go to dance." Toni said.

Once outside, the breeze cooled Lottie's face as she leaned against the wall. She grinned at one of the sturdy door people when they glanced her way, but something grabbed Lottie's attention. She narrowed her eyes at a cluster of men entering a strip club across the street. They wore leather jackets and jeans, and even at night, she could see who those leather jackets belonged to, with the brilliant white insignias adorned on the back.

They were the Diablo Disciples bikers.

But one caught Lottie's attention and stole her breath.

With a cigarette to his lips, Bash was walking into that strip club behind his friends.

And then her stomach dropped as they disappeared inside, the bouncers closing the doors behind the bikers. Why would he be going into a place like that? Obviously for the entertainment. He wanted to see tits and asses gyrating in his face.

Oh, god.

The drinks she'd gulped now felt like sea water in her stomach as she pictured Bash with random beautiful women. Women who were confident in their sexuality and didn't hold back from kissing him or grinding on his lap.

She'd worried he might be dating or casually hooking up with women. Since she didn't plan on making a move, she avoided discussing his love life. Preferring to keep her head buried in the sand.

Whose fault was it if he was looking for someone else? Those ladies were most likely brimming with confidence and sexiness. Complete opposite of a novice virgin.

She wanted that for Bash; she thought with a sinking heart. Not at all sick with jealousy at the idea of his rough hands all over someone else's hips.

With the dense rocks in her stomach and a drowning feeling in her chest, she turned when she heard Toni's approach. "I know just the place!" she announced, flipping her hair with a smile. "All the guys who hang out at this bar are sexy as fuck."

Ugh. It was agony for her. She couldn't stop thinking about Bash being wooed across the street. She didn't want to chill with hot guys. The only guy she found attractive was at a strip club, most likely with two blondes on his lap playing with his hair and showing off their breasts.

Lottie was never so glad that Toni bailed on once they got to the next bar. Toni was immediately set upon like vultures, and she'd gone along willingly to dance with a couple of guys. Lottie found a quiet spot to look at her phone and was disappointed by the lack of texts from Bash.

It wasn't unusual. They weren't regular texters, but she still felt a sharp stab of disappointment, and now her inebriated mind was verging on a jealous rage.

He must be getting his brains banged out.

Did strippers give happy finishes these days?

She could only hope the glitzy lighting would temporarily blind Bash, so he couldn't see the gyrating nakedness. Yeah, that was the best outcome, she thought with a sigh rushing around her chest. He had forty-year-old eyeballs. It wasn't unrealistic.

He had gorgeous eyes.

Bedroom eyes.

Intense eyes that promised uncharted things.

God, she loved his eyes. She didn't want him to be blind, but she didn't want him being horny for other women.

When Toni asked if it was okay if she took off with a guy, Lottie was glad because she jumped in a cab outside.

Blame it on the shots. Blame it on the edibles, blame it on her insane jealousy.

"Are you sure that's where you want to go, lady?" he asked, looking at her through the rearview mirror. Lottie nodded and laid her temple against the cooling window. It had been over an hour since she'd watched Bash walking into The Den. He might still be getting railed by a woman who knew how to send a man insane with lust.

That woman wasn't Lottie. She couldn't even touch Bash's arm without being queasy and overwhelmed.

But how dare he go into a club where women took their clothes off when he knew, *he knew*, he was her friend! He'd crossed a line, a sacred friendship oath, and she would remind him of his egregious error and offer him the chance to make it up to her with groveling and coffee gifts.

Especially the coffee.

Bash

The meeting with the Murphys at The Den was brief.

Afterward, Bash and the boys hopped on their bikes and returned to the clubhouse. Axel split off from them and hooked up Scarlett, carrying his old lady into the back office. Chains sat at the bar talking to his old lady on the phone. Tomb's wife was already at the club, so he went to play a game of pool with her.

Unwilling to watch everyone suck faces with each other, Bash headed down to their gym, changed into shorts and a muscle t-shirt, and did a chest workout for a while until his upper body burned with fatigue. Still, he felt good at the finish when he swiped a towel over his sweaty face.

His body was broken. Not physically. For forty, he was in the best shape of his life and intended to be for the foreseeable future. But with his sex drive, it wanted to own only one chestnut-haired beauty, with a sharp tongue and an addictive blush. His dick wouldn't work for anyone else, even if he'd wanted to. Which he didn't. But it fucking blew that he couldn't have Charlotte in his bed right now.

She plagued his mind day and night.

When he gave a passing glance to the dancers on the stripper poles, all he saw was her shy face dancing for him, and it made his craving growl even more to own her.

Worse still, needing her was screwing with his concentration. Bash was completely lost when Axel turned to him for his opinion earlier, because he was too focused on Charlotte and how he could see her that night.

He was acting like a lovesick kid.

The truth was, he was addicted to being around that woman.

Her laugh was a song. Her intellect was a bedtime story.

If she'd been a puzzle, Bash would have broken her open to see how she worked, just like he did with engines.

He'd experienced countless pleasures over the years. Kinky, vanilla, everything in between. But sitting next to her and sharing sandwiches, eating those cookies she baked especially for his sweet tooth, and listening to her cat stories was about the best time Bash ever had.

As good as all that was, he needed more.

It wasn't anything he could avoid.

Not that he'd tried to. The second he clapped eyes on Charlotte, Bash was determined to have her. But with any cautiously constructed plans, he couldn't have known she wouldn't feel that instant pull like he had.

He needed his fingerprints all over her little pristine body, and it was slowly driving Bash mad not to have her in his life, in the ways he craved to have her.

By his side. In his bed. On his lap. Eating lunch at a clubhouse bench in the backyard or cuddling into his ribs during a cookout bonfire. Relying on him. Needing him for everything. Having her on the back of his bike only once hadn't been enough. That sacred spot was reserved for women like her, and he couldn't wait any longer to feel Charlotte's arms latched around him as she rode backpack style.

When all the present-day brothers were still single, they'd sit around drinking whiskey in the backyard after a hard graft and speculate about who would take the plunge first and offer a woman his property patch. They considered it a joke, being staunch bachelors. Anyone in an MC will tell you that a biker is inundated with pussy every night.

And then, one by one, starting with Chains, Bash watched his brothers falling for their old ladies, and now those women wore property patches.

He'd never wanted it. He didn't oppose it, but didn't expect it to happen.

But for weeks now, he'd skim his gaze over her incredible body and wonder what she'd look like wearing only his *Property of Bash* patch on the back of a custom made cut and nothing else. *Fuck*, those images did a number on him. It was all he could think about, and most days, he had to jerk off to cool down.

Seeing Charlotte in a property cut, made especially for her, would be something he couldn't recover from. It would be the beginning of everything.

And on that insane, complicated thought, Bash pulled a grey hoodie on and then slipped back into his cut. Wearing it on clubhouse grounds was mandatory. But it was also a badge of honor. He was hungry and ready to devour a plate of whatever Denver had cooked on the grill earlier, if anything was left.

But then his phone started ringing, and Bash got annoyed when he saw it was the prospect at the gates.

"What is it, probie?"

"Yo, Bash. You need to come outside. There's a drunk chick here insisting we let her inside."

Packs of women would try to sneak in on non-party nights, so Bash rolled his eyes. He was about to tell those idiot prospects to deal with it, but then Dillion spoke. "She says she knows you."

It was clear to Bash that something was off. He didn't date long enough to have a woman stalking at his door. It had to be a sweet bottom wannabe trying to gain entry.

"Do your job and send them away, probie."

"You got it, boss," Dillion said, but then, in the background, he heard. "You tell Benjamin to come to this gate right now, or I swear I will put some whoop-ass on you, little boy, the likes of which you won't recover from. And I know how to set bones but also how to break them."

That voice was unmistakable.

Even if his brain hadn't recognized it, his gut would have because it flooded with lust, and he barked into the phone. "Make sure she doesn't leave, and don't lay a fucking finger on her, or you're dead meat."

"I wasn't gonna touch her," scoffed Dillion, amused. "She crazy."

"I am not crazy. You're crazy." He heard his girl say as Bash hung up, tossed his phone on the bed, and bolted through the clubhouse. It probably took him twenty seconds to walk to the gates, controlled by electronics and constantly guarded by a guy.

He couldn't think of why Charlotte would be at his club.

Not when she stuck steadfastly to her rules of only engaging with him in neutral territory. But he was elated when he signaled Dillion to open the gate, and there she was.

Holy fuck. His nurse was here, swaying gently on her heels while holding onto the fence.

"Finally." She huffed, glaring at him. "I've been waiting here for over an hour."

Shit, just hearing Charlotte's sugary voice made Bash rock hard. Her presence made every muscle in his body go stiff. There was little room to focus on anything but the screaming need for fast relief, preferably from Charlotte's hands or sweet lips.

She'd come to him.

Whatever her drunken reason, she was here for him. And that alone was enough to tip Bash over the edge.

Bash cocked an eyebrow at the prospect, ready to rearrange the little shit's face if he'd left Charlotte standing out here unguarded for an hour. But Dillion grinned and shook his head. "Three minutes, tops, boss."

"An hour, at least." She insisted. "Don't listen to this little boy. He's a known liar. Everyone says so."

Dillion chuckled at her accusation and mouthed, "She crazy."

Fuck, she was so sexily hammered. Bash smirked and stepped forward to slide an arm around Charlotte's waist.

"Come inside, little darling."

"That's what I've been trying to do." She hiccupped, leaning into him, light as a feather. "This boy said he didn't know me, but I said I knew *you*! I should rearrange his face."

"You can later." Chuckled Bash even as Charlotte pulled a face at the probie.

"Tell him you know me, Ben. Go on, tell him."

"I know you, baby."

"See." she pointed, all smug at the prospect. And then she got even cuter by sticking her tongue out at him.

"How did you get here, darling?"

"I was in a cab."

Shit. Bash frowned because it was a decent drive from town to the clubhouse. "By yourself?"

"Yep. Toni ditched me for a guy, and I needed some words with you, so here I am."

Some words? This he had to hear. His lips twitched around the edges at her chastising tone. Approaching the doorway, he tapped in the code and steered Charlotte through first, but he grabbed her hand once inside. A lot of his brothers were married, but a lot weren't, and he'd gouge out their eyes if they licked their chops when they got an eyeful of Charlotte in her tits-hugging shirt. If she'd rejected his hand, he was going to throw her over his shoulder, but she squeezed his fingers and it settled a beastly feeling inside of his torso.

Intent on leading her to the stairwell and up to the second floor where the primary patched brothers' bedrooms were located, she pulled on his hand, and he stopped.

"Wait. I want to have a look." She said, leaning deeper into his ribs. Bash understood it had more to do with how much hard liquor she'd drunk and not because she wanted to cuddle up to him. It didn't stop him from enjoying her closeness.

"You could have come anytime. It was your choice not to."

She swiveled her head and squinted at him. Bash bit the inside of his cheek and wondered how many of him she saw.

"Don't you start that, Benjamin Laurent."

Fuck. Full naming him? She even pulled her hand away to poke him in the chest, but then slid her fingers back into his. Only his mother used his full name, and she was happy living in New Mexico with his stepfather, so he hadn't heard it in person for months.

"Oh, I know her. She cuts my hair." Proclaimed Charlotte, not at all quiet, and she started waving at Nina, sitting on Tomb's lap. Tomb gave a grin and a chin lift. Nina called back, "Hey, sweetie."

"This place is so big," she said, her eyes everywhere while leaning on him. "I didn't know it would look so neat. It's so cute, Bash."

Cute. She thought his clubhouse was cute.

"Is Casey here?"

"Not tonight."

"Aww, bummer, I know her. Did I tell you I've had some drinks, Bash? My stomach is so full. I had some drinks and then so many shots because Toni pissed me off." Every other word she said ran into each other, but Bash caught the gist of what she was saying.

"Why did she piss you off?"

"She says I'm boring and no fun, and I need to bounce on a bunch of dicks, and then I won't be boring anymore. I ate some edibles, but I don't think they were real because I feel great. Maybe I'm immune."

Shit, not only drunk, but his girl was high, too?

Bash interrupted her by cradling Charlotte's face. "How many edibles, baby?"

"Um, like fifty." She said, and Bash nearly died on the spot. She was a nurse and must know not to do that shit, but then she giggled and almost head-butted his chest. "Four. But I feel good, like I could fly. Do you think I could fly, Bash? I bet I would beat you at flying."

"What's wrong with your chick, Bash?" asked the VP, approaching from the games room. His arm was around Monroe's shoulder, and two of her sisters towed at Chains' other side. It wasn't unusual to see the girls around. They'd taken to Chains like a big brother protector.

"She's high as a fucking kite," Bash said, tightness in his throat, and he hooked up her hand again even as Charlotte tilted into his shoulder and whispered, not so quietly. "Oh my god, does he have three wives? Do bikers do that? You better not have three wives, Ben."

Monroe burst out laughing, and her sisters pulled disgusted faces in unison.

"That's our cue to find popcorn. We'll be in the kitchen." One of them said, and they dashed away.

"He's only my hubby," Monroe told Charlotte and introduced herself.

"Oops. My bad. I'm just learning about bikers. There's so much stuff online. Have you seen? Fan clubs and blog posts are talking about these guys. Ruin is their favorite."

"Of course, that moody psycho is," griped Chains, and he shared a look with Bash, silently asking if Charlotte was okay by jutting his chin her way. Bash answered with a nod.

"Come on, baby, let's get you a coffee."

"I don't want a coffee. I want to scold you! Now I remember why I came. You distracted me."

"I know." He appeased, half-laughing, and started the walk to the stairwell.

"You were at a strip club, Bash. I saw you! Did you bring strippers home?" While scowling and poking him, she rambled with a soulful gaze and her eyebrows furrowed, causing a stirring feeling in his stomach.

She'd seen him earlier heading to their meeting and figured he was there for a stripper fun time? And now she'd tracked him down in a little jealous rage.

Bash couldn't hold back his grin.

Charlotte scowled deeper, and he thought of five ways to get her to smile at him. All of those ways involved his tongue on her body.

"Come with me," he said, guiding her. They took the stairs along the hallway, where Bash pushed open his door.

"Is this your bedroom?"

"Yeah, only when I stay at the club."

"But you have a house?" she asked, staying close to him. As Bash closed the door above her head, she glanced at the simple room. All that was in the room was a bed, a dresser, and an armchair. It was somewhere to stay overnight when he didn't feel like riding home, especially if they had late meetings. Sweet bottoms and the house mouse ensured the entire club was kept clean. Bash wasn't the neatest person; he dropped clothes where he took them off and left dishes on the counter at home, but the sweet bottoms had always taken care of the patched brothers' properties. Especially since Scarlett started a cleaning service so they could earn a paycheck.

"Yeah, darling, I have a house." One she refused invitations to.

Another little huff came from her, and Bash smiled. She smelled incredible. Like musk and temptation. The infamous forbidden fruit. He resisted dipping his nose into her glossy hair and inhaling her.

"I bet you take all the strippers there, don't you?"

He was fighting his hard-on with all of his will. Standing so close, if she brushed against him again, she would feel what her proximity did to him.

Charlotte wasn't doing anything but existing, and Bash was balancing his sanity, jonesing for her in the worst way.

Fuck it. Bash leaned down and pressed his nose to the beating pulse on her neck. Hearing how she gasped, he inhaled her scent. The battering of his heart matched that of his growing cock.

So that he didn't scare her away, Bash put his ass in the chair. Not that Charlotte noticed; she'd turned her back to him, waving her hands.

"And another thing…"

What was the first thing? He wondered with a smile.

Damn, he loved seeing wasted Charlotte.

She was letting rip with her unfiltered thoughts and loose tongue, and he wanted all of her so he didn't interrupt.

"You can't be hanging around strippers, okay?" she spun around and then slapped a hand on her forehead. "Woo, head rush. Yeah, anyway. No strippers for you, Benjamin. You're *my* friend, not theirs. I disapprove, and I hated seeing you going in there knowing gorgeous women would flock to you like… like, what flocks?" she gestured a dismissive hand in the air. "They'd be all over you, is what I mean. Oh, gosh, is it hot? Did you turn on the heat?"

She was staking a claim on him. Did she realize that?

Bash

Bash felt a rush of approval bubble up in his throat.

"Anyway, that's what I came to say. I should go now." She remained motionless. Bash wouldn't let it happen if she made a move toward the door. When he knifed out of the seat, her eyes got big, and she tilted her chin to look up at him.

"You are the tallest man on earth." She remarked breathlessly. Blinking slowly.

And then she did something that made his head explode when she popped open her jeans' button, unzipped them, and started pushing them down her gorgeous legs. Far from objecting, Bash would be thrilled by Charlotte giving him a striptease. He'd beg if he had to, but she'd made his tongue go dry, and now his heart triple-beat against his ribcage.

"Ah, god, that's better. I can breathe again." This was the same woman who got shy if she accidentally touched his hand while they shared food. And now she was wearing only a blouse and black briefs. The dirty bastard inside Bash lapped up the half-naked sight like he'd been sent an express gift from someone above who loved him.

Beautiful girl.

She was *exquisite*.

He licked his lower lip and tried to recall why he was a decent guy.

He was in so much trouble.

She was an oblivious cocktease, wiggling her ass to peel off the jeans. Bash was losing it, with blood pounding in his ears, ready to let out all the dirty thoughts he had about her.

"Where was I? Oh yes, I remember now. I was leaving."

"You can't leave while you're smashed, Charlotte. Sit down." He gave her a little nudge to put her ass on the edge of his bed. Then crouched down and started taking off her boots and the jeans hooked onto them.

"You could take me home on the bike. I want to do it so many times, it was so much fun."

"I'll take you out on the bike whenever you want to, but not tonight."

"Boo, you're no fun, Bash." She pouted and ran her fingers through his hair. The pleasure and agony conflicted within him, unsure of his feelings for this version of her. He wanted her to touch him when she was stone-cold sober, when she was his scowling little darling.

The purity in her innocent eyes instantly aroused Bash. So many unspoken truths hung in the air between them.

He was ready to get real, be upfront and see what Charlotte thought about it.

If she ran away from him, he'd chase her.

Clearly, he'd allowed his psycho passion out of the box because he was almost licking his chops as he watched Charlotte wandering around his room, touching everything as she did. He'd have to take her to his house so she could roll on his couches and bed, get her scent on everything. On the third lap, she stumbled, and Bash shot forward to catch the little darling before she face-planted the floor.

She giggled at his save and grabbed onto his forearms. "Caught me."

"Yeah, I did. You're a little brat when you're drunk." He hummed and held her steady before he sat down and put her on his lap. "Stay where I put you, Charlotte," Bash warned and watched her eyes haze over with lust. The heat was blatant and unmasked, and he was aware of the potential addiction it held.

"I'm hardly drunk," she made a *pft* sound in his face but followed it by playing with his hair again, murmuring how soft it was. "You should do that more often," she went on, rolling one fingertip to his smiling mouth. "This crooked smile is so cute, did you know that? Ugh, I bet strippers tell you all the time how hot and irresistible you are."

They didn't, but he wanted to hear more about her thoughts. He was downright greedy for them.

"Do you think I'm hot and irresistible?"

Charlotte groaned and laid her forehead on his shoulder. "I wish you didn't look like you. I was fine before you looked like you," she babbled.

Not fully understanding her drunk train of thought, Bash only hummed and gripped the side of her thigh. He was a man who knew when to keep his trap shut and let his lady do the talking.

"I never liked men." She huffed as she played with his hair and beard. The bottom of Bash's stomach fell out. If she was a lesbian, he would throw himself off the nearest roof. He couldn't be half in love with a woman he had no chance with. But then she continued. "I wasn't sexually attracted to anyone. There's a word for it, but I can't remember it now. Wow, my head is so fuzzy. Make the room stop spinning, Bash." She said, groaning, and she fisted his shirt.

Despite his love for having her close, he didn't want his sweet girl to suffer. His hand moved in a stroking motion around her nape. "You ate a pound of fucking cannabis, baby. You're going to spin for a while."

She made a noise of anguish, and Bash felt it in his chest.

He smoked weed but hadn't tried edibles. He was baffled by her behavior. She was the most level-headed person he knew.

Weeks after Tomb and Nina resolved their marital issues, Bash recalled seeing the old ladies being uncharacteristically rowdy. It was discovered that they'd bought edibles and were high as kites. His brothers showed up quickly once they discovered what their wives were up to. Only Axel entered the room like a whirlwind, lifting Scarlett onto his shoulder and carrying her upstairs to her former bedroom.

"Hold on to me, Charlotte, and I'll stop the room from spinning."

"See." She jabbed him in the ribs, her face nuzzling his hoodie. "You say lovely things. Why do you have to be the first person I'm attracted to? It's so complicated."

If she'd shot his ass full of bullets, Bash would have been less stunned as his smile grew. Fucking finally, she admitted it.

She settled into his chest after she caressed his hair and beard some more.

"Why is it complicated, darling?"

"Because I thought you were in a dangerous gang like Nora's Thorn, but you're not bad, Bash." She giggled and flopped over his arm, swinging her legs over the chair. "Bad Bash. Bad, bad, Bash, watch out, ladies, he has a gorgeous face that will make your tummy feel funny. But you can't look at him too long because his face is perfect. And all you think about is kissing him and tasting his lips."

Bash wasn't complaining about her confessions. It was more than he could have hoped for.

He was on fire, and so fucking turned on.

She had secretly wanted to kiss him.

For minutes, he luxuriated in having her snuggled into him while she babbled incoherently about her shit night. Also forbidding him to play with strippers—her words. All the while, Bash soothed his girl through the worst of her high comedown. When she said the dizziness was better, she purred into his neck as he rubbed her upper back with circles.

More declarations came out of her perfect lips.

She said she loved spending time with him and couldn't wait to see him each day.

"I think I'm addicted to you, Bash." Her sweet sigh made Bash nearly burst. He knew she was stoned, and he shouldn't take advantage.

He *wouldn't*.

But his blood was burning to take her taste into his mouth.

Ah, fuck it.

He was no saint. Couldn't even pretend to be one.

With a growl, as Charlotte teased the fuck out of him by licking her lower lip, he crushed her mouth, swallowing her gasp of surprise. But then she did the sweetest thing ever, and she melted and gave in to his kiss. Inviting him in by opening her mouth, she raked her nails through his hair and mewled, arching into his body, stretching for more.

If what she said was true and his little darling hadn't been sexually attracted to anyone until him, then he was going to show her what a kiss could do. She might be high now, but he was about to send her head into the fucking clouds as he pushed his tongue into her waiting mouth and then sucked on hers. The sounds she made had his dick harder than a spike. Bash knew he couldn't take it further—even as his body disagreed. But kissing her was the best damn thing he'd ever waited for.

Sometimes cravings don't live up to the hype.

The first beer.

The first time staying out past curfew.

Dating a cheerleader.

Getting head for the first time hadn't been as good as his younger self had thought. The chick had nearly bitten his dick off with her braces.

But kissing Charlotte was a dream come true.

"So fucking sweet." He groaned into her lips, going deeper, tasting her as fast as he could, just like a glutton would with a piece of cake. As he slowed down, barely touching her tongue with little licks, she was like a wild thing, obsessed with kissing and wanting more and more.

Bash was here and very willing to provide.

Eventually, their kissing came to a natural stop. Bash peppered smaller kisses to her wet lips and nearly came in his sweatpants when he watched her lick her lips like she was savoring the taste of cotton candy, her eyes all unfocused and dreamy.

"I'll remind you of every word you've said when you're sober tomorrow." He warned.

They'd crossed into an unknown terrain with infinite possibilities on the other side, so he wasn't letting his little nurse shy away from him now.

"Psh. I have a fantastic memory." She jabbed him, then let her head flop on his shoulder. "I knew Bash would kiss like a god. He's too perfect; he can't be real." She talked like she didn't even realize she was sitting on him, with his taste lingering in her mouth.

His raging cock was all too real, and so was his thudding heart. He was completely infatuated with her, on the verge of serenading her with Barry White's lyrics.

Bash was this side of desperate to be her scratching post. To let Charlotte play with him like her favorite toy. But there was a shred of decency in him not to do that while she was intoxicated. *Fuck his fucking decency*. He groaned in agony.

"This is the best dream yet," she purred, rubbing her face on his goatee. "So real."

"Little darling," he chuckled, waiting until she looked him in the eyes. "I am real, and this is real. You're grinding on my dick."

She slowly blinked. "Hmm. I rarely do that in my dreams. But it feels perfect to have Bash all to myself."

The top of his skull burned with the scrape of her nails. *Jesus*, this woman was killing him. He'd schemed to play dirty tricks and use all his ingenuity to get her to fall for him. He didn't know she was already there. What a dumbass for not realizing it earlier.

Charlotte's words repeated in his mind, and he was feral for the answer. Basking in her skin's softness, he brushed his thumb against her mouth, pulling the lower lip down to touch the inner wetness.

"Is that what you want, Charlotte? To have me all to yourself?"

She flashed him a serene smile and leaned in until their foreheads touched. She'd started pawing at his chest and neck, trying to get at his skin. Bash groaned and shoved her hand up into his hoodie. Rubbing his belly seemed to make her happy, but it made him want her even more when she scratched his abs.

"Answer me like a good girl."

"Ugh, I like that. Why do I like that so much? Bash's good girl. It's like this thirst in my throat I can't quench." Her head lolled on his shoulder, and her hand stilled on his stomach.

She wanted to be his good girl.

Dream. Coming. Fucking. True.

Bash grunted and pressed his face into the side of Charlotte's honey-scented neck, scraping his teeth only a little, not even to mark—not yet. But she gasped and reared her head back, blinking slowly.

"Did you bite me?"

"Do you want me to?"

She hesitated, nothing but burning lust looking out of those hazel eyes, and Bash realized how lucky he was to be the one seeing it happen as she nibbled cutely on her lip, before nodding her head shyly.

He'd leave his teeth marks all over her silken skin if she asked him nicely.

His girl was a gift.

If only she'd given him these confessions months ago.

But they didn't stop coming.

While stoned and cuddled in Bash's arms, Charlotte told him the sweetest secrets to make him the happiest fucking man on earth.

It was too bad if she thought she was dreaming or talking to herself. He wasn't forgetting a word of it.

"Little darling, tell me again how you want to keep me." He coaxed diabolically.

"You are wicked." She poked, chuckling coyly. But she shared all her fantasies and private thoughts, and Bash soaked in each one like the greediest monster.

It might have been an hour. She'd grown quieter, and Bash knew he should put Charlotte to bed; it was late, and he wasn't driving her home tonight. But he couldn't let her free from his arms yet. She felt incredible bundled into him.

She'd shared so much with him.

Everything he'd remind her of tomorrow. There was no hiding from it now he had her truth. He was fucking happy, even if she had come to him in a way she might regret.

He would own the body, soul, skin, and bones of Charlotte Martin. He would own her desires and make them happen. There would be no crevice of her innocent mind he wouldn't know personally.

And he couldn't wait.

When she mumbled his name, he reminded her she wasn't alone by stroking her back to clasp her nape.

Eventually, she'd gone up on her knees so she could straddle his lap. Now they were groin to groin, and Bash hadn't been aware he could stay hard for so long. He was a medical marvel.

"I've got you. You're in my hands now, darling. Your body, mind, and heart are all safe." Bash didn't want to freak out Charlotte by bringing up anything serious tonight, especially since she let her guard down. He'd keep it for the morning. "Wanna know what's on my mind? How crazy happy I am that you came to me tonight?"

She nodded, all cute, and he smiled, running his thumb against the edge of her pointed chin. And when she sighed contently and then nestled closer, hiding her face in the crook of his shoulder, her tits rubbing against Bash's front, he felt a stirring of satisfaction in his chest. That noise of frustration he'd been enduring for months suddenly was silent because he had Charlotte against his body. Meant to be there.

"I'm considering how quickly I could make you whimper from a little over-the-clothes touching. And I'd give every dollar I have to know how you sound when you come for me." Her breath stuttered, and then she purred like a little cat and rubbed her face on his shirt, her fingers digging into his back. A mix of frustration and excitement in the sound as Bash lazily continued to caress her. It was an addiction touching her. He knew this latest version of Charlotte was all to do with what she'd taken tonight. The effects of that combo had loosened her up to a degree even he couldn't have hoped for.

Was he a bastard for encouraging it? Sure was. But would he stop himself from going too far? If she kept grinding on him in the way she was, he couldn't say how strong his morals would continue to be. At best, they were crumbling at the edges. And at worst, he was a degenerate aching to lap up her moans and cries.

"Can you imagine that?"

They'd been platonic all this time.

In Charlotte's mind, they were only friends. Not Bash's, but he was willingly pushing the boundaries. Breaking down the walls she'd erected almost on sight. Breaking through those walls with stroking affection was dangerous territory, but he couldn't hold himself at a distance.

She was a compulsion of the highest caliber, and he'd been offered unlimited access.

Bash was far from a squeaky-clean hero. If anything, he related more to a villain. And now he'd been presented with paradise on a lickable plate. Every devil on his shoulder shouted for him to take, take, *take*.

She's yours. Take her. Own her.

"You're so vocal. And dirty." She whispered in a tone filled with shy awe.

"I'll make it clear how much I want you, Charlotte. You're a dream come true," He replied with honesty. Every word was firm with the force of his desire. "You have no idea what noises I'll make for you, little darling. Groaning your name like a chant when you wrap these sweet lips around my hopeful cock. Cursing to the ceiling as I jet my come in your fluttering pussy, and then groaning again, when I watch it run down your thighs, knowing how wet I'm making you." Bash pressed against the hollow of her neck while peppering her skin with whisper kisses. "I won't hold anything back now. Do you understand?"

"God, Bash. Yeah, I understand," she moaned in return, color hitching a ride on the higher portion of her cheeks. Her legs clasped tighter on either side of his knees.

"All you need to do is ask, and I'll show you," he implied, urging her to give him the word. Though he knew he was close to losing control and he would fuck Charlotte only when she was in her sober mind. It didn't stop him teasing her, though. And he rasped the most indecent things in her ear. She was so excited by his proposals that she rocked her hot core against his groin.

She puffed out air. "I need…" she stopped, like she couldn't find the words or was hesitant to say what she needed from him.

"Tell me what you need, baby." He demanded, getting his hands on her ass; she made Bash's eyeballs roll into the back of his skull as she started pumping her hips against him, going through the motions of humping him. She was killing him in the best way.

"I don't know why I feel this way." She panted against his neck. "I ache, Benjamin."

Fuck him. His name on her lips went right to his dick, and he decided right there she'd only use his real name when they were like this.

It was a bad idea to encourage her to grind on his thigh. She would hate his guts when she sobered up. But the compulsion felt like an electric shock.

Just once, his body was saying. Feel her come right now.

Bash dipped his mouth to her ear and rasped. "Can you picture me touching you, Charlotte? How good will it feel?"

She panted, the wheezing exhales sizzling the skin on his neck, her fingers all grasping at the hoodie.

"I want you to grind harder. Go on, it's only us here. Nothing you say or do will ever be the wrong thing. You know it'll feel good."

She pitched back and forth with each moan escaping from her lips, discovering how good it felt to have his solid thigh grazing up her tight little clit. Fuck, he was jealous of his leg getting the rub.

"*That's my good girl.* Now I want you to concentrate on my hands on your ass, forcefully rocking you, giving your clit the friction it needs."

It was dizzying to Bash how quickly she obeyed as if she were born to listen to his demands. If given half a chance, he'd put her body through many demands that would leave her sopping wet and exhausted.

Each roll of her hips became a little more unhinged in tempo, stronger than the last, and she panted so sweetly Bash was sure he would detonate.

"Benjamin. *Please.*" She stuttered, and it was almost his undoing as his brain trip wired and his hands fisted tighter on her plump ass, driving her to move faster on his willing body. She was as hungrily feral as he'd hoped she would be.

"Good girl. You are spectacular, Charlotte. Soak my leg right through your panties until you're dripping and shaking." His voice was only a whisper now as he felt how she slammed through a climax. He had to hold on to her hips, so she didn't buck right off his lap.

Never had Bash been a woman's sex toy to get off on, and he felt a strange bond toward Charlotte growing around them, fixing them together.

While she'd babbled all her thoughts and dreams of them being together, she'd reused the exact words several times.

Never done this before.

Haven't done that before.

My first time.

His mouth lowered down to her ear, and he felt the settling shudder going through her body. Every reverberation of her bones trembled underneath Bash's fingers, reacting to the slightest request. *Perfect.*

"Charlotte, are you a virgin?" he asked, not wanting the answer but craving her to say the words. He had no right to ache for her to be untouched in that way, that only his hands would ever wring pleasure from her core. But he wanted it anyway.

It didn't matter, even if she wasn't. Bash was well prepared to fuck every man she'd ever had out of her tight little cunt until all she knew was the shape of his cock.

She'd confessed already no one had ever made her come.

Charlotte could no longer claim that since the proof was a wet patch on her shorts. He nipped her ear before bringing her face up.

"I'm the oldest virgin in creation," she complained, rolling her eyes like it was a bad thing.

Bash could only hear the relentless drumming of his heart and feel the rush of possessiveness bubbling up in his throat.

Mine.

His little darling would be all his.

And so would her virginity.

Bash

After getting Charlotte out of her clothes and into his t-shirt and putting her in bed, there was only one place to go. Well, two, but sleeping beside her would come next.

There was a growing anger as Bash climbed off his bike after a brief ride to a quiet suburbia neighborhood. The two-story house was within a gated wall, newly built in the past months for safety measures. It boasted a keypad entrance and cameras around the estate. No part of the property was unguarded. And that included a prospect parked outside, leaning a hip on his bike seat. Bash waved over while texting Denver to open the gate.

As soon as the message was read, the gate whirled open, and he walked the short distance to the back door, which was unlocked for him.

There stood his friend with bare feet, relaxed out of club colors, in a football shirt and sweatpants. His hair was messy, like he'd been rolling around in bed for hours.

Bash was a familiar visitor to their house. If Denver's twin girls were awake, they would rush their Uncle Bash's legs and demand candy because he always brought them treats. He'd eaten at their table countless times. If he didn't visit his mom for the holidays, then his ass was parked at Denver and Casey's holiday table, made to feel like family.

Because they were family.

But as Bash's jaw ticked, his hands wanted to damage his closest friend's face.

"What's up, brother? Not your usual time for visiting." They didn't go further than the kitchen, and Denver leaned a hip on the counter.

"I've got Charlotte in my room at the club."

Denver showed his surprise with his eyebrows climbing into his shorn hairline, and a grin emerged. "Holy fuck, Bash, you made it happen, finally? Casey's gonna bust a gut when she hears this."

"She won't be happy once I rearrange your face," He warned, making Denver laugh.

"Getting it from the little nurse hasn't chilled you out, then?"

"She rocked up to the club, stoned out of her mind. She had a lot to share with me." All her private fantasies were Bash's only; he'd go to his grave without spilling those details to another living soul. But in the mix of those, she'd disclosed something that shed light on her distaste for Denver. She never expressed her dislike for him directly, but her reactions were loud. Tonight, he'd asked her why, and she'd told him about the blackmail.

"Tell me you haven't been extorting Charlotte. Tell me you didn't threaten to take her fucking job away from her if she didn't assist you with stealing shit from the hospital."

"It seems like you already know the answers." The bozo dared quip.

Bash reacted and grabbed Denver by the shirt, slamming him back against the sink unit. Nothing but untethered anger in his hands.

"You absolute fuck. It stops now. You don't approach Charlotte for anything, not even if you're bleeding out and need a Band-Aid. You got it?"

"If you boys are going to fight, let me kiss my husband goodnight first." They heard. Unfazed by the sight of Bash holding Denver, Casey entered the room. Next, she positioned herself in their way and lifted onto her tiptoes. Denver, not giving a crap about being grabbed, met her halfway and planted a kiss on her lips. "I'll be up soon, little bird."

"Okay. Goodnight, you two. Play nice in my clean kitchen, and don't dare wake the kids, or you'll deal with me." Then she strolled out of the room.

"You are a fucking jackass. You knew what she meant to me," Bash accused, pushing Denver away.

The realistic part was that if it had been anyone else, he wouldn't have cared how Denver got his medical provisions. But hearing that Denver had used Charlotte, who'd taken care of Denver and Ruin at separate times, boiled his fucking blood.

"You threatened her job." He grated through his teeth.

Denver, the calmest man on earth, was hard to rattle unless his family's safety was in question, and then he turned into a powder keg of destruction. With his own life, though? He didn't look like he gave a shit if Bash turned into his namesake and bashed his fucking brains in. Bash sighed and pulled out a stool, straddling it.

"I needed the supplies. You know I wouldn't do shit to hurt that girl. Casey would break my balls. She likes Lottie. My last hospital contact quit on me. I had to find a new one."

"Probably why they quit."

Denver rubbed his facial hair. "Nah, he got caught screwing a doctor on duty and was fired. The joker thought I would still pay him."

Bash narrowed his eyes. "Have you been paying Charlotte?"

"She wouldn't even hear me out about money."

That rang true, but it didn't make the situation any better. "She won't take it, even if I give it to her, so you're gonna give every cent to a charity she likes. Something to do with cats."

Denver dared huff a laugh, and Bash fired a glare. "This shit isn't over, Denver. You scared my fucking woman into thinking she'd be reported if she didn't help you."

His eyebrow winged up. "She's your woman, then? You should thank me. I always put a good word in for you. I probably warmed her up to your ugly face."

Right then, Bash couldn't see the funny side. The only reason his friend was still standing was because it was Denver. He would've taken down anyone else. He got up, ready to go back to her.

"This shit isn't right, Chris." He said, using Denver's legal name. "And it won't be right with me until you make it right with Charlotte. If she's too wary to be around you, then Casey won't get to be around her."

A grunt of agreement came from Denver. "Casey's already given me that warning."

At the back door, Denver asked. "You finally got her to agree to date you?"

"She's mine." That was all he'd say. He'd made her come tonight, but technically, she was still firmly in the *won't date a biker* camp.

Bash had no choice but to change her mind.

The mental image of how he'd left Charlotte was stuck in Bash's brain on the ride through the peaceful streets. Her body was smoking, seriously the most beautiful woman, and her eyes had so innocently watched him like he was her snack. They cut right through him down to the marrow, which made him hungry for something just out of reach. When she'd wriggled on his lap, appearing open to any depraved acts he desired, she'd gazed at him with a submissive offering, and it was nearly his undoing.

He was in deep trouble because he realized he had gone all in as his heart pounded out of his chest.

Back at the clubhouse, he left his bike in its usual parking spot and headed inside. In the late hour, there was only a skeleton crew around, but didn't hang back to chat. He strolled up the stairs to his locked room. Charlotte was right where he left her. Snuggled under the covers. The rooms at the club were kept basic, and the bed was tiny compared to the one at home, but for once, he couldn't wait to shuck his clothes and climb into it, knowing she was there waiting for him. Making sure he was quiet, he stripped down to his gray boxer briefs, but it took only one glance at Charlotte curled in his bed, and his cock throbbed. It would be indecent for him to sleep up against her when he was like this. So he headed down the hallway to the shower rooms and closed himself in one stall, setting the water to hot.

Relief was on Bash's mind, and he needed it now.

With groaning movements, he palmed his jutting cock, and the pleasure of that simple touch zinged down his spine.

It was all Charlotte's fault he couldn't control his body. He didn't get like this. That untouchable goddess and her slurred confessions spun around his mind like a chant.

She breathed, and it got him aroused. She existed, and his dick became an impossibly large spike in need of finding a home inside of her.

Fuck her.

Own her.

The thought of being in bed—touching her, and listening to Charlotte breathing was too much for Bash to deal with.

The boiling water from the strong showerhead fell over him, but Bash didn't focus on washing his body; he was too deep in his deranged thoughts, picturing Charlotte playing with his shaft. Dreaming of her lips stretching to take him and how she'd have tears streaming down her face when she choked, trying to take him right to the back of her tight throat.

Stroke after hard stroke, he fucked his hand and wished it was her tight cunt he was powering into. He fantasized about the sensation of her wet lips dribbled with his come. The pleasure grew, making Bash grunt and slap the other hand on the shower wall while he locked his knees in place and jerked off.

He'd been given a taste of the sounds she'd make when he fucked her. But now he craved to hear what indecent noises she'd make while he gripped her by that long ponytail and pumped into her impossibly deeper until her pussy hurt. The need to know what she'd look like coated with white bands of his come dripping from her chin, and those kiss-swollen lips plagued Bash's mind and curled lust like a virus throughout his lower body.

Precum leaked from the head of his cock, warning of the closeness of his climax, and with fast pumps, he grunted her name. His head dropped forward as ropes of his pleasure spilled out onto the floor, drained away by the water.

It took only minutes to dry and pull on a fresh pair of shorts in his room, and then he made the mistake of glancing at Charlotte. The lust returned tenfold like he hadn't just orgasmed his brains out minutes earlier.

Flipping off the light, he climbed into bed. Charlotte was sprawled on her back, emitting the cutest puffs of air through her nose. Unable to resist, he slid an arm underneath and brought her over to his chest. She immediately angled her leg over his knee and murmured in her sleep, "Ben..."

"I'm here, darling."

Nothing in his life had felt this good.

And Bash would do anything to keep it.

Charlotte

Charlotte could count on one hand, and have five fingers left over, for the number of times she'd woken up in a stranger's bed.

Being confused was an understatement as her eyelids flickered open and her familiar bedroom wasn't there.

Neither was the twenty-two pounds cat, whose routine was usually creeping up on her bed, reminding Charlotte, with great bellowing meows, it was way past breakfast. Prince would wither into stardust if he didn't get his special homemade food at a specific time. For a cat who didn't wear a watch and couldn't read a clock, his belly always sensed when she was a minute over mealtimes.

Her groggy mind started functioning one cog at a time while Lottie rubbed at her tired eyes. Her head was banging like a tambourine, the throbbing pain traveling from one temple to the other, as she realized where she was.

She would have accepted if she had no memory of last night. Sometimes it was better not to know, like when you went all psycho with jealousy at some guy's place.

In a hurry, all the shameful information was downloaded. She was mortified, from bothering the gate guy to accusing Bash of hanging out with strippers.

For such a controlled person, she'd been off the scale last night.

She glanced to the other side of the bed, regretting it when her head went on a vertigo tour and caused nausea to ripple up into her throat. But she was alone in the bed. The pillow appeared to have been used, leading her to believe that Bash had also slept there.

Bash. Oh, dear heavenly angels. She moaned, lying there like a lump of mortified jello.

Please let it all be a dream.

Forcing herself to move, she swung her legs over the side of the bed and realized she was only wearing an oversized t-shirt. Heat burned her cheeks, knowing she was wearing Bash's clothing. A swift scan around the room failed to reveal the whereabouts of her clothes.

Right on the heels of that emergency came another one, when her bladder made itself known in a screaming way. Lottie crossed her knees and prayed she could hang on, but that was looking less likely as the minutes crawled by.

Speaking of which, what was the time? Her purse sat on a chair, and she lunged for it. A sweep of relief when she found her phone inside and saw it was after ten a.m.

There were several texts from Toni on the locked screen, but her head was pounding, and she didn't have the mental bandwidth to deal with her friend yet, so she put the phone down. It was no good; she needed to use a restroom.

She unlocked the door from within and cautiously peered outside. The landing appeared calm, and there was a door at the end with a bathroom symbol. *Hallelujah, rejoice. Hold on, bladder.*

In Lottie's wildest dreams, she never thought she would have to do the hundred-yard tiptoe run in a foreign hallway, dressed in a man's t-shirt.

But here she was.

It was by the grace of fate that the bathroom was unoccupied. It smelled of pine and bleach and had a row of sinks plus four stalls. Without haste, she hot-footed into one, locked it behind her, and did her business.

Lottie wondered about the chaos Prince must be causing at home. Despite her cat's aloof personality, he didn't always enjoy being alone. When she was at home, he sought her out and would sprawl on the floor, acting like he didn't care one iota for her. Yet, Prince would trail behind whenever she moved rooms, searching for a new place to relax.

The aim was to find her clothes and escape without being seen. That meant calling a cab and Lottie was so deep in her thoughts that when she flushed and exited the stall and headed to wash her hands, she came to a screeching stop when the door suddenly swung open.

Whereas she was horrified to be found barely dressed, the guy looked her up and down, grinning.

"Hi," he said, "Did you sleep well, Lottie?"

Crap! He knew her. If her brain cylinders were functioning properly, she would recognize his face.

"I slept fine." She answered and turned on the faucet to wash her hands. After drying with a paper towel she threw into the nearby trashcan, she headed for the door without another word to the guy. But he was hot on her heels.

"Wait up. If you're looking for Bash, he's…"

She spun around so fast and crashed into the hard male chest behind her, almost squishing her nose.

"Ouch, goddamn." She cursed as he grabbed her arms while she rubbed her sore nose. She wasn't even put right on her feet when she heard the best sound ever.

"Splice, brother. Is there a reason you have your fucking hands on my girl?"

The warning timber of Bash's powerful voice was a gift from god, and all of Lottie's former embarrassment fled the scene when she saw him charging down the hallway. Looking like a mixture of thunder and paradise. All she wanted to do was run and hide behind him.

She'd never done the morning-after walk of shame. There was no blueprint for how she should act. She'd already run through the body checks; nothing felt sore or used. She was fairly certain they hadn't had sex.

But trying to sneak out of the MC was pointless because Bash's eyes devoured until he loomed over her. He reached out and pulled her close, wrapping his arm around her. On reflex, Lottie's arm sneaked around his back, and she felt Bash inhale until it stretched his shirt. However, his gaze remained fixed on Splice. Ahh, yes. His face came back to her now. He'd tried flirting at the hospital to provoke Bash.

"It was my fault. I turned and bumped into him."

"See, not my fault."

"You were in the same fucking bathroom as her." Accused a growling Bash. For one thrilling moment, Lottie thought how sexy it was that he was protective over another man touching her.

"Man, I didn't know she was there until I arrived. I can't see through doors."

She nearly giggled at his response and saw Splice's eyes turn her way and glint with amusement.

Splice's lack of X-ray vision didn't appease the growling biker because he went on. "You should have left as soon as you saw her in my fucking shirt."

Oh, boy. She *was* in his clothes and very little of them. Her embarrassment returned, and she squeezed his waist, interrupting him before Bash turned into a caveman and threw his friend into a wall. They could wrestle later, but she needed her clothes.

"Bash, I need my clothes."

His head dropped and all the visible signs of his aggression at Splice disappeared when he smiled at her.

"Come with me, little darling," he spoke roughly. Lottie felt the invite tugging low in her abdomen.

Splice turned to push open the bathroom door, and she heard him muttering. "Another one bites the dust. May the sucker rest in peace."

"Fuck off, Splice," Bash answered. Once they were in his room, she blushed as he checked her out.

Last night, Bash had been casually dressed. Today, he wore his MC garb. He looked every inch the formidable biker she was used to. But nothing about how he was staring at her stopped her stomach from whipping up a nervous storm.

What could she say?

Lottie didn't know where to start, so it all blurted in a mad rush. "I'm sorry for coming here last night. I wasn't in my right mind, and I didn't have any right to say the things I said about the strippers or what you do with them. I'm sorry if I embarrassed you in front of your people. I'm trying not to die of mortification when I remember everything I said to you."

His eyes slit to narrow lines. "You remember everything you told me?"

"My head is hurting, but I think I remember most things. I'm never drinking again." It had been blatant stupidity. And it would serve as a lesson for Lottie to never let herself get pushed into acting recklessly again.

Before Lottie realized what was happening, Bash took her into his arms, put himself on the side of the bed, and then placed her on his lap. She didn't know what to do, but she was definitely swooning.

"I brought water and some pain pills." It showed her weakened state when she opened her mouth for the unknown pills as he dropped them onto her tongue and then uncapped the water for her to sip.

"If you've just drugged me after the night I had, I will do some fantastic martial arts on you," she warned, only for Bash to chuckle and brush a kiss on her forehead.

"I had a great night, too."

With quickness, Lottie arranged through the train of proceedings. From scarfing those stupid edibles, taking a cab to the MC and finding Bash, then stripping off in front of him… oh, shit, she'd done that! Her face bloomed. In addition to that, she had shared a lot of personal information, then slept in his bed, and now was sitting on his lap.

Considering that, why wasn't she feeling more freaked out? It was a lot of emotionally based things all at once, and yet, she was at ease on his lap with his face right there, if she dared to turn her head to look at him.

"You have to look at me sometime, Charlotte." His voice was thick with laughter, like he was reading her racing thoughts.

"Nuh huh," she replied, and he nuzzled her cheek with his beard. Bash was nuzzling her!

"Since when do we get touchy?" But she knew the answer and was dying a thousand squirmy deaths.

"Since you had your tongue in my mouth, baby."

"You kissed me!" she accused, finally looking at the smiling biker. "My tongue was trying to fight you out of my mouth, but I was very drunk, and you exploited my weakened state."

Another hot little nuzzle. His abrasive facial hair tickled her skin. She had no idea how touchy-feely Bash could be, and her senses were trying to catch up with her feelings.

"Is that the stance you're taking, hm?" his voice smiled, and when she looked up through her lashes, his eyes were intense with color. "Oh, little darling, these next minutes will be so fun for me. You might wanna hold on to my shoulders, dig your nails in if you have to."

She was instantly on high alert, as if she thought a giraffe family might storm in. She took a deep breath and asked nervously. "What does that mean?"

"Besides how much you love kissing me, I'm gonna remind you of everything you said last night."

"Nooooo." she wailed, smacking a hand over his smiley mouth. "Don't you dare, Benjamin Laurent. I know the opposite of CPR."

"That's murder," he laughed, mumbling behind her hand, and then the devil licked her palm, and she pulled it back. "And I know for certain you don't want me dead. But the first thing I need to say. If you keep calling me Benjamin, I'm gonna fuck you. I had no idea how hearing you say it would affect me in the dirtiest, hottest way, and you said it about a hundred fucking times last night, until I had to jerk off before climbing into bed with you. From now on, be a good girl and only use it when you want me worshipping between your thighs, okay?"

Lottie had no words. Speechless. Struck dumb. There she perched on a devilish biker, listening to instructions to only to call him by his real name when she wanted fucking. For the first time, no words would come.

"You weren't tongue-tied last night, my little chatterbox." He chuckled diabolically, reminding Lottie of how open she'd been with the TMI.

"Forget everything. It was all lies. I'm infamous for storytelling."

"Nice try, darling," he smirked. Lottie's heart felt airy, as if his nearness was causing her motherboard check engine lights to flash madly.

There was no explanation for why she felt as relaxed as she did, considering the current *wearing no panties yet sitting on a man's lap* situation.

"Can I put on my panties before you remind me of last night? I assume you have my underwear…"

The darkening passion that entered Bash's eyes threatened her lungs with early retirement. The lust hit her low, directly in her core. Lottie couldn't look away from his magnificent eyes.

Not when she was feeling the same thing mirrored back at her.

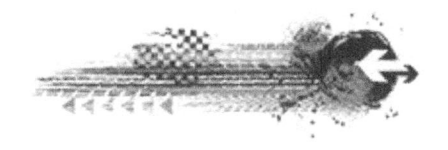

Bash produced her clothes, all neatly folded and smelling fresh.

Knowing he'd laundered her clothes put a warm feeling in her chest. No one had shown her such a small yet profoundly caring gesture in a long time.

When he sat on his bed and reached for a packet of smokes and a silver lighter, Lottie gaped at him.

"I don't suppose I'm getting privacy to dress…"

Bash lit up, watching her from under his heavily hooded eyelids like he had no place else in the world he wanted to be.

Something loosened in Lottie's belly, and she took his silent dare. If he wanted to watch her getting dressed, the biker could.

Fearlessly, she inserted her legs into the holes of the panties, smoothly pulling them under the t-shirt. When putting on the bra, Lottie turned her back, throwing his t-shirt over her shoulder. She heard Bash catch it, and then he groaned. "Fuck, my clothes smell like you."

Her head whipped around. And yep, he had the white material up to his nose, inhaling like a pervert. Every part of Lottie's cheeks flamed. The rest of her clothes were put on faster, and she finally faced him.

"I don't like you smoking," she scowled, watching as he tugged on the cigarette and then blew out the smoke. "It's bad for you."

"A lot of things are bad for me, Charlotte," he said, resting the hand holding the half-smoked cigarette on his thigh.

"You should quit."

"Who's asking, little darling? Just a health professional or my woman?"

Would this man ever stop stunning words out of her?

I think I'm addicted to you, Bash. The memory of saying that saturated her mind, and Lottie's backside found the chair behind her so she could step into her boots. *Being Bash's good girl* was something else she'd said to him during her drunkenness.

"You never talk to me like this." She breathed around erratic heartbeats. Unable to draw her gaze away from Bash.

"Then it's about time I did. Things changed between us last night, Charlotte. We can't go back to how it was."

Her forehead puckered. "What does that mean? You won't be my friend any longer?"

"If you need me to be your friend, I'm your friend. But we're gonna be so much more."

A hot pulsation darted through her.

She had no rebuttal words for that, not after her confessional session was out in the open.

As Bash leaned over to stub out the cigarette into an ashtray, his t-shirt rode up, and she spied part of his washboard stomach. Every inch of mouth wetness dried up, and she was still dreamily staring when his head rose and found her looking at him. The smirk he flashed Lottie said he knew exactly what she was doing, and he liked it.

"Ah, little darling, you're the most beautiful thing I've ever seen." He said as his eyes ate her up with a gaze so lewd her inner thighs squeezed together to stop her panties from disintegrating.

"You don't have to flatter me," even as her cheeks bloomed with happiness. It was a weird sensation. She didn't seek validation through compliments. But it seemed her system had gone through a factory reset for this man. Each time Bash heaped compliments on her, she fell into a series of modest euphoria flutters that were impossible to control.

Bash crouched in front of her. Lottie's nerves eased when he grabbed her chin with a finger and thumb.

"Do we need to work on your self-esteem?"

Lottie chuffed a laugh. "Hardly. I have plenty of that, thank you."

"Then believe what I say. You are fucking *stunning*. Even when you wear those plain scrubs that make your ass so fucking hot, I can't even think about anything else when we eat lunch together. Once I savor every inch of you, you'll understand how irresistible you are."

"Bash." She breathed, scandalized, and turned on. "You can't say things like that."

"Yes, I fucking can." He smirked. "You're addicted to me, little darling. You want me all to yourself." He added.

"A biker who smokes and swears too much," she muttered, rolling her eyes, but Bash only grinned at her in return. "Lucky girl."

Yeah, she was.

But she was also terrified of going to the next stage with him.

She'd grown comfortable with him in the friendzone. She could handle him in *that* zone. But now he'd stepped out of it, forcibly dragging her along. She didn't have the manual for handling *this* version of Bash. He was unleashed and scaring her hormones into quivering all over the place.

"You need to slow down a bit."

"No," he answered, climbing to his feet. He dropped a kiss to the top of her head and thankfully put some space between them so Lottie's poor lungs could inflate without stuttering. "We're happening, Charlotte. You already feel it changing, don't you?"

What could she say? The truth was all that was needed. "Yes. But it doesn't mean we have to move at warped speed. I was high last night for the first time, and things happened, and I slept in a bed with you without my underwear! And now you're all smoldering, bossy biker, and I can't catch my breath. You need to give me time to catch up to where you are."

"Ah, my little darling, you are so cute." He soothed, and she wanted to kick him in the leg for that cute remark. She would rather he went back to calling her stunning. "You are in the same place, Charlotte. You hid how you felt about me. I was hatching plans like a madman, trying to get you to fall for me, and you already had. There's no way we're staying static now."

Lottie gaped. His words reverberated around her head. "You... you were hatching plans." She smiled. God, he was adorable. "Now, who's being cute? Bash and his cute little plans."

"Keep working that mouth, Charlotte. You'll get the same thing as last night, but you won't work it out on my leg this time."

Heat as hot as a Floridian summer blasted her all over. His meaning was clear, reminding her of how she'd had an orgasm on his lap. Before she could utter a word, Bash went on. It was embarrassing enough to know last night happened without rehashing it minute-by-minute.

"If you remember all those fantasies, you whispered into my chest. Trusted I'd keep them between us. Then you remember what I promised you, Charlotte. You're safe with me. All of you. Your heart and soul. I've wanted you for so fucking long, and now I know you feel the same. I'm not pumping the brakes, baby. I'm the man to give you everything you confessed you wanted between us, but was too frightened to reach out. There's no need to be afraid now. I'll take over."

Oh, wow.

His words became a key, springing open a lonely place within Lottie's chest.

This patient man claimed her, even though she was as far removed from any biker as a woman could be. He wanted her.

Sifting through her feelings, which had grown impossibly larger over the months, she knew it in the structure of her bones and the very breath. There was no putting her thoughts back under lock and key. Not when she'd poured them into his hands.

"Before Bash." She started, and he cocked a curious eyebrow. "That's how I categorize everything I was before I met you. I say and do things now I never have, and didn't want to. I don't know if I'm good at this, Bash." She gestured a hand between her and him.

There was an urgent part of her that wanted his control. To free her from all decisions. She wanted his attention, *desperately*. It ate at her all the time, and those pockets of time spent with him felt like an oasis she couldn't wait to return to when they were apart.

Though the unknown scared her silly, she craved to explore the part of him that was raw and animalistic, the side of Bash that made him look at her like she was a piece of cheesecake. For months, she'd been around his softer side. The side of him who was her friend only. But now they'd shifted dynamics. Lottie couldn't disguise wanting to experience the primal side of Bash. That was the in-charge man who'd talked her through an orgasm.

Without warning, he sprang forward and pulled her up to her feet, cupping her face; he wore a look of awe. "Look what you keep giving me, little darling. I'm gonna eat you a-fucking-live."

"Oh, wow." If she knew more about relationships, she might have expected him to be this intense and swoony. But she was in unfamiliar waters with a shark who scented her blood, and all Lottie could think of was to swim closer.

She dropped her gaze to his mouth, and Bash groaned. She couldn't forget how much she enjoyed his kisses and how addictive his taste was.

"Charlotte. Don't look so hungry at me, or we won't leave this room for a month, and I'm trying so hard to give you a good experience with your first fuck."

"*Oh, god.*" She buried her face, but he wouldn't let her hide.

"You just remembered that part, huh? I've thought about it all night while you wriggled on my chest."

"Stop." she warned. "I'm going to die of embarrassment. Can you forget everything I said?"

"Not happening, baby, but I will stop mentioning it." *Whew*. And then Bash showed how diabolical he was. "For now." He added and laughed when she socked him in the gut.

"I'm leaving."

"I'll take you home to the cat, baby. And then we'll grab some food."

Surprisingly, her headache had lessened, and now her stomach reminded Lottie that she was hungry.

"If Prince has wrecked the house, it'll be your fault. You should have sent me home last night."

"And pass up the chance to hear how handsome and hot as fuck you think I am?" his eyes twinkled with saucy evilness, and Lottie considered socking him again.

"You are mean, and I don't think I like you, Bash."

"Yeah, baby, you do. You're fucking crazy about me."

"I'm leaving." She huffed, shooting through the door, but the biker was behind her with longer strides. He guided her toward the exit, but she fell short when everyone in the central area noticed her. Bash wrapped his arm around her waist, his lips touching her ear.

"Be my confident little nurse."

"Hey, guys. Do you want coffee?" called out a pixie-cut redhead with a friendly smile.

"No thanks, Scarlett, I'm taking Charlotte home."

Charlotte remembered this was the president's wife, and Lottie smiled at her.

"This is the worst walk of shame I've ever done." She mumbled only for his ears when the boy at the gate last night walked by with the biggest grin and winked at her.

"We'll talk about how many you've done when I get you home." He growled playfully, and Lottie burst out laughing and jabbing him. "This is my first."

"Mmm, all these firsts I get." He made it sound dirty, and she flushed as Chains straddled a bar stool.

"Hey, brother. And Bash's woman, Lottie." He called out, wearing a half-smirk. "My harem of wives are at home, if you were wondering."

"Strike me down now." Half hiding her face against Bash, she groaned.

"Chains is teasing, darling. He thought that shit was funny."

"So that you know, I'm never coming back."

"Yes, you are." And then, thankfully, he led her outside into the fresh air.

He was so sweet, helping her into his jacket and his bucket helmet. Bash slid a pair of shades over his eyes, pulled a black gaiter mask over his nose, and climbed on in front of her. Lord, he looked like a true outlaw, and her thighs shook with pleasure to be so closely curled around his body. Nothing was the same as it was twenty-four hours ago.

For the first time, she acted impulsively and headed to an unspecified destination without a map.

The destination was Bash. And the journey was unknown.

But she was nervously excited.

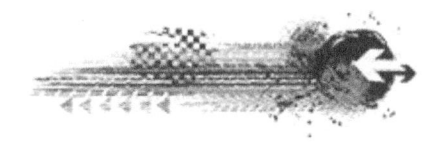

By the time Bash returned from picking up some takeout food, Lottie had showered, tidied her hair and dressed in fresh clothes, fed the sulking cat some treats, and was now sitting on the floor grooming him with his special brush.

She heard Bash coming through the door, having left it unlocked for him, and that anxious tickle in her stomach returned hearing him walking into her house. It intensified when he appeared. He'd toed off his boots, leaving him in socks, and tossed his jacket over the newel post.

"I got breakfast burritos and coffee."

"Oh, bless you. I'll finish with his lordship before I eat, but can you hand me the coffee? My brain needs it today."

Bash held the incredible smelling coffee out of reach when he was closer. Lottie scowled at him. "You know not to play around with my coffee, Ben."

Bash suddenly dropped to his haunches in front of Lottie with an unmistakable expression. He looked ready to fuck fifteen babies into her while tying her to the ceiling fan and making her beg for mercy. Her hand faltered on Prince's coat, and the cat howled because Prince loved his pampering time like a Stepford housewife. It was the only time he allowed affection.

Lottie blinked, her mouth dry and her breasts heaving under the fitted t-shirt. Suddenly, she felt very exposed under Bash's lust-drenched scrutiny, and she didn't know what had made him react.

"What did I tell you about saying my name, Charlotte?"

"Oh, shit."

"Oh, shit is right. You use my name if you want to be fucked. Does my little darling need fucking right now before she's had coffee or breakfast? Because I'm ready to go."

He's. Ready. To. Go.

Did that mean he was aroused?

"I didn't think you meant it."

"I meant it, so use it wisely, baby." Then her friendly Bash, the one she knew so well, returned, giving her a wink. He rose to his feet, but lowered his head. "Give me a kiss for this coffee." He held it out of reach.

"That's extortion!" She accused. "You never make me pay for coffee."

"That was before you were my woman."

Whoosh. Her heart rolled over.

"Okay, just because I need the caffeine." And his kiss. *Ughn*, she wanted his kisses again, those greedy kisses that turned her on so much her pussy was doing Kegels like crazy. She went up on her knees and Lottie shyly tapped his mouth. He hummed, then handed over the coffee. And because she was so nosy and curiosity wouldn't kill her cat because Prince fought like a sloth, she buried her mouth on the lip of the cup, while she stole a glance at Bash and saw... and saw...

His bulge was massive, pushing against the crotch of his jeans.

Yep. Very aroused, and now her stomach flipped with nervous excitement.

That man was going to annihilate her. Virgins weren't meant to ride oversized dicks for their first outing. She might have to take a week off from work when she slept with him to recover from the wreckage he'd leave behind.

"Bash, my gag reflex is fine, but I might need time to work up to blowjobs. I don't want to disappoint you." She exclaimed. Her tongue had gone AWOL. She swore it wasn't even a thought a moment ago.

How was that honesty for a woman who wasn't in a relationship yesterday but appeared to be in a serious one today?

Placing the takeout cup far enough away from Prince's swatting paw, she buried her burning embarrassment by brushing his coat, making his silver fur shine, while he lazed with his eyes closed, uncaring that his mistress's life was upside down.

"You always surprise me," coughed Bash. "As for sucking my dick, that's up to you, darling. Nothing will disappoint me, but it won't stop me from licking between your thighs until you rip the hair out of my skull."

Game. Set. Match to Bash.

"You are so mean." She made a face.

"Being honest, baby." He relaxed into the armchair. "Because I'm a greedy fucker where you're concerned and want to know what those plump lips feel wrapped around my dick. If you ever want to try it, let me know. I'll be an excellent teacher."

Lottie's lungs had been through a lot in a few brief hours, and if she didn't get her irregular breathing under control, she might pass out.

Bash sipped his black coffee like he hadn't just made a scandalous proposition.

But now she was considering it.

Bash

There was a small part of Bash that wondered if he was about to fuck up Charlotte's life by bringing her into his world. Especially now when that world was charged with new enemies.

He had witnessed firsthand how diligently his brothers protected their families. How much Axel worried about keeping his queen safe, constantly worrying she would be picked off the street and used for ransom.

It meant Bash was now concerned about the implications of Charlotte being his woman. It made her a target, and it scared the shit out of him.

But there was no way to pump the brakes.

He was already in too deep. Too selfish not to keep her.

Already so addicted to that woman and everything she was.

Even now, Bash had one eye on the time, waiting to see her again. Even though they'd been hanging out for the past two days, he still couldn't get enough of her.

That morning, the club was a busy hive as he kicked back on a stool at the bar to do paperwork. It never ended, especially now that the club was adding new investments, which meant Bash had an even more significant number of properties to keep track of. Sweet bottoms were milling around, bringing trays of catered food and liquor carts, all chatting excitedly about who would be at the cookout. They threw cookouts on their property a few times a year.

On certain occasions, such as today, other MCs would be arriving.

Part fun, part business.

Those talks would take place around the bonfire with bourbon and shared resources. As nomadic as the Riot Brothers were, they were forming a pattern by infiltrating smaller businesses around the country, using tactics of violence and intimidation. It all made sense once the MC network started talking and sharing info.

Their progress had been slow lately because Ruin took out their investor, who was bothering Tomb's wife, Nina. They were trying to rally the troops and get back into Utah.

And that wasn't something the Diablos would roll over for.

Going to war with any faction wasn't ideal. Bash wanted a quieter life, especially now he had Charlotte to consider. The thought of her being used against them kept him up at night.

The logical decision would have been to leave her alone.

But it would have been easier for him to slit his own throat.

He was drawn to her like he'd never been to another living person. The need to be near her clawed at his gut. Bash wasn't sure if he was any better, considering how she felt about the trouble her sister caused. He would protect her no matter what, with all the Diablos behind him.

"Hey Bash, got a second?" he heard and looked up from the paperwork to see Axel coming from the direction of his office.

"Sure, what's up? Don't say war. It's only eight a.m.," he joked as Axel parked in a seat next to him and sighed, scraping both hands through his long hair.

"I want to run some logistics by you about tonight. Scarlett and her cleaning crew are preparing the bunkhouses for the Apollo Kingsmen to crash in while they're around."

Last summer, the club queen came up with the idea of building two bunkhouses in their backyard. It made sense to have a place for the new hangarounds and prospects to sleep, and to keep the upstairs rooms for patched brothers. The other bunkhouse was suggested for the sweet bottoms. The club queen might not be too happy that some of those women had slept with her man before she came along, but she was nice enough to help them find housing and jobs.

Now, traditional barracks-like buildings housing twelve bunks each and shower rooms with a small kitchenette in each were on the property, and it would be the first time any other MC would use them as a flop on their visit through Utah. It made sense; it meant more face-to-face meetings and not over the phone when anyone could tap them.

"How many of them are we expecting?"

"About twenty, Jamie said. They're bringing their sweet bottoms."

Bash chuckled low. "You know, out-of-town women make our sweet bottoms act like hissing cats."

"Scarlett will keep them in line," Axel smirked.

"They know not to cause shit tonight. They can have their fun, but if they start trouble, Scarlett knows what to do." And then. "I was talking to Chains about inviting Harvey."

Bash's head whipped up. "Seriously? We're gonna ask the man who wants to ruin us to break bread at our table?"

Axel tapped his ringed fingers on the bar top. "Chains had about the same reaction. But I'm sick as fuck talking to that guy over the phone. I wanna look at the whites of his eyes."

"What if he doesn't come?"

"He'll come," Axel said confidently. "He's determined to join forces with anyone with power, and he's finding out that sucking up to the mayor doesn't get him as much as he thought it would."

"Denver will hit the roof if Albie comes with him. Not where Casey and the kids are. This is supposed to be a friendly cookout," reminded Bash. For fuck's sake, he couldn't bring Charlotte if guns would be drawn. He wanted her to like him, not run for the fucking hills.

"It is a friendly cookout. I only want to talk to him. Harvey wouldn't be dumb enough to bring Albie. According to him, he's neutralized that dumbfuck. But we know different since he's been spotted nearby."

Albie, Denver's sinister brother-in-law, had been the one to stab Denver and had been sending Casey threatening notes. Denver beefed up their home security like a royal palace for that reason.

"I'll extend the invite to Harvey's Mrs, if he has one. That way, he knows I won't try to kill him." Another flash of a smirk.

It was a risky move to bring a fox into the henhouse, but the Diablos didn't get to the position they were now without ballsy moves.

"What do you need me to do?"

"Just keep watch. He'll bring a lieutenant with him, I'd expect that, but none of his other goons will be allowed in. We're putting extra security at the gates, around the perimeters, and about a mile from the club to check if Harvey stations his men anywhere near." Axel made a disagreeable sound. "He's made enough noise that he wants to iron out any differences, and we'll see what he has to say for himself." Then he added. "I'm giving Denver the heads up if he wants to stay at home with Casey."

"Denver won't stay home, Prez."

Axel half smiled. "I know he won't. That's why I need you to monitor him."

"Fuck, this might not be the best time to bring Charlotte. I wanted to impress her, not watch me throw myself on Denver like a fucking grenade if he kicks off."

Bash's complaint caused Axel to chuckle. "You're bringing the nurse?"

"She's weary about clubs. It stems from her sister getting in with a gang. But I don't think she'll think we're any different if we brawl."

"Nah, it'll be fine, brother. Bring your woman. You know the others will look after her."

The others were the mob of old ladies who traveled in a pack and conspired like crazy, sometimes including Ruin as their honorary member against his will.

"How do you do it, Prez?"

"Do what?"

"Protect your old lady in our world."

"If you're lucky, my brother, you find a woman who's your equal. Not a fighter, but somewhere soft for you to land after you've done your fighting. She's your sounding board when you have too many voices all speaking at once. She's there to help carry the load you have on your shoulders. Protecting her and the life you forge together doesn't become a separate entity. It fuses over time. It becomes like breathing." Axel climbed to his feet, giving Bash a contemplative smile. "When it's the right woman, she's your balance, like you're hers. And if dangerous shit comes along, as it inevitably does, knowing you're combatting for a reason gives you the strength and determination, to always come home alive to your soft place."

It gave Bash a lot of shit to think about. He only nodded, grateful for Axel's advice.

Axel clapped him on the arm. "Invite your Charlotte. We could always use a nurse at the club." Then tacked on. "But you know, Bash, if she doesn't fit in with the MC…"

Shit, Axel was implying they would veto her.

That law hadn't been used in decades, never in recent history, and he braced to fight a fucking lion because he wasn't giving Charlotte up for anything, for anyone.

His throat worked with a hard swallow, and he glared at his boss and friend, the man he'd pledged an oath to walk into fire with, and felt a split down the middle of his torso, a definite shift in his priorities happening organically without explanation, he felt it.

"Relax, Bash, you look like you wanna throw me over the bar," laughed the prez. "If the nurse doesn't like us, she can always be a civilian old lady."

Bash frowned. He hadn't even considered that because that, too, hadn't happened... ever. But it was in their bylaws that if an old lady caused too much shit within the ranks of the club members or she didn't vibe well with the MC culture, she could be kept separate, she would live somewhere off the property, would never wear a property patch and couldn't ever come to any club events.

"Would that work?" he spoke aloud, almost to himself.

"If that's what you wanted, you'd make it work. But I have a feeling once the old ladies get their mitts on your woman, she'll soon be ingratiated like a native. My old lady has a way of making people feel at ease."

It gave Bash a lot to think about.

And as Axel walked off, Bash's phone vibrated on top of the bar. He turned the screen over and frowned.

CHARLOTTE: Bash, I got called in for a shift. I won't be able to see you later.

CHARLOTTE: <sad emoji face> I'm sorry, hotness. (I'm trying out nicknames, don't laugh!) I really wanted to see you.

Bash snickered. She was too fucking cute.

And there was no way he wasn't seeing her for twelve hours. Gathering up the paperwork, he dropped it off at the office, locked away the private files he'd been working through.

BASH: I'll be outside waiting for you on your break. See you soon, little darling.

When he later arrived outside the hospital, he still had time to kill, so he parked and went to their bench. He'd shoot some texts to the Diablo nomads, checking in as he did weekly as part of his secretary duties. Currently, the club had three nomads.

Atom was in Wyoming working on a club venture. He rolled into town sporadically but always got on the road again within days. The last time he was at the clubhouse was for Axel's wedding. He drank, he celebrated, and then he left.

Bash had only heard stories about Drifter. He'd never seen the man in all his years with the Diablos. He was a myth and a legend nowadays, talked about in chronicles that Bash wasn't sure were true. He'd been part of the old crew but remained loyal to Axel when he took over. He kept his patch, left his council role, but decided on a wanderer's life instead. Though never seeing him in person, Drifter always replied to Bash's texts.

Their third nomad was Silver. The last time Bash texted him, the guy gathered useful intel down south about Harvey. The Riot Brothers had left Alabama in a rush, leaving bad debts and worse enemies.

As the saying goes, the enemy of my enemy is now my friend.

Shortly after sending the messages, Bash received two replies confirming that there was nothing of note to report. The reply from Drifter always took hours—days, sometimes, but it would come. There were contingencies for if the nomads died while away from the club. Word would reach Axel through their network. So he didn't think the guy was dead yet.

A delicate scent caught on the mid-afternoon breeze caused Bash to raise his head and look toward the entranceway. She was too far away for him to smell her honey, but Bash was convinced he could still catch a hint. He moved like he was totally in sync with her, charging to meet her with long strides. As soon as Charlotte laid eyes on him, she smiled, affecting his heart.

The urgency to touch her felt like madness clawing at the inside of his skull, and it only settled once his hands were around her waist and his face buried in her neck, so he could inhale her.

"I smell of work," she giggled, wrapping her arms around his shoulders.

"You smell fucking delicious." She was still smiling when Bash took her beautiful face in his hands. "Missed you, little darling."

"I missed you, too." She replied, more shyly. He grabbed her hand and went over to their bench. He didn't have to play platonic anymore, so he pulled Charlotte into his side with his hand around her back, holding her low on her hip, squeezing possessively. *Mine*. Every part of him agreed. She was his woman.

"You didn't have to come, you know?"

"Charlotte, I'm not going without seeing you all day."

She dipped her head, but he still saw her pleased smile.

"I thought our lunches might stop now that—"

"Now that you're mine? You've always been mine, only now you know it, too." He smirked. "Did you think I'd lose interest in spending time with you, Charlotte? That wasn't for show. How I feel is still fucking real. Only now, I get to taste you." He would fuck her so soon while she blushed, he decided. He loved seeing her turn pink because of things he said.

And he'd been tame so far.

"Speaking of. You've been here for two minutes, and I still haven't had that mouth. Give it to me."

Charlotte took a second too long because she was still shy around him, though she'd been in his lap most of last night while they watched a movie. She watched the film, and Bash watched her. He got his mouth and hands on her as much as he could. Now that he was out of her friendzone, the need to maul his woman was a dark thirst. Making her moan for hours underneath his hands was a pleasure he didn't know he craved.

With Charlotte, he could touch her for hours, driving her insane with orgasms, and not expect anything back, because being part of her pleasure was more than enough. The look of unguarded lust in her eyes was his paradise. And he lived for her sexy little whimpers. All he wanted to do was taste and strum her into crying down his throat.

So that's what he'd been doing for the past two days. Gorging on Charlotte's pleasure. His mouth on her neck, and a hand down the front of her pants, working her up into a dripping mess for hours.

Unhinged, unmoored, he'd defiled Charlotte's body, touching her with worshipping hands while she cuddled on his lap and drove him wild with her tongue in his mouth, giving off the sexiest little mewls.

Bash reached a hand to the base of her neck and helped her come forward a few inches. "Missed this mouth," he groaned and then took it, encouraging her to open it by licking the seam with the tip of his tongue. When he moved inside, Charlotte softened, kissing him with enthusiasm.

"My sweetest little virgin." He grunted against her lips, and she answered by poking him.

"You're mean," she half-smiled, "does it bother you?" she asked seriously, and Bash grabbed up her hand, laying it across his upper thigh, right where his cock was hard and ready.

"I feel like whatever answer I give, it's a trick question," he smirked, and she smacked him again.

"It's not a trick question. I was fine with being the oldest virgin in the world."

Dramatic little thing. Bash grabbed the white sack of food he'd brought her. "Eat, baby."

"Okay, I'll eat, you talk."

"Your virginity is going to be something I savor for the rest of my life." He answered honestly. "Knowing I'm the only man who gets to see you naked. To be the one who pries your legs open to taste you. Have you sliding all over me because I've made you addicted to getting my dick inside you so often. Making you sweat and beg is more than I can fucking take."

Charlotte gaped. A sugared grape she paused halfway to her lips.

Bash wasn't finished.

She needed to grasp the extent of what was on his mind since she'd confessed she'd had no other man before him.

The wait to fuck her was agony.

It was also paradise.

"Your virginity isn't nothing, darling. It's a gift I will treasure. I will eat, suck, lick, and fucking devour it until it coats my lips. And once my cock gets into you, I'll wear it like a goddamn crown, dripping all over me."

Bash leaned in to kiss the base of his shy, speechless girl's neck where the pulse was quivering so deliciously he could easily bite down and mark her.

But that was too deranged.

He'd save that for the bedroom.

"Eat your lunch, darling. You'll need your energy."

He meant for the next hours of her shift, but damn him if he didn't get a dirty kick out of watching Charlotte turn the reddest red when she interpreted it to mean he was going to fuck her. Maybe tonight.

She shoved grape after grape into her mouth, nibbled on her favorite salty crackers, and it was comfortable minutes later, she said. "I liked your dirty talk, Bash. But I don't think I'll be brilliant with sex acrobatics. Don't forget, I'm a novice. Even with foreplay! I'm going to mess it up, and you'll go back to your biker babes and strippers who know how to suck and ride and twist and do all the fancy stuff to turn a biker on."

His little darling was fretting over nothing, and she looked so sweet with her soulful eyes raised to his. He wanted to eat her alive.

"You turn me on by existing, Charlotte." Didn't she get that yet? "You get this little hitch of breath in your throat when I kiss you, and it makes me want to fucking maul you like a deranged lion."

"Bash," she laughed, her worried features easing.

"I mean it. That's the last thing you need to worry about. Anything you need to learn or try, you'll do it with me. Yeah?"

She nodded shyly, popping a grape between her plump lips. Lucky fucking grape.

"Are you gonna be my good girl?"

Her free hand tightened on his thigh, and Bash grunted from his chest. He wasn't into public sex, but he could make an exception on their bench if she continued touching him.

"I'm not a patient man, Charlotte. Tell me what I want to hear. Will you be my good girl?"

"Oh, my god, yes," she said in a hushed tone, and checked to see if anyone was eavesdropping. That would never happen. Even while entirely focused on Charlotte, Bash was aware of their surroundings and had marked the number of people who'd left the main entrance.

"Yes, what, Charlotte?" he pushed, smirking.

"Yes, I'll be your good girl." She huffed like a beautiful queen, glaring at him, but her eyes were heavily glazed with lust.

Charlotte wanted to be his good girl as much as he needed it. Maybe more. She just didn't know what she was agreeing to yet.

"Now you've made me lose my appetite," she grumbled dramatically, sighing and huffing as she leaned into his side.

"Finish your lunch, Charlotte." He insisted.

She snapped her gaze to him and then smiled. "I guess I should. For all this energy, I'll need to do the sex acrobats."

A laugh bubbled out of Bash's chest at her antics.

He couldn't fucking wait.

Bash

With Tomb by his side, Bash observed the meeting, confirming that the frontman of the Riot Brothers was a narcissistic prick.

Harvey and his younger brother, Kurtis, had arrived an hour ago.

The brothers were in their mid-fifties, while the girls they brought seemed to be in their late teens at most. As Harvey instructed the women to play, Bash glanced at Tomb, who responded with a silent expression of disgust by raising his eyebrow. Scarlett stepped out of Axel's arm and took them over to the buffet table.

Last night's bonfire went fine, with the out-of-townies arriving to settle in. The cookout was set to start right after the meeting.

Harvey did most of the talking, Bash noted. Bragging like an idiot. And even when Kurtis tried to interject, Harvey cut him off. Was there a dispute amongst the ranks?

"We are all entrepreneurs, Axel." Harvey simpered, puffing on a thick Cuban cigar, a scotch in his other hand. They'd come dressed in three-piece suits and dripping in gold, like they wanted to give the impression of respectability. "It's only out of respect for you we're here today. I think our organizations could run very well side-by-side. You help me, we help you."

Axel took a slow sip of coffee.

Some men would have gone toe-to-toe by drinking liquor, regardless of the time of day. But as Bash knew about Axel, the prez didn't need to live up to anyone's expectations, and he had enough ego not to give a shit about other's opinions about his choices.

It was like watching a salmon being reeled in on a fishing line as Axel scrutinized him.

"What do you think I need help with, Harvey?"

Another puff of the cigar. The man smirked and gestured around him. "You tell me. I have many resources at my disposal. I could be good for this place with the right cash injection." The way Harvey said it was an obvious diss, and Bash saw Axel's lips curl as he sat silently, regarding the enemy in their midst.

Anyone Axel invited to the club for a meeting would have instantly realized his statement was bait. Harvey answered in the wrong fucking way, letting his ego speak. Only a stupid man would come with a pocketful of insults.

"Here's how it's going to go," Stated Axel. "If your organization doesn't stop trying to take what's ours, including every business in town and beyond, and those you've tried to extort for protection money; we're going to end you. You personally at first, and then each one under your ruling," announced Axel in a tone so stark, Bash was glad he was on the right side.

"I've offered you plenty of opportunities to make the correct decision here. And at each turn, Harvey, you've chosen the wrong fucking way. That ends today. No exceptions. Your investor had a nasty end, if you recall. You don't want the same outcome."

"We had no idea he was involved in that protection racket." Butted in Kurtis, red-faced. "That isn't how we operate."

Harvey was seething across the table, staring down Axel. Chains remained stoic, but Bash knew their VP would be ready to flip some fucker over a table at any time.

Around them, people kept their distance from the meeting.

"Let me remind you that the Diablos, compared to your mere fifty members, are much larger," Axel confirmed. "We're much more aggressive and have influence beyond this country. We know each of you and have no qualms interrupting our day to finish you."

That had been one of Drifter's tasks, and he'd come through big time. Right now, that history database of the Riot Brothers sat in Bash's safe.

"You never intended to take this seriously, did you?" spat Harvey. "We came here in good faith."

"You came because you thought the Diablos were an easy take. Do I need to remind you that one of your hotheads stabbed one of mine?"

Arrogant as ever and still so sure of himself, Harvey snapped. "That's been sorted. Albie acted on his own; it wasn't on my command. Why the fuck would we want to stab a Diablo when we're trying to form a business connection?"

With a glance at his silver wristwatch, Bash felt a surge of anticipation, knowing his girl would join him at the club soon. He was dying to have her sit on his lap, feeding her all her favorite treats.

"I get it, Harvey. I know you're trying to make a good impression on your minions by begging for my approval. All the others kicked you out of their doors, right? Yeah, we heard the stories. But you see, measuring whose balls are bigger has never tickled my fancy, you get me? You're not even close to being influential enough to worry us. And I don't do deals with people who have attempted, on more than one fucking occasion, to disrespect us and step on my big balls."

Chains and Diamond chuckled.

"Find somewhere else to make your patch because it won't be here. And as a final nail in the coffin, in case you still have grandiose ideas to ignore my word, you should be aware I'm in close contact with your Alabama foes. They don't know where you and your brother are. Yet. It can stay that way, but it's up to you."

Because Harvey jumped to his feet, Kurtis followed suit. The men and their women had been searched before they'd been allowed in, and so had their vehicle, but Bash braced anyway for the hint either of them was carrying a weapon.

"You fucking cunts just wasted my goddamn time." Harvey hissed.

"Looks like." Axel rose and smiled and then called over to his wife. "Scarlett." She knew the signal to bring their women over. They appeared more relaxed than egotistical Harvey did, Bash noticed, as they smiled at Scarlett.

"Thanks for the advice, Scarlett." One told her.

"Put down the fucking plate," Harvey told his woman, "we're leaving." And then to Axel, he said. "You'll regret this, Tucker. I came here in good faith. You just fucked that out of the water."

Axel only stared and directed his following words to Diamond. "See them off the property."

"Got it, Prez."

A minute later, their Mercedes screeched out of the forecourt. Chains chuckled. "You enjoyed that far too much."

"I wanted to put a bullet in his fucking brains, but I promised Scarlett no guns today."

"Thank you, honey." She beamed at her husband.

Reno, Kylie, and their kid came through the entryway right then. Kylie was carrying a large food Tupperware.

"I hope that's your gorgeous spinach dip." An excited Scarlett squealed.

"It might be." Smiled Kylie, under Reno's arm.

Reno gave a chin lift, holding Michele in his arms. His stepdaughter was a cute pill. "Better put your strong panties on, guys. I got word from Ruin that he and Rory are coming in. You know he turns into a Doberman watching over her when we're all around."

Ruin's old lady had agoraphobia and didn't attend many club occasions, but when she did, he hovered like a papa bear hunting for rabbits. Most of the time, Rory assured her old man she was fine, but Ruin was still vigilant for the sign someone might say the wrong thing to upset her. Only the famous popstar could control Ruin, and seeing their enforcer totally soft for his woman was always a sight. Bash couldn't blame Ruin for being fanatical about her protection and wellbeing. He treated his old lady like a queen. If given the chance, Bash would do the same for Charlotte.

"Hey, you could bring out your guitar, Bash," Chains said with a smirk. "That would wind Ruin up if you asked Rory to sing with you."

"I'm not trying to die tonight, VP." He pushed off the bar and grabbed his jacket, swinging it on. "I'm off to pick up Charlotte. If you ass-clowns could behave tonight…" he left the rest hanging as everyone burst out laughing, and Bash grumbled as he strode out the door.

The Diablos didn't have behaving in their vocabulary.

Charlotte

"Kiss me, Charlotte."

Lottie answered Bash's demand by leaning into his unyielding body and gently pressing her lips to his. She was still baffled about why she enjoyed how he demanded affection from her. Her body snapped to attention each time, begging to obey and *please* him.

The kiss started slowly, his lips tenderly tempting hers, savoring the moment.

Gentle yet *assertive*.

Giving her no doubt that Bash was in control of her mouth. *Entirely*.

She hummed against those soft lips. Then, she angled her head to the right as Bash's incredible tongue slipped inside her mouth, taking control, and he emitted a groan so sexy her fingers dug into his veined forearms so she didn't wither to the floor.

Bash was amazing at kissing.

Was it possible to become addicted to someone's mouth?

If she was on better terms with Toni, she'd ask her the question. But right now, she was keeping her distance despite Toni's efforts to make amends.

His hand held the side of her face possessively, keeping her mouth hostage under the skill of his tongue as he tangled it around hers. Lottie moaned into Bash's mouth and rode her hands up the front of his chest, unable to resist touching him.

Another addiction, she realized. Touching him was stimulating, and he never stopped her curious fingers.

His mouth pressed against hers urgently. *Demanding.* Using his thumbs on her jawline so her mouth opened wider.

He acted starved, with bites and licks that almost curled her poker-straight hair in a ponytail. It was as if kissing her was the sole thought occupying his mind throughout the day. Lottie inched nearer until her stomach grazed his crotch, and the breath was ripped out of her, feeling how powerful he was.

Arousal hit her from all corners.

That buzz of attraction was ever growing. Turned on by her boyfriend, she didn't even know who she was anymore.

Fused at the hips, he touched the front of her neck in a dominant move, causing her to shudder with anticipation before he wound her ponytail around his hand.

"I dream of this hair." He husked against her lips. "Using it like a rope while I take this mouth, so I can seduce these innocent lips into wrapping around my cock."

Oh, wow. When Bash said those hot words, she imagined it all, and damn, it made her even more turned on, thinking he'd take control of her actions. And how good at it he'd be.

He tugged on her ponytail and slanted her head, kissing down the column of her throat.

Plundered. It was the only word for it.

It was charged, risky, and filled with enticing promises.

With a rapid heartbeat, she moved away from him when their kiss eventually slowed, trying to catch her breath. Recalling their location outside of the Diablos' entryway.

Even before that, when she'd heard his black Dodge outside her house, she'd felt the overwhelming need for his mouth. She acted impulsively and caught Bash off guard by jumping into his arms.

He collected her in his car because she'd insisted she couldn't go to a cookout empty-handed. She'd carefully placed a jumbo container of devilled eggs on the back seat. Her secret ingredient was finely chopped jalapenos and chive mayo mixed with the yolks. They were always a big hit when she took them to work potlucks.

Now, all Lottie wanted was to be alone with this man and kiss him until her lips were numb. The idea of walking inside and being social for however long, while she felt twisted up inside, wasn't appealing at all.

"Kissing you is the sexiest thing in the world." He shared, his voice all rough and heavy with longing. She was learning to pick up his cues better, and how he looked at her was not masked. Bash wanted to be alone with her, too.

"We could always drop off the devilled eggs and skip out..." she suggested, hoping he'd say yes—a little scared he'd say yes.

As horny as he was making her feel, Lottie wasn't sure yet if she was ready to jump on a massive biker cock and lose her virginity. And Bash wasn't pushing her. She used to think guys had manly tantrums if they didn't get enough sex, but he was so sweet and patient, and she loved him even more for it. She *liked* him even more for it. *Liked*.

"Ah, baby. You don't know how badly I want that. But I want you at my club. Do you understand? I want you to see it's not as bad as you imagine."

Lottie nodded. She couldn't put it off forever. And deep down, she knew the Diablos were nothing like Thorn's gang. Bash made it clear what kind of man he was.

He was overloading her awakened hormonal system, replacing everything she'd known with feelings of longing that only his mouth and hands could appease.

His head stayed close until she could look at the deepening color of his irises. Such a handsome man. She could gaze at him endlessly, without wanting to tear her eyes away.

"I don't know what you see in me, Ben. I'm odd. But I sure love kissing you." When his eyes flashed darker, she realized what she'd said and burned all over as he pressed his chest to hers. "*Bash*. I meant to say Bash!"

"If you wanna be odd, then be fucking odd, darling. I'm still gonna be into you. I'm still gonna drag you into dark corners and feel you up and make you moan."

He had the upper hand in every aspect of their relationship.

And truth be told, she preferred it that way.

Every time Bash took control or shoved into her comfort zone, she grew warm and sticky inside and softened for him, anticipating what he would say or do next.

The man had no filter, and she secretly loved it.

Say my real name when you want fucking.

She heard it repeated in her head and realized that's what Bash was doing. He was waiting for her to tell him when she wanted it.

"If you keep looking at me like that, we won't make it across the door. I'll fuck you in the back seat of my car." He growled against Lottie's neck and then stepped back, but hooked up her hand to keep her close.

Lottie laughed airily and tugged on his hand, reminding him about the eggs in his car. "I can't help having eyeballs, Be... *Bash*."

His gaze snapped to hers when she nearly slipped with his name again, and something syrupy unfurled in the lowest region of her abdomen, where all her sexual appetites were waking up and listening only to his command.

"You can't help having a sexy little body, either. Let's head inside before I devour it."

Thank goodness for Bash's crude tongue. It kept her mind so discombobulated that she didn't worry about being nervous when introducing her to many faces. The man at her side had already swept the nerves out of her and replaced them with a savage longing for him.

Lottie didn't yet have a soda in her hand when she gasped loudly, thankful for the heavy rock music pumping through wall speakers, so no one else caught it. She latched onto Bash's bare arm, where the Henley was pushed up his muscular tatted forearm, with the ribbon of veins on the underside, and she shook him for his attention.

She stared across the room like she was seeing things.

"Bash. Bash! Omg. *Omg*! Be cool." She whispered when he dipped his head to her mouth. "Don't look now, but *The Rory Kidd* is over there."

She had loved Rory Kidd's music for as long as she could remember. The woman had a voice gifted by the angels, because she could sing any genre of music, and make it sound as though she was singing to you personally.

At her side, her boyfriend chuckled and handed Lottie a glass of Pepsi, with a lot of ice clinking against the glass and a black straw stuck in the top. Still, all her concentration was watching the woman in the flowery maxi dress sitting with her biker husband, who looked as sullen and scary as a man could be. But Rory Kidd smiled lovingly as she played with the biker's fingers.

"I told you Aurora was married to Ruin, yeah? And I told you about the antics of their teacup pig," reminded an amused Bash.

Lottie was too busy hyperventilating to take notice of his masculine logic. Pft, who had time for that when she was having a fangirl moment?

"Hearing that you *know* her and *seeing* her with my eyeballs are two different things, Bash." She breathed, unable to contain the electric excitement zipping around her chest. "I think I'm sweating. Have I turned red?"

"I think I want to know why you don't get this excited over me, little darling," he smirked, tapping a fingertip on the edge of her nose.

"Hey, I get plenty excited for you in a different way. But this is Rory Kidd. I've loved her music for ages. You've seen all my CDs! I even collected the limited edition ones her record company put out last year, even though she's been retired a long time."

"I know, little darling," he flashed that sinful smirk again, and she tuned back into Bash's frequency, shuddering when he slid a hand to hold her low on the hip. "Do you wanna meet her?"

"Meet her?" she shrieked, wide-eyed, nerves bumping all over Lottie. "Like in person? With my face?"

"Baby." He chuckled and tapped a kiss on her lips. "You are fucking adorable. Yes, in person, that's how it usually goes. You can't be any worse than Casey, who screamed right in Rory's face when she met her."

"Oh, god. I have to be cooler than that then." She heaved in a calming breath and took the longest sip of the soda. "Is she nice? I'm sure she is. You can tell with some famous people that they're as nice as you want them to be." She gibbered.

Yep. Rory Kidd was even lovelier in person when Bash nearly carried her across the room so Lottie could meet her musical idol. It felt like a dream, and Lottie floated on air.

Most everyone was outside because of the sunny day. The grill had been fired up, and the smells of charred meat permeated the air. And a bounce house was set up for the kids attending with their families. But one by one, more of the bikers' wives drifted over to Lottie and Rory Kidd. There was Scarlett, Monroe, and Casey, who she thankfully knew more than the others. Then Kylie and Kelly came over, and last, Nina. Bash rose to his feet and dipped his head to kiss her. Lottie took it shyly, feeling her cheeks heat.

"I'm gonna leave you with the girls while I grab you a plate of everything. You good with that?"

"Of course," she smiled gratefully and tugged on his collar to kiss him again. Bash's eyes darkened, and he put his mouth on her ear. "My good girl." Then, to the other biker, he said, "You wanna escape with me, Ruin?"

Ruin grunted. He hadn't said a word since Lottie had sat down, but he was watchful, especially over his wife. The guy was about as intense as it came. "Are you okay, beauty?"

"Yeah, love. Get some food. You didn't eat earlier."

Ruin frowned. "I'll be back soon. What will you do if you need me?"

"I will scream *Jesse!* at the top of my lungs," Rory Kidd chuckled and wasn't shy when she smacked a kiss on her husband. "I promise I'm fine."

"She's fine, Ruin." Piped Scarlett, wearing the cutest cut-off shorts and red sandals to match her fire-red hair. "Or you could stay and gossip with us."

Ruin rose to his feet and kissed Rory again. Then, with Bash, they both strode off toward the back of the building.

"Whoa, your husband is intense, if you don't mind me saying," Lottie remarked, and Rory beamed.

It was Nina who said. "Girl, you have seen nothing yet, so stick around; you'll see intense in abundance."

"He's mad at me because I forgot my property patch." Explained Rory and Lottie's brow creased with confusion.

"What's that?"

"When we're at these things, the guys like us to wear a *Property Of* patch, so other men know we're taken and don't hit on us." Said Monroe, and that's when Lottie noticed all the women, apart from Rory Kidd, were wearing similar leather vests to what the guys wore. Each one was a different color. The patches on the back said which man they belonged to.

"Mine is pink." Stated Rory, "But it doesn't go with my dress, so Jesse is scowling."

"No one would dare even look at you, Rory. They know he'd spoon their eyes out." Informed Kylie, holding a glass of clear liquid. The woman had a riot of tight curled hair bouncing on her shoulders and was wearing hot pink nail varnish.

All the biker's wives were incredibly gorgeous.

"I told him this rock he put on my finger was enough claiming, but you know how he is." Lottie got the impression she loved her husband's passion.

In her chest, she felt a pinch of envy.

Not for another biker, but for what those women wore.

They'd been claimed. They belonged to someone.

As archaic as it was, it felt like they were part of something huge.

An unbreakable partnership.

And Lottie experienced a twinge of envy, wondering if Bash would want her to wear his Property Of patch. Or if another woman before her already had worn it.

Was it a reusable patch?

But it was wild to even think about it right now.

They weren't there *yet*.

Charlotte

As panicky as Lottie had been about attending the MC party, she shouldn't have worried because the biker women welcomed her like they'd always been friends.

As they moved outside, her eyes immediately sought Bash and found him watching her.

Those anxious butterflies quivered in her stomach.

Dying to go to him, to feel those strong arms band around her and never let her go.

Before she could, her phone pinged with a message, and she frowned, looking at the unknown number. It was from Nora, asking to talk.

Without a reply, Lottie deleted it and set the phone to silent.

The picnic tables were set up close enough so people could converse with each other. Bash grabbed her hand when she was near and dropped his mouth to hers. His lips tasted of potent liquor and everything masculine that he was.

"How was it?" he asked, and she melted to see he was interested in her answer.

"Meeting Rory Kidd was everything I hoped it would be. But they're all so nice. I've had fun talking with them."

His smile lit her up.

"I'm glad, Charlotte. So, you'll come back?"

"Hm, maybe." She answered, trying to be all cool and coy as she batted her lashes. "If you ask me nicely."

"You know how nice I can be." His undertone was clear.

Boy. His tactics of niceness left her wet and needy for his territorial touch, especially his attention.

Every day, it got a little worse.

"You're a chameleon, aren't you, Bash?" she asked, always genuinely intrigued by his fascinating layers. They'd chosen a picnic table by themselves, but plenty of people were around having fun. However, Lottie only had eyes for her man, who was straddling a bench. "You've been patient with me. Kind and generous with your time. You make me laugh more than anyone. And I relax around you. But there's this other thing about you…"

"What's that, darling?" he asked, a dark smirk kicked up the corner of his lip.

"It's like you're holding yourself in check."

"I don't hide shit from you, Charlotte."

"No, I didn't mean it like that. You use your friendly gloves on me because you think I might bolt if you show me who you are."

Bash's eyebrow lifted. "Are you thinking about bolting?"

Lottie snorted. "Hardly. I enjoy kissing you."

"And other things." He reminded her flirtily. She ought to have known there wasn't an inch of Bash, which was gentlemanly. Of course, he'd bring up how easily he could make her come.

"Yes," she tapped his chest in a chastising motion, "and other things."

The only man she registered on a chemical level was him. Something about him immediately drew her in, even when she'd tried to avoid him.

That feeling was the driving force of all her recent decisions.

"Whatever you think or feel, you don't have to water down for me." She shared. "Even if we're not on the same page yet, I'd like an open dialog between us."

"I can do that," he agreed. "Does that mean I can tell you I'm dying to put you on my lap, so I can feel how wet you are, before I make you cry an orgasm into my mouth?"

Every inch of Lottie's hair was set ablaze. Not *literally*, because she'd seen the ramifications of hair being on fire, and it was not something she wished for. But no part of her body was unaffected by his words. In her mind, she could see herself climbing onto Bash's lap, almost hearing herself moaning as he slipped past her panties to check out her dripping arousal.

"You're mean." She complained playfully. The way Bash's eyes would flare with passion when she told him she needed something from him. She was certain he'd do it right there.

He knew he'd flustered her and he flashed her a little smirk. "Just truthful, darling."

The following hours flew by quickly.

She ate a wide variety of foods until she felt like she would explode.

She laughed so much at everyone's stories. Learning more about Bash as he cradled her hand. Quite a few times, if she was left alone for any time, men who weren't Diablos asked who she belonged to, and there was a slash of warmth through her chest every time she gave Bash's name.

By the fourth time she was asked, Lottie was nearly high on endorphins, declaring that Bash was her man. She'd left him in the backyard, building the bonfire, and went to find a bathroom. She ran into Scarlett and asked for directions.

"Oh, girl, I have a key for our bathroom. We don't want any gross boys in there." She produced a key from her back pocket and showed Lottie where to go. Scarlett stayed in the four-stall bathroom until she was finished and washed up. "The best thing I asked Axel to build." She said. "I'm all for equality, but a girl doesn't need to see the gross bathroom habits men have."

"You asked your husband to build you a separate bathroom in his club? And he did?"

"Yep."

"Wow." Lottie was impressed that this pint-sized woman had such influence in a male environment. "Why do I think that's romantic? It's so practical, my type of gift."

"I know, right? I want a hot tub next, but Axel won't install one at the club. He said he'd shoot anyone in the face if they saw me without clothes." Scarlett looked delighted recounting her man's words, and Lottie couldn't help but laugh.

They remained talking for several more minutes.

"Okay, I think I've distracted you long enough. Are you ready for your surprise, Lottie?" With a radiant glow, the woman locked up and linked arms with Lottie.

"Surprise? What surprise?"

"Oh, you'll see, but you're gonna die."

And you know what? Lottie almost died when they stepped outside again. Everyone was hanging out around the massive bonfire in different groups. It wasn't pitch black yet. She searched for the one face she liked the best in a sea of bikers.

When she spotted him, she stumbled and froze like she'd been zapped with a freeze-ray gun.

"Surprise, Lottie," Scarlett whispered, as she nudged her and then took off to sit with Axel. But all Lottie saw and heard was Rory Kidd singing.

Her favorite artist of all time was not only the sweetest person ever in real life, but was singing right there!

If it had only been that, Lottie would have been ecstatic.

But there was more.

Her boyfriend chilling beside her, accompanying Rory by strumming an acoustic guitar. His fingers danced on the strings as Rory sang her famous lyrics.

She didn't even know he played an instrument! And look how crazily good he was with his head dipped over it, never missing a note of Rory's song "*Flowers of Sugar Dreams*." It was a slow, sultry song, and Rory's voice was incredible, giving Lottie chills on the back of her neck.

But there was more.

After Rory's song ended, she smiled at Bash. He kept playing, but the tune transformed into something else.

And then the guy of her dreams started singing.

It wasn't some random mumbling or him goofing around.

Bash had some serious singing skills.

His voice was so raspy and sexy, and he didn't miss a single note. The sound flowed from his throat like he'd been singing for years. His voice had a rough, whiskey-drenched quality, making certain words come out gravelly.

Lottie's emotions amplified, and her feet wanted to run because she couldn't process how extraordinarily huge those feelings were when Bash's gaze held firm.

The song was by Luke Combs, and as Bash powered through the lyrics, '*When she gets that come-get-me look in her eyes, well, it kinda scares me the way she drives me wild.*' Lottie's hands went up to hold her beaming cheeks, as that heart of hers threatened to thump right out of her chest. His voice was a replica for Teddy Swims.

There was no space to catch a breath for the sexiness she was hearing.

She was tempted to crawl to him on hands and knees until she was curled around his legs. Lottie couldn't look away as another layer of her biker boyfriend was revealed.

He was *electric*. So dynamic. She was having an out-of-body experience, transfixed by him.

He was the type of guy she never thought she'd be into. Strong and *extremely* dominant. But there was no denying her feelings or the connection they shared.

As the song progressed, Rory Kidd chimed in with a few lines. Their blended voices sounded perfect together. Bash was looking directly at her while he sang a love song.

Once it finished, the rest of the group whooped and hollered, clapping for them both.

Lottie realized she hadn't moved an inch, kept spellbound by her biker boyfriend with the singing voice of a sex god.

The world could have imploded at that moment, and nothing would have pulled Lottie's focus away from Bash as he carefully put down the guitar, and started through the crowd toward her.

His stride ate up the space, his eyes burned into hers, and Lottie nearly expired.

She felt excitement and fear, her heart racing uncontrollably as if he had instantly bared his soul to her. She was so excited, she unglued her feet and met Bash halfway.

"You didn't tell me you could sing."

He half smiled. "I can't, not really."

"Shut up. You were fantastic, Bash. I nearly died. Rory Kidd singing right in front of my eyes. But then you started singing, and I wanted to explode into glitter. It was so good. No, it wasn't good. It was freaking *incredible*." Unable to stop her joy from spilling all over.

She was too shy to ask if he'd sang it for her.

But there was no need, not really, not when Bash cupped the side of her face and leaned in to kiss her. Lottie immediately went up on her tiptoes, feeling how his tongue gained entry to her mouth, and the boil of lust whispered between them.

His kiss made Lottie realize she didn't want to go back to being alone. As they kissed more passionately, she came to a decision and knew it was the right choice.

She was going to say his full name, and Bash would know what she was asking for.

Despite the roughness, she loved how he handled her ponytail. She enjoyed it all, his biting and groaning into her mouth. Lottie needed him to take her somewhere, she didn't care where.

But then she was ripped from his mouth when she heard someone yell, "Prez!" there was panic in the scream as everyone looked toward the back door.

The bikers all shot to their feet and headed over to the younger guy wearing the prospect vest.

"We need Denver, Prez. Dillion got hit badly. He's slashed up."

"Who the fuck by?" growled Axel, already striding inside. Bash was the only one who didn't follow the other bikers. With a frown, he held onto her arm. "I'll take you home, Charlotte."

"Denver isn't here, Bash, remember? He took Casey home."

"They'll call him in. Come on, we'll walk around to the front." Again, he tried to direct her, but Lottie shrugged off his hand.

"I can help."

"Baby, no." he frowned. "I don't want you around this shit."

Lottie gained insight into his thoughts from his tone. He attempted to shield her from the trouble at the Diablos' door. He wanted her to see the Diablos in the most positive way possible, so she wouldn't end their relationship. Everything she'd told him about her apprehensions about dating in the past year was valid.

But it was also different now.

The Diablos weren't the monsters she thought they might be.

And she was stronger than Bash was giving her credit for. Putting on her nursing attitude, she faced him. "I can help. Take me inside?"

He gusted a sigh, but grabbed her hand.

It wasn't quite pandemonium inside the clubhouse, but Lottie could have cut the tension with a knife. Axel was asking questions of the uninjured guy. From what she'd gleaned, the two prospects had been sent out to do a pickup and were jumped by masked men. Dillion coming off worse.

"Axel, Charlotte can look at the probie," Bash spoke, and all those bikers turned her way.

Axel didn't hesitate. "Are you sure?"

She nodded. "Does Denver have a room to work in?"

The boy was lying on a medical grade table when Axel showed her to their medical room. He was shirtless, and there was a thick towel wrapped around his arm, stained red with his blood. He looked around her age, maybe a little younger, and his face was taut with pain, draining of color until he was pale as flour.

Thankfully, Lottie's training kicked in and gave her a sense of calmness.

"I need everyone out to give me space." She issued and heard feet moving as she walked to the wall-to-ceiling storage unit, crammed with every paraphernalia needed for a medical room.

"I guess I know where Denver's blackmailing went to." She mumbled and caught the sound of deep male laughter from behind her. As she looked around, her gaze landed on Axel standing in the doorway.

"What's your name?" she asked the injured guy, sterilizing her hands and donning a plastic apron and gloves.

"Dillion," he groaned, thankfully still stubbornly alert. "Is it bad?"

"Let's look, shall we? Why didn't you go to the hospital, Dillion?"

His eyes flicked behind her. She saw Axel staring back with his stoic face, and the older man spoke. "That doesn't matter, babe. Can you help him?"

She would try.

The wound was severe. Despite needing stitches, Dillion retained full movement in his fingers, and fortunately, the artery was not damaged. It would've been a more dire emergency, and Lottie wasn't a surgeon.

She found what she needed from well-organized and labeled drawers and had a syringe of pain reliever loaded.

"Are you okay if I touch you, Dillion?"

"Yeah, yeah, babe, go for it, please." He grimaced, white as a ghost and sweating.

"I don't have the full equipment to treat him properly," she directed toward Axel, "he ought to have an X-ray."

"Just do your best, babe." The president of the club told her.

"I'm giving you some pain relief first before I clean and stitch you up."

"Thank fuck, yeah, gimme it all, babe. I'll love you so fucking much." The man groaned with a half-smile.

But all Lottie heard was the growl coming from behind her. "Watch your fucking mouth, probie." Warned Bash. Her man acting like an unhinged demon, watching her every move. She brushed it off, blaming the situation while the bikers watched in the doorway.

"You're gonna be fine, Dill," said the other prospect. He was the one who looked most worried. "Bash's nurse is gonna fix you."

Bash's nurse. That's who she was now. She'd smile about it later when she had time to reflect.

Once she got Dillion all drugged and calm, she started fixing his arm. It was bad, and he surely would have scars once healed. She didn't get why he didn't go to the hospital. The plastic surgeon would've done a way better job than her.

As Dillion reached out to say something, Bash abruptly surged forward, preventing her from answering the patient.

"Bash, you need to give me some space."

"You do not fucking touch her." He hissed.

That was it. She spun around with her hands full of medical tools and told him, "Out, I need you out, Bash. You're not helping right now. I mean it."

Her man stood there, staring as he dropped his head. "Does he need to be half-naked, Charlotte?"

She got less annoyed because her guy was jealous she was touching someone, even if it wasn't sexual. *He was so jealous*, she wanted to do giddy backflips. Note to self: learn how to backflip.

"Yes, now out, please. This is what I do, Bash. I'm helping your people." She reminded him. Bash gusted a sigh, shot the prospect a stare, and stepped out of the room but didn't go far, positioning himself with Axel and Chains.

"You keep your hands on that table where I can see them, probie." Cautioned Bash.

"You got it, boss, hands are right here."

"If he cuts them off, I'll try to sew them back on the right arms," she told Dillion, giving him a teasing grin, and he laughed. "Thanks, I think."

Charlotte

It was sometime later, when Denver arrived, she was finally finished, and Dillion's arm was stitched and bandaged. The bikers scattered when they saw she knew her stuff. Only Bash and Axel remained with the other prospect—whose name she forgot.

"Shit, look at you, probie, being taken care of by the best," he remarked. She snapped off the apron and balled it up to throw in the trash can. "Everything okay here, Lottie?"

Lottie was still half salty with that biker, but she'd be civil. "Yes, he needed forty stitches. I've given him antibiotics from your supplies. Make sure he takes the entire course and changes the dressing regularly, or that arm will need amputating."

"What?" Dillion jack-knifed to a sitting position, his eyes growing wide.

Both Lottie and Denver laughed.

"She's yanking your chain, probie."

"Oh, thank fuck. I need my arm, babe."

She started for the door where Bash was waiting, but Denver gently caught her arm. "Thanks for this, Lottie. You took care of one of ours. It means a lot."

"It's no problem."

"And what else?" Bash said, staring so severely that Lottie shivered from how attractive he was. His question was directed at Denver. Bash's closest friend let out a small laugh before directing his gaze towards her.

"And I'm sorry for blackmailing you into letting me take this stuff. I never would have ratted you out." Denver's eyes gave Lottie a coherent message - he would do whatever it takes. And after being around the men here, she understood that, weirdly.

"Apology accepted."

"He's not gonna do that shit again, are you, Denver?" advised Bash, in his oh-so-seriously, pantie-melting rough voice.

"Nope." He smirked, kinda meaning it.

"I appreciate that," she told him. "If you'd asked me first, I could have connected you with a medical supply company. It's like Costco, only cheaper and tax deductible, practically free, which is your preferred price." She said, tongue-in-cheek. Denver laughed. Bash didn't.

He was already advancing into the room to take her hand. "Are you finished here?"

"Yeah, unless Dillion wants that amputation now?"

"Hell no." The guy jumped off the table. "Thanks, Bash's nurse. I owe you big time."

She expected Bash to take her home after the excitement, but he led her to his room through the hallways and stairwell.

Lottie's stomach muscles tightened like a vise, and every hair on her body rose, anticipating his next move. While he unlocked the door, he put her in front of him. With his free hand, he latched onto her ponytail, and zips of pleasure went down Lottie's arms.

"Say nothing yet, baby. I'm hanging on by a thread." He issued a fiery warning.

He encouraged her into the room, flipped on a light, locking them into his club bedroom.

The air was palpable, whipping heat around them like a typhoon.

She remained static, her heart banging out of her chest, and her pussy was aching for the attention of only one man. The intensity of his gaze was so fiery that it was a wonder his bedroom didn't catch fire.

Bash shrugged out of his club vest, placing it on a hook on the back of the door.

Of course, she remembered this room, where it all started for them, yet nothing held her attention like he did.

Bash exuded an incredibly masculine energy. His captivating appearance caused every part of her body to ache from only a glimpse. From his tousled brown hair to the shadowed tattoos on his skin. The thick silver rings on almost every finger, including his thumb, thrilled her. His well-worn jeans hugged his perfectly sculpted rear end like a work of art.

That man had an ass worth posting about on social media.

"Do you realize how fucking incredible you were taking care of the probie?" His pride in her made emotion bubble in her stomach. But he wasn't finished with his praise. "I watched you that day saving the boy's life on the roadside, and I was so turned on by you, I could have punched through the road to get at you, but I couldn't do anything then. But I can now. Take off your clothes, Charlotte."

He spoke his demand in a thick and unmistakable timber.

Lottie's thighs tingled, and she had the urge to rub them together like a stick insect because of what he was doing to her.

"I want to watch you undress for me, baby. But if you need me to do it for you…"

Didn't that boost her confidence?

Overwhelmed with exhilaration.

She was desired.

She was *wanted*.

Bash was completely into her and he didn't even try to hide it.

She was nothing but erratic breaths and sexual longing as she toed off her sandals and snapped open the buttons of her prim white shorts. Bash didn't miss a thing as his eyelids fell to half-mast. It was *exciting* to have him watching her.

"That's right, my good girl."

His praise spirited right between her legs, and her clit frantically pulsed, craving his fingers to make the ache stop.

Bash hadn't missed her reaction as she stepped out of her shorts. "You like that, don't you? Being my good girl."

"I think I do, yeah."

He smirked in return and came forward. Before he reached her, Lottie whipped the t-shirt over her head, leaving her only in a cute turquoise bra and panties set, decorated in delicate flowers around the edges.

The way Bash's stare flamed, you would have thought she was a lingerie model flaunting her seductive lace.

His breathing increased, similar to Lottie's.

She couldn't stand the distance any longer. "Will you touch me now? *Please.*"

Bash charged at Lottie like a bull, grabbing her around the waist.

"I'm thirteen years older than you, little darling, yet I know this body was made to be mine." He expressed so much confidence in his gruff way.

She couldn't disagree. Not when he was the only man she felt this way about.

"The first time I saw you," Bash said. One hand rolled up between her aching breasts, and he latched those fingers around her throat like a rope. "You stole the breath out of me. You took charge of the situation and then handled a bunch of asshole bikers like kindergarteners. And there I was, gaping at you like my whole fucking life just changed."

Oh.

OH.

"You're in that same place as me now, aren't you, little darling?" he husked, a smile striking his features. His fingers made a necklace around her throat.

"Yeah, I'm there now, too." She answered truthfully. "I just like to take my time."

Bash chuckled. Before she knew it, he'd thrown her down on the bed with a bounce and a surprised squeal from her lips.

"You're about to experience what my mouth can do. It's my turn to take my time." Bash nuzzled his mouth into the side of her neck, scraping with his teeth until she wanted to writhe underneath him. "I really want you to beg."

Her head felt light, her body was heavy with lust. Begging she could do. She was about to beg like a frantic animal.

She'd never stood a chance against him. While Bash may have been ready for a relationship before her, Lottie was ready now.

Lottie most likely wouldn't have admitted her feelings for him if it was up to her. She would have remained friends with him, enduring the suffering of unrequited longing until he found someone new.

Something deep inside her reacted to Bash in a way that felt so carnal, so real. A part of her soul was yawning awake and begging him to keep her.

It sounded ridiculous, especially for a woman who couldn't wax poetically. She didn't even know if she possessed a romantic side yet, but she was willing to jump in with both feet if it meant she kept feeling these incredible, pulsing sensations whenever Bash touched her.

A tsunami-like wave of arousal surged through her veins. It was so strong that it robbed her of sanity.

She not only wanted him. She *needed* him.

How was he naturally dominant in making her lose her mind with the slightest touch? As his lips roamed across her cheek to find her mouth for a fast, over-too-soon kiss, then that wicked mouth moved down her chest, she stroked her fingers through his hair and trembled.

"Need to warm my girl up first." He claimed, raising his head to take her mouth possessively, forcing his tongue inside until Lottie moaned in ecstasy.

Get her warm? Was the biker insane? Couldn't he tell she was almost combusting?

But then his hand slid into her panties, and she dissolved into a moaning wreck as soon as his seeking fingers focused on her clit, and started strumming with precise movements.

Lottie's hips bucked, and she whimpered into his mouth, pleading for more.

She was plenty 'warm' in moments as she rushed to a climax so powerful she thought she might have broken her back. She had to pull away from Bash's mouth mid-moan.

After days of experiencing a preview of sex, she craved it even more. The more he tormented her with his mouth and hands, she thought she might turn into a nymphomaniac.

Shaking with remnants of an orgasm, she focused on Bash, who was watching her, and whispered against his mouth, "Please. Again?"

Bash jack-knifed to his feet but didn't go far, and he used her ankles to yank Lottie to the edge of the bed, where he leaned in and buried his nose against the crotch of her underwear.

She nearly died on the spot. Attempting to crush his head by snapping her thighs closed, but he forced them wider, to run his nose up and down the dampened crotch. Sniffing her.

Oh heavens above, she was dying as every inch of skin became pink.

"Fuck, Charlotte. You are incredible. Look at you spread open for me. My sweet begging girl, this is the way I've needed to taste you."

He yanked her underwear off and jammed them into his back pocket.

"Beautiful girl." He dropped to his knees like he was going to worship. Lottie angled up to her elbows so she could see him better. When he traced a fingertip along her slit, then brought that finger to his lips, he groaned. "This perfect pussy is going to get to know my mouth, baby. I'm gonna need it often." *Oh, please.*

Regarding sexual experience, Lottie trailed behind Bash, but she knew what she wanted, and it was him all over her.

She yearned to map her hands over the hot valleys and dips on that perfect specimen of a man. And to make him grunt noises the same way he ripped sounds out of her.

She wanted to kiss him until she died from lack of oxygen, and then to come back to life so she could see how masculine his skin tasted.

Lottie was insatiable for him.

He'd been the perfect boyfriend for weeks.

Attentive.

Caring.

And downright seductive.

Now Lottie needed him to be the dirtiest.

"About to be, baby." He told her, and she realized, in her hazy lust, that she had spoken her fantasy aloud. "I'm gonna take my good girl for a walk on the filthy side."

He showed her how by keeping her legs forced open with his hands, he blew air over her mound, gave it the tiniest lick along her slit, and then... *ohhh*, Lottie moaned like she thought they did in porn films when Bash—the sweetest, kindest man on earth—ate her pussy like a starved, unhinged man.

He was lewd with it, lashing his tongue from side to side until he edged into her lips, and then he licked some more, seeking her screaming clit—throbbing for the attention. He didn't make her wait before he latched his mouth on like a demon and sucked.

Oh, god, he *sucked* so hard.

Lottie bent forward, one hand fisted into Bash's hair, and tumbled into a tailspin with building pleasure she'd never felt before. Why hadn't she anticipated how wonderful oral sex would feel?

Made better with the way he rasped filthy words against her sex while he ate her and grunted sex-like noises.

"Beautiful pussy."

"Drown me, baby."

"Let me have it, Charlotte. That orgasm you're holding onto belongs to me. *I want it now.*"

His words absorbed into Lottie's skin and occupied every crevice with mushy satisfaction.

Those last words were pressed against her aching center as Bash rode two long fingers into her and curled them in a way that destroyed her.

Lottie instantly flatlined.

Charlotte

Breath gone.

Eyes rolled into the back of Lottie's head, and she emitted stuttered, baying noises.

The man she was crazy about had his head buried between her legs. She was having the most fevered maladaptive daydream, or life was treating her so well.

All she embodied was passion and bliss. And Bash.

"*Fuck*, you've got to be quiet, baby," he groaned against her pussy, looking up at her through lust-saturated eyes, and his lips were glistening from her pleasure. "Or I'll need to end whoever hears my girl orgasming all over my face."

Lottie's world tilted even as she tried to laugh at his joke. Her core liquified, tightening her walls first and then releasing on an exhale. The pleasure was too much. She completely fell apart as his tongue explored intensely, making her have an orgasm that went on and on in the steamiest way.

Dazed and resembling a reanimated corpse, Lottie was positioned on Bash's lap and cuddled into his arms, however long later.

The obscene way he lazily licked her from his lips melted her entirely.

"Was I quiet?" Lottie thought she might have gone deaf there at the end. If she'd screamed the place down, he would have to squeeze her out of a window because she was not doing the walk of shame twice.

"If my mouth hadn't been between your legs, I would have eaten those sexy as fuck noises out of your throat, baby." He told her. "When I get inside you, you'll cry down my throat."

Okay. Wow.

"Won't you, my little darling?" he pressed with what she now recognized as his dominant voice. And her body listened.

"Yes."

"That's my good girl." Bash kissed her.

Was this how it felt to be so obsessed with someone you'd do anything for them? When Lottie waited for a flicker of shame to sprout, none came. She hummed her contentedness and wrapped her arms around him.

"When do you, *erm*… have a turn?"

She knew well that he gave so much to her and had taken nothing in return.

"It's unfair to you I get all the goodies."

"Goodies," he chuckled, roping her throat with his palm again. His frame engulfed hers, but not to make her feel small. "It's not about turns, baby. Making you come is the greatest fucking privilege. That's what I get out of it. Seeing you react to my touch is my pleasure."

"I want to make you feel as good as I do, Bash. If you tell me what to do for you."

A shudder went through him as he lowered his face to the crook of her neck. "I'm hanging on by a thread, Charlotte. If you want your hands all over me…" he left the rest of the words hanging. *Expectedly*. "You know what you need to say."

Ben.

Benjamin.

The tremble zipped along Lottie's neck, where Bash still held, right down to her toes, not missing an inch between.

Nerves rattled in her veins with a warm whisper.

She wanted him.

But her worries were stacked on top of each other. As meticulous as Bash was at making her come, and his insistence he *enjoyed* it as much as she did, she had enough ego to want the man she was dating to have the same level of pleasure, and for her to be the best woman he'd ever been with. To make him burn and become so addicted to what she did to his body.

However, as the days and weeks went by without them having full sex, the doubts crept in and found crevices in Lottie's overthinking mind; knowing she could never compare to the more sexually experienced women he'd been with.

Even tonight, she'd seen the type of single women through the clubhouse, enjoying the company of the bikers, and she knew she couldn't compete with their confident sexuality.

For a perfectionist-wannabe, that was a hard pill to swallow—to believe she would lack somehow once she got into bed with Bash.

It was why she felt comforted when he took complete control.

"You're quiet, little darling." His fingers caressed her softly, and she stared into his eyes. "Are you ready to go home?"

Lottie nodded, stroking the hair back from his face.

She was basking in Bash.

Thinking how lucky she was. How foolish she'd been to hold off from him for so long.

He was seriously beautiful. Inside and out.

Pushing off the bed, after he'd kissed her lips, leaving them tingling, she watched Bash grab her shorts; he anchored them to her feet, helping her into them. No panties, then? Guess he was keeping them. *Dirty boy.* Then he went across the room for her shirt. When he turned around, he caught her red-handed, lapping him up with salacious eyes.

He was still hard in his jeans, and Lottie's mouth dried up.

"If you keep staring at my cock that way and licking your lips, I'm gonna think you want it shoved down your throat, sweet darling, and I need to come inside you the first time."

Look, Lottie wasn't prideful. She didn't have an overzealous ego, lying to herself that she was the bee's knees. If she didn't know something, she made it her business to learn.

Mixing that with how she strived to be a perfectionist made for a weird couple of days of research. Her search history would never recover from the digital trauma. And god forbid, if the FBI were monitoring her, she'd have to apologize for what she made them watch, too. What she'd told Bash about blowjobs still stood. She was unsure if that was something she could do. But she'd wanted the knowledge marinating in her brain for if it came up.

She would take it to her grave, how she'd been practicing on varying sizes of fruit and vegetables, to see how her gag reflex would react. Pretty good was the outcome. But then she'd abused her iPad. It would never recover from the porn clips she'd watched for tips and tricks.

Switching her gaze from Bash's crotch, she flashed him a modest smile, and lifted her arms for him to slip the shirt over her head.

"You make it sound like I'm teasing you, Bash." Ben. Ben. Ben.

"Woman, you exist, don't you?" he growled passionately, hooking her around the waist, his thumbs brushing the underside of her breasts, before bringing her to her feet so she could step into her sandals. "So yeah, you're fucking teasing me. All the time."

Well then.

She trailed her fingers across his t-shirt until she stroked the edge of his goatee.

"That's good to know."

Another reactive growl that made her laugh. He reached for his Diablos cut.

Then Lottie had a thought and blurted out the question, not holding back like she usually would.

"Has anyone else slept in this bed?"

Bash looked *pleased*, and he fastened an arm around her hips. "Your jealousy tastes fucking delicious, baby," he pressed his lips to her cheek and hummed. "No other woman has had the power to make me feel like you do, Charlotte."

"But the bed..."

"Is new. I haven't stayed here that many times. As soon as I knew I wanted to keep you, my sweet, innocent, *good girl*, I bought a new one."

"Oh." She felt shy. And she appreciated his diplomacy for not mentioning other women. She didn't want to know Bash's tally or she really would get stage fright about going further with him. "Okay."

For a moment, Bash's thumb played with Lottie's lower lip, dragging it down and releasing it. A quiet, vigorous concentration in his stare.

"You don't get it yet. The hold you have over me. You could ask me for anything, and I'd get it without question, do anything for you."

Whoa, that was some power rush.

She felt like he was saying something big without giving the words

"Charlotte, you torment me. You know it, don't you?" His hands palmed her butt, and she rested her fingers on the back of his belt. "You've consumed me since that very first day. And now you're completely mine." The smirk fanned the flames of attachment that grew ever stronger the longer she was around Bash. "Let's go home, little darling."

Goodbyes were given to those still around. She'd even exchanged numbers with the ladies to get together soon.

Did it make her a biker old lady?

Or was that a title only for those who were married?

Bash walked her to his motorcycle, zipping her into his jacket and a spare helmet. Before he climbed on in front of her, Bash pinched her chin, directing her head back so he could kiss her so hot she lost all coherency.

"Beautiful girl. I love turning you on."

The atmosphere was so charged between them that breathing became less critical. His eyes, filled with desire, affected Lottie's stomach muscles. That one intense glance made her emotions go haywire.

Once Bash got on the bike, she tucked her hands into his belt and nuzzled against his back. He only wore the Henley and leather cut because she had his jacket, and his cologne smelled amazing.

"Ready, darling?"

Oh, yeah. She was *so* ready.

And she showed how ready she was by running her hand across his stomach until she was between his legs. She gave the solid pipe a good squeeze and was almost overwhelmed by the thrill of touching him there for the first time.

"*Charlotte.*" He groaned but didn't pull her hand away, so she fondled him some more, shaping him with her curious fingers.

"Take me home... *Benjamin*. And if you could be quick about it, that would be fabulous."

The neediest thrill nearly buzzed her clit right off.

The truth was undeniably clear. She had been holding onto it for a while, just waiting to speak up. Lottie needed him in an insane, old-fashioned, almost obsessive way.

"Now?" he growled, looking back at her as Lottie grinned innocently. "You tell me this *now*, Charlotte?"

Once she'd said it and the message was clear, she wanted sex—to be fucked by him. Lottie was light as air and intoxicated by her obsession with him. She was nothing but smiles and grabby hands.

"Yes, now. Let's go, Benjamin."

"Jesus, woman. Killing me," he grunted, his heavy, sexually dripping voice caressed over Lottie. And it was the sound of a devil falling from heaven.

She couldn't wait to know how he felt inside her.

"You better hold on, little darling. We're stopping for no one." He warned, and she laughed into his back.

The bike roared.

And Lottie teased him the entire journey.

Why didn't she know sooner that having a biker under her thrall would be so invigorating?

Bash

"Does my girl need me inside her? *Tell me, Charlotte.*"

Bash was a coiled livewire of frustrated arousal, with Charlotte trapped between him and a wall, her little hips bumping forward, telling him without words what she ached for.

He badly needed relief from her body. *Only hers.*

He didn't plan to push Charlotte forcefully against the hallway wall as soon as she unlocked the door, even before turning on the lights, but his instincts took over to assert his possession of her.

"Yes, that's what I need, Ben."

He saw nothing but gorgeous green lights of consent in her gaze as she shyly slacked her lips and made them wet. Inviting him home.

"Tip your head back and kiss me, little darling."

After that, he was going to ruin her.

Own her.

Make his little darling as insane about him as he was for her.

It felt only fair.

She made a noise so sexual his dick pulsed.

And then she shocked him, kissing him first, rushing up to her tiptoes, grabbing the front of his shirt. She kissed him boldly, not shying away from giving him her tongue, letting Bash know where her head was at—and thank fuck, it was on the same page. He was bursting open, wanting her. His teasing darling knew what she was doing when she pulled away and left him dragging in breaths.

What a gorgeous little treat she was.

Bash was in hell. Or heaven. Depending on what agony he focused on first.

He wanted to fuck her like an animal right there on her hallway floor. Just mount and rut despicably rough. Though Bash was fighting to hold on to civility, to make her first time memorable.

He tried to move them to a better place, a room with a bed at least, but Charlotte's roving hands did nothing to dampen his spirits. They made him weak, turning him on even harder until all he tasted in the back of his throat was her steaming arousal.

This moment was all about her.

Making her fly apart under his hands.

"Baby, you're holding your breath. Exhale while I play with this plump little clit. So slippery already, aren't you? This tight pussy is going to stretch to take my cock. It's going to feel like you're strangling me in the best way."

She gasped when he rode his fingers at a maddening pace up against her G-spot. Bash didn't have teasing her in mind this time.

The aim was for her to drip sexy cream all down his hand in the fastest way possible. "Will you tell me what to do?"

It would be his pleasure.

He needed her drenched and softly relaxed before he fucked her.

This woman was already underneath his skin.

She owned the real estate to his every waking thought.

There was no way a man of his age should wake with a rigid bat of a dick every morning, after the most vulgar dreams of fucking her throat, until she could only whisper afterward. But she'd achieved the impossible and turned him into a man that comprised primarily of filthy thoughts, and horny schemes to make her fall for him.

It wasn't only sex between them.

They'd build foundations to last a lifetime.

But at the moment, it was sex they were chasing.

She was a drug of choice, and Bash gorged on her sweet lips, sucked her tongue until she mewled and clawed at him, all but ripping the shirt over his head, and he indulged his wild yet innocent woman in everything she wanted from him.

"What do you need from me, Charlotte?" he dotted small kisses on her lips, relishing in how she surged forward, trying to take more, but the hand he had locked around the front of her throat prohibited that and he loved to see her straining, *needing it*.

"Only you. I need only you," she confessed, and his mouth went bone dry and his dick harder than ever.

Bash was about to give it to her.

And she would fall in love with him.

Bash was *certain*.

It wasn't boastful to think his cock could work miracles, but he knew what he was working with and how to use it. He wanted nothing more than for Charlotte to fall hopelessly in love with his dick and need it inside of her every hour of the day. *Fuck*, he'd love to sleep with his cock buried in her warmth all night long.

Was it selfish to want her addicted to him? To rely on him for everything? He didn't care. That was his aim all along.

Their foreplay had been enough.

Teaching Charlotte about what her untouched body could experience, at the height of pleasure, was mind-blowing. Now they needed more.

With the simplest sweep of her fingertips on his jawline, Bash was ready to unzip and shove so hard into her, until she screamed into his throat.

But there were other things his tongue hungered for, and once he'd nearly ripped the clothes off her, leaving her naked for his savage eyes to feast on, he lowered and found her wet and so fucking hot between her legs.

Her moans buckled him and made him slurp deeper, tasting paradise with a fast, flicking tongue.

"So sweet. That's it. You're doing so well. Come for your man, Charlotte. If I don't get a soaked face, then I'm not making my girl come hard enough."

She half laughed, taking fistfuls of his hair, driving her pussy into his face. "Ben. *God. Ohhhhh*, that's nice. I'm going to…" his girl exploded.

She was trembling as he continued with the clit play until she told him she was too sensitive for more.

He broke away and climbed to his feet, savoring how sweet she was, and he crushed a kiss on his girl. Letting her taste herself in his mouth just long enough to unzip his jeans. Pushing them only so far to free himself and then rolling the condom down his length before her hand replaced his to stroke him.

Tight and *testing*. From the base to the tip, like she'd found a new toy she was interested in. Bash wanted to spill over her delicate fingers. His soul let out an aching groan.

"Baby," wanting more than anything to fuck into her hands. "There will be time to play with my cock. Now I gotta fuck you."

"Do you promise?" she batted her lashes, stroking harder. His eyes rolled into his skull, fighting not to come.

She could have the world.

As he lifted her in the air, her legs caught around his waist, perfectly adjusting to his stature.

His cock nudged against her softness, and she whimpered low in her throat.

"I have you, little darling. You ready for your man?"

"So ready, you don't even know." She stared at him dead in the eye, and he understood because he was there in the moment with her. "Come on, Benjamin, give it to me already." She teased. "I'm not brittle."

But she was to him.

She was a precious jewel, and he vowed to do anything in his power to always see her safe, *well fucked* and happy.

Hurting her was inevitable this first time. She was so small, and he was *not*. But he promised he'd lick all her soreness away until she thrashed against his mouth.

He had just the medicine for his little darling's sexual aches.

With a shared inhale, he took hold of himself and notched into place. Her fiery center was going to become his heaven, he knew that, but nothing prepared Bash for how incredibly hot her compact cunt would feel, trying to suck the very tip of him inside.

Charlotte was so agitated, pumping him with her hips, clawing up the skin on his neck, and panting little breaths in his face. Her eyes were obscured with lust. Her arousal matching his.

She angled her leg higher on his hip, and Bash slid another inch inside her tightness, and they groaned together.

"Fuck me," he cursed.

"No, *you* fuck *me*," she returned, and Bash gripped her by the ass and drove into his woman with one thrust.

"*Fuck*," he breathed, settling deep within her clenching pussy.

Heat exploded through his groin, and Charlotte locked her nails into his shoulders, her head thrown back as she inhaled brokenly.

"I got you, baby." He rasped against her lips, keeping still until she was used to him. Her pussy walls eventually softened around his length. "Relax for me. That's my good girl. You're so soft, Charlotte, and you feel like paradise."

"*Benjamin, oh, god.*"

"I know, darling," he spoke into her lips and licked inside when she opened for him. He kissed his Charlotte with every inch of pounding desire drilling through his bloodstream.

It was a fucking madness he wanted no cure for.

"God, look at you, baby. You're *beautiful*."

She was such a sight with her pussy stuffed with his cock, stretching around him. Taking him better than he'd imagined.

"You're so big. I expected it, but… are you breaking my vagina?" she whimpered softly in Bash's mouth, even while she tested by circling her hips.

Her pussy choked his cock, the pressure so acute that if he moved now, he'd embarrass himself because the orgasm was boiling at the base of his spine, threatening to jet out of him.

"I would never break this sexy little cunt. But I will fuck it until it gushes all over me."

Anchoring Charlotte's leg to his side, opening her wider, Bash tested a slow thrust and swallowed her stuttered inhale, licking the noise like a collector of her sexual sounds. He sank further, but was still only about halfway inside her.

"Try to relax. Come on, show me you're my good girl and can take me. Start fluttering those sexy little pussy muscles, baby."

"I am," she panted. "Keep going."

Bash was new to easing a woman into sex, and his heart was roaring with pride for his woman taking him so well.

At first, he only gave Charlotte the easiest thrusts, using his hands underneath her ass to move her on and off him, nice and slow, until she started mewling into his mouth.

"Ohh. Ohhhh. *Benjamin*."

Fuck, yeah. He'd warmed his girl up.

Her pussy was so slick that when he looked between them, there was a ring of her cream around the condom, and it caused him to shove up with a harder thrust.

"*Please*," she breathed. "Please just fuck me, Ben."

"Say that again."

Her eyes flared. "Please, will you fuck me, Benjamin?"

It was a bomb of need going off inside Bash's head to please her, to provide everything his girl wanted from him.

When he started shoving upward with his pelvis, it was nothing you'd give to an innocent virgin. He fucked with a frenzy, eating the kisses and moans out of Charlotte.

"I wanted to give you slow, baby." He worked his cock as far deep into her as he could reach, and the bliss was immense, wrapping around him. She was so soft in his arms and so fucking wet they could hear the suction noises as her walls locked on.

"I planned to be the perfect first fuck for you, but you've turned me into an animal. I need to rut and force the orgasms out of you."

"It is perfect. *Oh, my god, Ben*, it's so perfect. Don't stop." She chanted.

A sopping gasp puffed out of Charlotte's lips. She canted her head on the wall and went stiff all over; no noise came with her tremors, but he felt how she spasmed with every part of her little body.

"Ah, damn, baby. Don't squeeze so hard. You're killing me in the best way."

With her legs around him and Bash's body keeping Charlotte against the wall, he could hold her around the neck, controlling the fevered way she kissed him while he pumped and *pumped*, going harder than he should have, but he wasn't lying when he told her she was killing him with her fisted grasp.

"This pussy is mine." Another thrust. "Mine to take when it needs a good fuck." A deeper thrust. "Tell me I own your pussy, Charlotte. *Tell me.*"

"It's yours."

Bash was rewarded with the best view by holding Charlotte's throat as he fucked her with a frenzy. They were a collision of kisses and moving parts.

"You take me so well, baby. You were shaped to handle my cock, weren't you?" He murmured as she went after his tongue.

His little savage came alive under his praise. Bash was on the edge of a climax but refused to let himself lose his control until she came one more time. Their lips collided in a tasting battle when he demanded, "Come on, give it to me. Show me how good you can drench me all over."

She did.

Panting into his obsessed kisses.

He swallowed all her pleas, ramming uncompromisingly into her soft wetness.

Bash followed right after with savage slams.

As he slowed to a stop, he roamed kisses up her pink cheek and down to her neck. Completely wrecked by her.

The best fuck of his life, if he were being honest.

"Christ, baby. I didn't even wait to get my clothes off, or to put you on a bed." He exhaled and felt her shaking with laughter. Unable to feel any regret because, holy fuck, that had been fantastic.

Bash didn't know if he believed one fuck could change his whole outcome, because he'd been that way ever since he met Charlotte. But he felt altered.

He'd wanted to own her for so long now.

It had been his aim, his mission, however sneaky he had to get.

He hadn't factored in how Charlotte owned him right back. Probably even more.

If he had any strength left in his legs, he'd drop to his knees and worship his little darling for the rest of his life.

He angled his head for her when he felt tiny kisses inching toward his mouth.

"You get me naked and remained clothed. I see how it is, Benjamin Laurent." She clicked her tongue, smiling brightly as though she had a light inside her.

Instead, it was his lucky cock.

He threw his hips forward and brushed against her clit. Immediately, the smile dropped from her lips, and she clasped onto his face, panting.

"Oh, that was mean."

Bash smirked.

She was incredible. An absolute fucking queen of a woman. *His queen*.

And he felt euphoric by her drugging touches.

"You are more beautiful than I've ever seen you," he shared.

She flushed and put their foreheads together. "What happens now? Do we stay like this forever? Attached and carried everywhere?"

He wished.

"I would do it in a heartbeat, baby. You look perfect on my cock. I'm gonna have your legs spread so wide so often, you'll think you live on my cock, anyway."

She laughed and slapped a hand on his mouth. "Ben, stop."

"You keep saying my name, and we won't leave this hallway."

He meant that as a promise.

She had little idea yet how under her spell he was.

If his girl needed five orgasms for breakfast, and six at dinner with a plate of tacos, he was her man to deliver.

They were so slicked from their joined pleasure, not ready to disconnect yet, but knowing he'd have to in a minute, Bash trekked up the stairs, giving her little bounces on his still hard length. She whined the whole way.

Bash was gentle and took his time as he carefully removed himself from her body. This woman had changed him with her drugging kisses, addictive laughter, and her incredible mind. She was everything he didn't know he'd been missing, and Bash was determined not to fuck it up.

He was keeping Charlotte.

"One fuck done, little darling," he rasped in her ear, sitting her on the bathroom counter. The red streaks on the condom fueled his over-the-top possessiveness.

Mine. She is mine. "How many will it take to get you addicted?" he smirked.

Charlotte exploded with laughter, blushing all over her naked body. "*Oh, my god.*"

Charlotte

A lot of factors normally played into waking Lottie every morning.

Usually, it was her bladder, demanding attention.

Most often, Prince howled from the doorway, so disgruntled that his human servant wasn't catering to his every whim.

Never once had a hand come through the sheets to touch her. She came out of sleep with her heart racing hard, and her eyes pinged open, in fight-or-flight mode, ready to face a murderer.

On reflection, she probably screamed too loudly. It was the type of noise you'd hear on a 911 call, but in her defense, she hadn't expected to see someone's head lying next to her.

With a startled shriek, Lottie snapped her eyes closed, as a violent shudder electrified straight down her spine. She could be forgiven for forgetting a man was in her bed last night. It wasn't as though it was a weekly, or *ever,* occurrence. Bash emitted a manly chuckle.

Was her hair a mess? Who knew?

Morning breath? Not too bad.

But she was entirely *naked* in bed with a naked boy.

That naked boy was lying on his stomach. His head turned her way, and his hand was palmed warmly on her quivering belly, stroking upward until he was holding her left breast.

"You have to open your eyes eventually, Charlotte."

As Lottie's eyes fluttered open, she was met with Bash's gaze.

He broke into a smile. "There's my girl."

"I forgot you were here." She confessed, breathless at the gorgeous sight of him.

Whereas Lottie probably looked like she'd slept inside a restaurant dumpster, Bash was beautiful, with a little more stubble than last night.

"I figured that when you squealed." He played with her nipple, and Lottie had to think around the blissful sparks. "We have a problem, Charlotte." He said gravely, and her heart sank.

Oh, no. He was already regretting their night together. He was going to give her a zero out of ten, did not recommend. Wasn't he?

With the death grip on the bedsheet to keep her modesty, not that it mattered since Bash was fondling her beneath it, she bravely asked. "What's the problem?"

"Two, really."

She popped up her eyebrow and waited for the answer.

"First, I hope you have coffee because I need one."

Whew. That she could do. Lottie was a coffee snob. If she ever treated herself to new gadgets, they were always coffee adjacent.

"And the second problem?"

"I'm trapped underneath a woolly mammoth." Lottie cracked up laughing. Sure enough, when she rose from the pillow, there was her Prince, lying the full length on Bash's back.

"When did that happen?" she giggled, unable to restrain it.

"About an hour ago. I didn't want to wake you. I think he's trying to suffocate me, Charlotte."

The goateed biker was freaking adorable.

And he looked so relaxed in her queen-sized bed with his sharp, beautiful eyes watching her.

"He likes you, Bash. I don't have any other data to base it on since he's never sprawled across me in bed."

"He's jealous and wants to murder me."

She giggled again, turning on her side to face him.

"You look cute." It was the wrong thing to say because Bash tweaked her nipple, and she shrieked.

"Woman, you're actively watching my slow slaughter, and you call me cute? I should spank you."

"If you weren't trapped under my beasty, you could." She moaned as her nipple endured the pain once more. Then Lottie tapped the bed. "Come on, get off Bash. He doesn't want to play cat and mouse. You won, my clever boy."

Prince twitched his pointed ears, staring at her as he nuzzled the back of Bash's head. Seeing her moody cat being so fond of someone was so bizarre.

But she couldn't blame him, since she wanted to rub all over Bash, too. After more coaxing, the cat moved to the bottom of the bed to clean his paw.

"I saved your life. Now you owe me."

She felt shy under his scrutiny, wishing to see into his thoughts.

"I'm not used to men in my bed." She shared, randomly.

"Good." He lunged forward to press his face into the side of her neck. His face scruff tickled and Lottie giggled. "You only need one man in your bed. I'm that man, Charlotte."

She was weak and full of girlie endorphins. "Yeah, I got that."

Prince was highly disgusted by their playful antics, and he swished his bushy tail, jumped down, and pranced out of the bedroom.

"I'm guessing you must be sore, so I will resist fucking you, baby," Bash stated, just like that, no filter in sight, making Lottie blush to the high heavens. Because yeah, she was tender as hell between her legs, like she'd straddled a submarine all night. "Though I want to be inside you again. But I need a kiss. Give me this mouth, Charlotte." He demanded.

Of course, she gave him it. She nearly head butted him in her haste to kiss him good morning. When Bash groaned, he fisted a hand in the side of her hair and swept into her mouth with his tongue, giving Lottie the type of morning kiss she'd only ever read about.

Right away, the pleasure depended utterly on him.

She chased it, ached for it.

Just like a cellist would monitor the conductor and follow his lead, she responded to Bash's sinful signals as he intensified the kiss, delicately biting, causing her to let out a soft whimper into Bash's mouth.

Last night had been more than incredible.

Bash had taken such good care of her before, during and especially after.

A biker in her bed, what a way to wake up, she thought. But now that biker was in her mouth, doing wicked things around her tongue, and Lottie drowned in him.

Until recently, Lottie was ruled by her analytical mind. No decision in her life has ever been made spontaneously. In the last weeks, that version of Lottie had all but disappeared. She reacted now and relied on emotional impulse. It was uncertain if her former self was taking a much-deserved break or if she had retired permanently.

He tasted like dark chocolate. Like spilled sin and wrong yet *good for you* decisions.

Bash took with dominance and overpowered Lottie with his signature seductiveness.

His kiss conquered.

Stamped a claim all over her.

Falling into him was as quick as falling into a black hole.

But then, like fate wanted to Bash-block, his phone rang, and he cursed, snatching it from the nightstand to look at the screen.

"Sorry, baby, gotta take this." Then he answered, "Yeah? Can it wait? I'm about twenty minutes away. Yeah, fine. I'll let you know. Later." Then he hung up.

Because of the late hour, nearly nine a.m., practically mid-afternoon for Lottie, she reckoned he was already late for work. When

Bash looked her way, his pupils were dilating to suffocate the color from his irises.

"Something important?"

"Not as important as you, but it's a job I need to get to soon."

There was silence as Bash toyed with the ends of her hair.

"This morning after thing is awkward, isn't it?" she huffed. "I need to use the toilet, but I'm not wearing anything. How do people just bounce out of bed buck naked?"

Bash's attempt to prove his hotness was a success as he uncovered and rolled out of bed.

Absolutely gloriously naked.

Standing there like his cock wasn't at face level with her burning cheeks, so brazen for staring at the weapon that was pounding inside her hours ago. If she could walk today, it would be a miracle.

"You are shameless," she chuckled, half hiding her face.

The air was both lacking and smothering. And Lottie was avoiding the inevitable, because who wouldn't want to be naked in front of this man? He'd worshipped her body like he couldn't get enough.

"Come on, baby, climb out of bed. Show me your stunning body."

Lottie was mortified, dying to pee, and sexually frazzled.

Going easy on her shyness, he went to use the bathroom. She heard him wash his hands before strolling back. Still comfortably naked.

He pulled on his clothes, and she watched, entertained. Masculinity rolled off him in poised waves. Bash had proven to be a seduction wizard even when pulling up his jeans — going commando — and covering up his perfectly bare ass.

Everything about the man was a disruption.

One Lottie welcomed with open arms.

"Charlotte, you're starting something you can't finish," he caught her.

Before she knew it, he pulled back the covers and yanked her into his arms, bride style.

"*Fuck it*. I can't put my dick in you, but I can let my mouth apologize to your sore little pussy. Let's get in the shower, woman."

Shower? With him? *Naked*?

She was going to pass away.

She hoped her tombstone declared how thoroughly satisfied she'd been at the end.

"But… you're already dressed." She nibbled on her thumbnail, eyeing him.

"Then you can undress me."

Oh. Yeah. She loved that idea.

And that's what they did.

Showering with Bash was checked off a bucket list she recently made up. He was attentive as he was careful with her, but every stroke of his soapy hands built a frothy need inside, and when he dropped to his knees to apologize between her thighs, as he told her he would, she was *wrecked*.

No longer a virgin, and she'd also experienced shower shenanigans with a biker.

There was no topping this week, Lottie was certain.

Bash

Leaving Charlotte so Bash could be Axel's proxy in a meeting had been the hardest thing to do.

She could quickly build her walls again if he gave her too much space to think.

No way was he giving up the woman of his dreams and the best sex ever.

Charlotte was gasoline on his fire.

The breath in his lungs.

Every thought he had lately centered on owning her and getting her hooked on him.

Charlotte had been such a shy thing about kissing him at the door, even after she'd taken his rampant fuck last night. She'd wholly owned his cock.

He learned that once a man found the woman he's obsessed with, the one who gave his life meaning, he wanted nothing screwing that up.

How had he lived without her tormenting his existence?

Give her up? Walk away? Go at her slower pace? It was impossible.

His girl was a blank canvas, and he planned to paint her with his filth.

Discovering what would make her scream and beg was his vocation.

The abandoned way she'd yanked his hair and fucked his face earlier in the shower. He knew he was closer to getting his woman hooked on him already.

That made his stride all the smugger, as he walked into the open doorway of a hay barn, two towns over from Laketon. Splice was monitoring the outside. Diamond and Devil were with Bash. They'd gotten word through a source that Harvey was trying to rent nearby farms for cannabis cultivation—otherwise known as a weed-growing farm.

Even if it hadn't been Harvey and one local with a fresh business enterprise, it wasn't what Axel would allow in Utah. Weed farms brought too much attention from the law. They'd be everywhere if they thought the town was going into cultivating cannabis.

Yeah, it brought a lot of revenue, and it was something the old faction of Diablos dabbled in before Axel mainstreamed the club, to better hide their dirty money in legitimate properties. But the cons far outweighed the pros.

"How heavy do you want me to be?" asked Diamond, looking distracted when he'd turned up, but he had his game face on now.

"Let's play it by ear," Smirked Devil.

"Good afternoon, gentlemen," Bash announced their presence, and six pairs of eyes turned their way.

Four farmers, plus Harvey and his simpleton brother.

"Turn around and fuck off." Harvey hissed.

"I guess our invite was lost in the mail, Josh?" he directed the question to one farmer. All four were known to the Diablos. Axel had asked Bash to create a database of all the companies in their surrounding areas years ago. A lot of them they knew personally.

"Bash. Hey, guys. How's it going?" he looked guilty, did farmer Josh.

The Diablos didn't play the heavy. If no one fucked with them, they didn't fuck back. It took a small, weak man to bully. His MC wasn't about that.

Right then, his phone vibrated, and he slipped it out to read the text.

SPLICE: SUV just pulled in alongside Harvey's car. Three Riot Brothers and a chick with bangable tits.

Bash told him to keep watch.

"We'll cut to the chase because Diamond here hasn't had his fourth snack yet, and my brother gets hangry."

All eyes pinged toward the bodybuilder biker.

"Word on the street is you're trying to lease their farms to turn it into a weed ranch. Axel sent me to let you all know that isn't happening. Today or any other day. With these farmers or any other."

"You can't fucking do that!" seethed Harvey. "What shit I do has nothing to do with your fucking MC. I tried to appeal to your better nature and found you had none."

"That's right." Bash smiled, "We're uncouth motherfuckers, and you best remember that. We don't play fair and never will with your kind. Gentlemen," he turned to the farmers. "What's going on?"

They looked from one to the other.

It was Josh who chose to be the spokesperson.

"You know times are hard, Bash. Crops aren't growing as fast as we need to sell, the fucking weather is against us, and inflation is making our produce almost free. We can't keep going on like this." Frustration was thick in the air, as the man raked a hand through his wheat-colored hair.

These men had families and kids to feed. Bash understood the dilemma. He couldn't say that, in the same situation, he wouldn't choose the lesser of two evils to do business with. If it earned them enough money to get through the winter months.

But two wrongs didn't make a right.

"This isn't what we wanted to do." Another farmer spoke up.

"But that's what you're doing." Bash pointed out. "Did you know it's a maximum prison sentence of forty years to life if you're caught with only a thousand cannabis plants? And how many acres are your farms? Four? You have six acres, right, Silas? Your grandmother kept it afloat during the war, and now your ailing parents live with you and the Mrs, yeah?" he sprinkled in the personal deets and saw Silas' eyes widen.

"You're taking all the risk for Harvey, and for what? A few grand to keep the banks off your backs? You get caught, and you will, because have you smelled the plants? That scent goes for miles. He won't wait around to tell the cops that you rented out the land because you're broke. Nah, he'll hang you out to dry, and while you get used to prison food, your families are evicted, he'll have already found new idiots to con."

Harvey should've figured out by now that the Diablos wouldn't let him off the hook, if he had any brains left. He was whispering with his not-so-smart sibling, probably coming up with a different plan.

Bash wasn't worried.

He faced all four farmers and let the silence stretch.

"We don't have a damn choice here, man." One snapped. "You got no fucking idea what it's like for us. One more season like this, and we'll have to sell up."

Bash understood being broke.

He hadn't grown up with a silver spoon in his mouth. His mom did her best. He got a job to help as soon as he could. As soon as he could earn a lot of money, he helped more. Even now, though his stepfather was a proud man and took care of Bash's mother, Bash still liked to treat her. She deserved it. So, he understood the despair of not having anything, the fear of losing what you had.

"That's where you're wrong." He started. "There was a choice. You could have talked with Axel. Did you consider that?"

They fired him perplexed glances.

"What do you mean?"

"You guys shop on Main Street, yeah? All those thriving businesses along that way. Not one storefront is empty now, like it was five years ago. The Diablos are responsible for that. We supported those people until they started earning money. What you're forgetting, gentlemen, is that this is our state and our town; we want our people to succeed."

Bash heard Harvey snort. "Utter bullshit. These fuckers would burn you if you step out of line."

"Diamond, it's time to show these bozos to the door."

"Gladly." Smiled Diamond and stalked over. He didn't even need to act menacing. He walked like a hungry wolf. The MC brother was tall and imposing, and Diamond's presence instilled fear in others effortlessly. There was no need for them to know he was a kind-hearted giant who enjoyed baking.

Despite Harvey's loud protests, Bash carried on after Harvey left. "All you had to do was ask Axel for help. My friend Devil here, you know the Devil? He's gonna stay back and chat with you; he's our money man, there's nothing he doesn't know about turning a profit. If you need a loan, we can do that, too."

The farmers looked stunned and also skeptical.

It wasn't altruistic of the Diablos. Far from it. They weren't charitable men. Ultimately, it just made more sense financially to avoid unnecessary police involvement.

As soon as Bash stepped outside, leaving Devil to do his money spiel, he noticed the Mercedes and SUV were still parked with engines running. He gave Harvey a finger gun sign as he walked to the bikes. Something grabbed his attention. It was brown hair, at first glance. And as he put on some shades to shield his eyes, he inspected the SUV.

What the fuck?

He could've sworn that was his Charlotte in the back seat. Bash's stomach dropped when he saw the side profile. He frowned, his brow creasing.

She kinda looked like her, but the mouth was way off. This woman's mouth wasn't as soft as his woman's, and her face was longer. She also had bangs covering her forehead.

Besides that, she was a cheap knockoff replica of his Charlotte.

A man in the SUV exited, leaving the back door open while switching seats with the person in the front. The guy climbing into the back yelled, "Shut the fuck up, Nora! I won't deal with your crap like he does." And then he slammed the door.

Once the vehicles were gone, he hopped on the bike seat and made a phone call.

"Hey," she said, a smile in her voice.

"Hi, darling. I know you're at work, I won't keep you. Listen, you have a sister, don't you? Does she live in Utah?"

"Erm, that came out of left field," she laughed a little. "No, as far as I know, she hasn't returned to Utah in however long. She moves around, but we don't speak, remember? Why do you ask?"

"I'll get to that in a minute. You said she was in with a rough crowd, yeah? That's why you hesitated to get involved with me; you thought I would be like your sister's man."

"I did…" she paused. "I thought we were past that, Bash? I told you I was wrong about you."

She was such a cautious little thing. He was going to kiss the fuck out of her later and then teach her to live a little dangerously with him. Naturally, he'd protect her like a dragon would its hoard. He was finally getting the picture as clear as day, and nothing would touch his woman. Not her crappy sister or the men she'd aligned with.

"We are. I'm asking for a reason. So this gang, do they call themselves the Riot Brothers?"

Her inhale was answer enough. "Yes, how did you know?"

"I think I just saw your sister. She looks enough like you I thought it was you from a distance."

"Nora is here?" her voice going up an octave. Then. "Crap."

Bash went on alert. "Does that mean something bad for you, Charlotte?"

"No, not really. But I'm not in the mood for Nora's drama. She's my sister. I'll always love her, but she's draining. I told her years back that as long as she was hanging out with those people, I wanted nothing to do with her. They're bad news."

"I know, darling."

"Listen, can we talk about this later? I have to go. Bye, hotness." She whispered the last part, and Bash chuckled. She was so fucking cute.

What a small world, he thought, sitting on his bike, waiting for Devil to come out of the barn. The Diablos' enemies were connected to someone who's linked to Charlotte.

Was that a coincidence?

Bash's mind was spinning with questions, leaving him with a heavy feeling in his gut.

Did Harvey know about Charlotte?

And would Nora try to use her?

No way he'd allow that.

Charlotte

Lottie found out her sister was in Utah four days ago.

When she saw Bash later that night, she recounted all the details she could recall about the Riot Brothers' gang.

She found it odd about the connection.

She prayed Nora would leave town without contacting her.

Whatever trouble she was bringing with her, Lottie wouldn't buy tickets. Not her monkey, and no longer her circus.

There was a time she would have looked at her sister's social media, to know she was at least alive. Nora was fully engrossed in it, posting pictures of her supposed life to elicit envy from her high school friends.

Her memories of Nora weren't all colored with bad things, but those good times ceased happening years ago. And she still hadn't truly figured out why Nora blamed her for every wrong thing in *her* life.

Both of them had a terrible upbringing. But Nora acted like she was the only one who got a raw deal. It got so bad that Lottie had no choice but to go no contact with her sister.

Despite being caught up in the euphoria of Bash, she still had concerns about Nora being in town.

They had dinner with Denver and Casey last night, and then she stayed at Bash's house for the first time. When she was beneath Bash, all her worries disappeared. He made certain. He was like a hurricane, commanding her focus. His mouth was a menace. When he kissed her, all she could think about was his dominance.

And because of that, she was smiling during a hectic shift.

She had partially patched things up with Toni. Their friendship had entered a new era, and she was fine with that.

Some people were a season, a reason, or a lifetime.

Perhaps Toni's presence in her life had a purpose, despite her cruelty, since she'd pushed Lottie out of her comfort zone.

She wanted Bash to be a lifetime. Only time would tell about that.

As Lottie was moving paperwork to another department, a coworker informed her that someone was at the reception desk looking for her. There was pep in her step, hoping it might be her hot muffin biker. He was so sweet. Since they couldn't do lunch yesterday, he had food delivered. She'd sent him a kissy-face text as thanks, and he'd replied that he would own her mouth as soon as he saw her. And he'd kept to his word.

Bash wasn't waiting for her, and Lottie took a deep breath, seeing her sibling leaning on the desk. She always looked so pretty with her perfectly wavy hair. The summer mini-dress looked great on her slender body.

"Nora." She spoke, and her sister twirled around, smiling.

That should have been the first clue this was no friendly visit, but an ambush.

"Long time no see, sis. How are you?"

To avoid making a scene, she gestured for Nora to follow, and took her to a private room where they talked to relatives of recently deceased patients.

"I'm at work, Nora."

"You look good. We could grab some lunch together and catch up." She looked hopeful, and Lottie felt a tug of guilt because the last thing she wanted was to spend any time with Nora.

"I can't. Maybe another time," she said to be polite, but there was no chance of it happening. "What are you doing in Utah? When you left, you said you were never coming back."

"Oh, that." She laughed, waving a manicured hand and tossing her glossy hair over her shoulder. "You know I never mean what I say. Thorn is in town on business, so I tagged along, hoping to talk to you."

Business. She could only assume what that entailed.

"I've been trying to call you lately."

"Nora, nothing's changed since our last chat."

Nora's smile dimmed. "So that means we can't be sisters?"

"Are you working?"

"What does that have to do with anything?" she snapped, her lovely façade slipping.

"That's why we can't see each other, Nora, because you expect too much from me."

"I haven't asked for anything, have I? Thorn gives me whatever I want. He takes good care of me, Lottie. We've changed."

Did Lottie want to believe that? It sucked not having any close family.

The women from the Diablos were way cooler and friendlier to Lottie than her sister ever was. Days later, they were still texting Lottie to hang out soon.

"So, if we can grab a coffee soon, that would be great, sis."

Did she dare hope Nora had changed?

And then.

"I have this great opportunity I think you'll love. Like really."

And there it was.

Lottie inhaled and let it out slowly. "That will be a no. No to everything, Nora."

Her sister blinked. "What do you mean by that? You haven't heard what it is yet. It's a no risk investment."

"Everything about you is a risk; I want no part of it."

"You've got such a fucking double standard, you know that, Lottie? Risk? Yet you're hanging with bikers after all the sanctimonious shit you spewed on me about Thorn and his friends. Holier than thou Lottie is doing the same thing."

Lottie's gaze sharpened. How did she know that? Unless Nora or Thorn had been watching her house. The thought of it creeped her out.

"The Riot Brothers are bad news. You've always known it. So whatever this opportunity is, that's your mess, not mine."

"You've always thought you were better than me." Nora glowered.

She didn't want to ask if Nora was taking drugs to explain how erratic she was, but it was a good possibility.

"I don't think. I *know* I am," Lottie told her.

She no longer sugar-coated her sister's feelings. For once, she could take the hard truth with a tall glass of milk. It wasn't as though she'd ever listen, anyway.

Nora, as predictable as ever, spat expletives at Lottie.

"You act like the world owes you a favor. Like I owe you a favor, Nora. But what have you ever put into the world besides a lot of bitching? I worked two jobs through college and have the career I earned myself. You hitched your wagon to a worthless piece of shit, expecting his wonder dick to fix your problems, and when he inevitably proves he's useless, you come crying to me without ever trying to change."

"You know what you did." Her eyes were filled with hate, which used to hurt Lottie. But no longer. She'd hardened her heart against her sister years ago.

"What invisible crime have you made up in your mind to make you hate me? The last time I checked, Nora, we had the same childhood. Your shit wasn't worse than my shit. But I've made something of my life, and you can't stand that."

"You're fucking boring. Who wants that life?"

"Me, I do. I achieved something on my own. Instead of doing the same, you wasted time with drug-using losers. Men with bigger egos than their intelligence."

"Shut your mouth, you know nothing."

"Don't I? I know they're criminals. You're tarred with the same deadbeat brush."

"And what of your bikers? I could tell you some shit about them."

It was too late for Nora. Lottie knew that.

She had been with the Riot Brothers for years, fully involved in their activities. Lottie had made plenty of unsuccessful attempts to reason with Nora in the past.

"Look, I'm sorry, okay? They're my family." Nora softened her voice, but Lottie wasn't fooled. She never stopped pretending.

"That's fine, but keep out of my way. I blocked you for a reason."

"Oh, shut your fucking mouth, miss high and mighty, control freak."

Lottie's smile was devoid of any humor. "And? You're not telling me anything I don't know. I took control of my life, Nora. You're pissing yours away. So we're both fucked up, huh?"

"Listen, I need a short-term loan."

"Congratulations, I hear there are jobs that help with that."

"Don't be smart. I need money now, and you owe me."

Lottie scoffed. "For what? These invisible crimes against you? I'm so sorry I fed and clothed you for years when I barely had enough to get me through college. I'm so sorry I was the one who signed for your first apartment and car. I'm so sorry for bailing you out—how many times? Countless. These so-called crimes are all of your own making."

Nora's mask dropped, revealing her true self to Lottie. An enraged, impulsive, and indulged woman. She was a toddler in a grown-up body.

For years, Lottie had justified her sisters' behavior by attributing it to their deprived upbringing. There was a juncture where today's decisions could not be held accountable for an awful childhood. It was tough to deal with, especially because she wanted to see the best in Nora.

"I might be pregnant. I need money, sis."

"Congratulations." That poor kid.

"It won't hurt you to give me a loan."

Loan. Ha. Her definition of a loan involved giving with no repayment.

"How do you know what I have?"

"Look at the car you drive."

"It's on finance."

"You've got a house."

"It's called a mortgage, not liquid money. I work for the things I have."

Nora popped out a skinny hip and rolled her eyes behind the fake lashes. "I know you. You've probably saved a bunch, haven't you? Having kids isn't cheap, you know? Oh, you wouldn't know that, would you? When was the last time you got laid, sis? Or are you still carrying the cherry around?"

Wouldn't she be surprised if she told Nora it was this morning? Her inner thighs were still aching from being held on Bash's shoulders all that time while he pummelled orgasms out of her.

"That's none of your business."

Nora cackled, and her eyes gleamed. "I thought so. If you gave me a loan, I could set you up with someone."

"Thanks, but no thanks. I'd rather dip myself in a bowl of herpes than date men you know."

Nora's eyes flared. "You *bitch*. You're no better than me."

Sighing, Lottie rubbed her forehead. "This is where we came in, so I'm wrapping up this futile conversation."

"I need it! You're not going to help me, seriously?"

Lottie gave her sister a withering look. "Do you know how much it costs to have a baby? If you are pregnant, which I doubt, you wouldn't allow something else to take your spotlight. A few hundred bucks won't dent what you need to prepare for it."

"I need more than a few hundred, Lottie. I'll pay you back."

"How will you pay me back?"

Her voice became more whine-like, like old times. "I'll pay you back. You know I will."

"No, I don't know that. Of all the times I've loaned you money, tell me how many times you've paid me back. Go on, guess." When Nora only glared, Lottie continued. "It's zero times. Ask your king of a boyfriend. You just said he pampers you."

"Thorn is strapped for cash right now, but he has a few things coming up that's gonna get us big. I need something to keep us going."

Thorn was a redneck loser from the deep south. He should've been swallowed instead of born because he's done nothing meaningful. He was a freeloading jerk who spent more time in jail than anywhere else.

"Isn't that what he's been telling you for years? Do yourself a favor and find someone better."

Nora's face took on a nastier appearance as she narrowed her eyes into darker slits. "So you can have him? You already tried that, remember? It's why you owe me. I forgave you for that shit."

Lottie nearly choked on her spit. "Is that the lie he's feeding you? I wouldn't have Thorn if he came attached to Chris Pine's dick. I told you back then, the same as I'm telling you now, he tried it on with me more than once while you weren't around, and I put the asshole in his place. He made up lies to cut you off from your family. You ate it all up and started attacking me."

Nora huffed. "I don't wanna discuss that. It's in the past."

"Yeah, you're right, Nora. I'm asking you one last time; don't contact me again."

With that, Lottie walked out of the room, never looking back. She then returned to the ER floor to do what she did best.

Taking care of other people's problems.

Charlotte

Dating a biker was exhausting.

Sleep seemed to be a distant memory.

Something old Lottie would do regularly, at least eight glorious hours a night. Now the new Lottie, the rebooted version, barely slept because a horny biker was always banging her.

It was such a hardship.

Oh, who was she kidding?

Being fucked by Bash was far better than REM sleep.

The weeks flew by in no time. Lottie was living a dream she hadn't known was in her heart, until the biker made her open her eyes. He had a profound impact on her life, opening it up significantly. She broadened her social circle and expanded her horizons, not just in intimate settings (such as the shower, in the garage, and those two occasions on his kitchen table) but also through fresh adventures and saying yes to things she normally wouldn't have said yes to in the past. During her day off, they rode to Colorado on his bike last weekend to visit another MC, the Renegade Souls. They were only there for less than an hour before they grabbed some food and headed back home. Lottie had no regrets, even though her legs were in pain. Bash was his usual sweet self, rubbing the top of her thighs in the bath and then, being the romantic, he pulled her onto his lap and taught Lottie how to ride him.

Bash was the true romantic in their relationship. Lottie was getting better at researching and chatting with the Diablo girls for advice.

She found out those ladies didn't hold back when talking about their bikers, and she loved being part of the girl gang.

If Lottie believed Bash would ease up on being so extreme and possessive, now they were officially an item. She was so wrong.

If anything, his attention to detail was even more focused.

Their lunch dates continued. He texted her all the time. They cooked together and enjoyed hanging out and getting to know each other. He was fun and funny. Had great wisdom. And he wasn't too bad to look at, either.

"What are you smiling about?" his rusty sleep voice asked. Lottie tilted her head and grinned at her awake boyfriend. Personal space wasn't a concept he believed in. He couldn't help but pull Lottie onto his lap on the couch, always wanting her close. He either sprawled over her back in bed or cuddled her against his chest to sleep. That's where she was positioned now, and she traced his shoulder tattoo with her finger.

"Oh, you know, just thinking about how sweet and romantic my biker boyfriend is."

"Is that so?" he flashed his trademark smirk, making butterflies dance in her belly. Her heart swelled, and she knew the feeling was something big. Something that wouldn't fade. There was no doubt she wanted to keep Bash forever.

She just hadn't said it in actual words.

But he had to know she was completely smitten with him.

He had to feel how she came alive when he walked through the door. Each smile from Bash was stored in her heart and savored like a favorite candy.

It was midnight, and they were slumped in his bed after getting home from a date. He'd fucked her once in the hallway, quick and satisfying. Then he put Lottie to bed and went to get Prince because he said he couldn't sleep without her, and the cat would need to adjust to having two homes.

He was just so sweet all the time. He purchased double of everything Prince had at Lottie's place just to make her cat comfortable in his house.

Her heart beat for that man.

And now he smirked like he knew every thought and feeling she had screaming in her chest.

"Yes, that's so." She said, stroking the hair off his forehead. His eyes flared, and before she knew it, Bash was on top of her, and Lottie was squealing with laughter.

"I'm about to show you some more sweetness, Charlotte. You better grab on to something and hold on."

Her eyes went wide, and her body grew wetter.

"A third time, Ben?" she teased, scraping her nails up his tanned chest. "Are you sure? We don't want to wear you out. You are… *forty*." She stage-whispered the last part and dissolved into fits of giggles when his fingers dug into her sides, tickling her like a maniac.

"Woman, you're gonna get it."

Oh, boy. She got it.

She got it so good two more times before they collapsed, and she called for mercy.

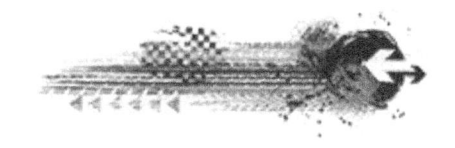

Bash

Her back bowed with the last ram of his dick, and Charlotte let loose a hoarse groan, setting off a cataclysmic wave of pleasure inside his body, now that he'd made his woman come. He fucked her relentlessly, only stopping when she finally released him from the soul-sucking tight grip from her inner walls.

Bash's detonation was just as ferocious.

Sex with Charlotte was nothing he'd ever experienced. Each time he was inside her snug pussy, it was heaven on earth.

If his soul had been snatched by her eyes, then Bash's body belonged to Charlotte just as much. When she wanted it, he provided.

His no-longer-a-virgin woman was a dream come true for teaching her what she enjoyed. She was stubborn until he got her naked and wet. Then she turned into this beautiful, begging little submissive that spoke to his baser self to provide and please.

"Your perfect pussy has wrecked me, little darling," he grunted.

She might be shy in some ways, but her enthusiasm more than eclipsed that. He was learning his darling was a perfectionist. Talking her through how to give him a handjob had been an experience until Bash thought his eyeballs would explode out of his skull. After coming twice, she still wanted to keep going. "I can do better, Ben." she'd whined all pouty. He'd had to tell her if she got any better, she'd kill him. Her beaming smile shot heat to his heart. His girl was a praise goblin, and Bash loved heaping praise on her.

Bash was suspended in that blissful moment as his hands fixed tight on Charlotte's more-than-a-handful-hips, holding her down and keeping her speared on his erupting cock as he filled the latex, wishing he was spilling every drop of come into her fluttering pussy, so he could watch it drip down her thighs, before pushing it back inside her where his come belonged. The overwhelming urge for that was a growl in the back of Bash's head—to claim her in all ways.

One day soon, he promised himself.

After the clean-up, he cuddled Charlotte into his side, ready to rock her to sleep, when his phone beeped. It was only ever club-related this late.

SPLICE: I know you're getting some on the regular now from the sexy little nurse, and your old man hips must be at risk of disintegrating, but can you be at the docks in an hour?

Little bastard.

BASH: My old man hips will outlast your herpes dick, brother. I'll be there.
BASH: And don't call Charlotte sexy if you want to keep your dick for seducing your married cougars.
SPLICE: I think she's sexy!
BASH: You're a dead man walking, Ryan.
SPLICE: HAHA. Give the sexy little nurse a kiss from me right on the mouth. With tongues, I always use my tongue.

Having peeked at the text, Charlotte giggled.

"Don't get charmed by that asshat, Charlotte."

"Aww, but he's sweet. Be nice to him. I think Splice is lonely."

"Lonely?" Bash rolled his eyes. "How did you come to that conclusion?"

"It's just a feeling I have. Last week, when we stopped in at the club after our date, it was only couples around and Splice. He looked lonely, Bash. Maybe he wants a girlfriend."

Bash snorted. His little darling was a sweetheart. But she was wrong.

"Splice is inundated with female company. He's the least lonely person."

"Having lots of sex, dating, or in a serious relationship are all different categories. Nina thinks the same as I do."

"God save us from the old lady girl gang."

Charlotte sucker-punched him, and he laughed. He grabbed her fist and kissed it.

Bash kept her mouth busy after that. There was no room to think of any man but him.

Just how he'd planned it all along.

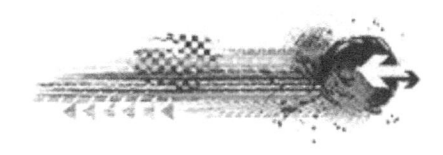

Charlotte

It had been an entire month since she officially became Bash's woman, and Lottie was inducted into the Diablos girl gang.

Scarlett and the other girls were persuasive in the group chat.

But Lottie was not too proud to admit the deciding factor was when Rory—*the Rory Kidd*, who Lottie would forever fangirl over, even if they were friends now—gave Lottie a video call to invite her over to the townhouse with the girls. She'd nearly expired in Bash's living room.

It took her two hours to decide what to wear.

Bash was useless, just chilling on the edge of the bed, grinning at her crazy shenanigans. And he kept grabbing her and giving her sloppy kisses.

"I can't go to Rory Kidd's house with your come drying on my skin, Bash. I absolutely refuse." She had a big smile on her face while he pinned her and whispered the raunchiest things in her ear about what they could do in half an hour, before she had to leave.

She loved getting naked with Bash. He had a body made for sexually objectifying and worshipping with her mouth and hands. And putting his come on her skin seemed to be his kink.

But not when she was about to go on a girl date with sophisticated women.

Lottie was taken aback when Ruin, dressed in a black tracksuit, opened the door. His unsmiling face and brooding eyebrows focused on her.

"Oh. Hey, Ruin. I'm on time, right?"

He widened the door and gestured with his chin, inviting her inside.

Rory greeted her, then told her husband. "Someone is here now, love. You can go to the club."

Lottie watched Ruin crowd against Rory, her friend's face beaming up at him like Ruin hung the moon, bringing her every star in the sky. His head dropped, and his voice was so rusty that Lottie shivered a little.

"Sure? I can sit in the yard until everyone leaves."

"I love you, Jesse, but I'm fine, I promise."

Lottie occupied herself, looking at the ceiling while they kissed goodbye.

"He's worried. I had a rough therapy session, and he likes to stick close." Explained Rory, who ushered Lottie through to their sizable lounge area.

"If you're not feeling up for visitors, we can reschedule for another night."

"Girl, no. I want to see you all. Doing exposure therapy always takes it out of me, but get some wine into me, and I'll be great again."

"Do you mind if I say you two are so lovely together?"

Rory smiled again, pouring the drinks. "Isn't he cute?"

"A bit scary too," half-laughed Lottie, with Rory agreeing with hearts in her eyes.

"Wait until I tell you how I stalked him."

What? The Rory Kidd stalking? No way. This she had to hear.

The rest of the girls came, and their night of fun and gossip kicked off.

Over drinks and platters of nibble foods, they shared stories and advised on how to handle the club women. Luckily, Lottie had yet to encounter them and hoped it would stay that way.

As the night ended, Monroe devised a clever plan to send provocative texts to their partners and test their response time.

Bets were made. More wine was shared. They didn't even hesitate before snatching up their phones.

"The only rule is that we ignore them if they text or call. The bet is to see which biker arrives first. Get your ten dollars out!" announced Scarlett.

"No fair," whined Lottie, sitting on the floor with her back to the sofa, staring at her text thread with Bash, concentrating hard on what to write. "I was a virgin until recently. I don't know how to send sex texts."

"Girl, really? Well then, we have to help our girl out, ladies. No biker bitch left behind." Chuckled Nina.

"Half of my relationship with Ruin was through texts." Rory said dreamily. "Talk about how much you want him right now, Lottie."

"And mention his dick. They love when we talk about their dicks." Added Monroe.

"I told Axel I'm drunk, and he needs to put a baby in me," laughed Scarlett, with the teacup pig, dressed in duck PJs, asleep on her lap. "His head will explode, or he'll break the speed limit, since we're not having kids."

"Chains goes feral if he knows I need something," Monroe said, typing on her phone, smiling. "I told him I'm thinking of his big, capable body and wish I was laid underneath it."

The other ladies fanned themselves.

Lottie was taking notes for future sexting with Bash.

"I let Devil know he's out of the doghouse and I need his colossal body." Smirked Kelly. She was such a demure soccer-mom but with an unfiltered mind.

"Mine is sent," Kylie announced. "I told Reno I forgot to put panties on."

Lottie dissolved into giggles. That was a good one to remember. "Nina, what did you put?"

"My man is simple to seduce." She smirked and turned her phone screen around for the girls to read her text. It said, "Do you want to fuck your wife?"

Lottie's cheeks flamed red. But that was a good one, too.

She had to be fast, or Bash wouldn't receive his text in time to get into the race.

With the girls calling out salacious suggestions, she let her imagination go wild.

LOTTIE: I was thinking me and your big, fantastic cock could have a special playdate soon.

She sent it and then died of embarrassment, covering her burning face.

"You're a natural. You didn't need help at all." Nina announced with pride.

"And now we wait." Grinned Monroe, clicking her nails on her glass.

It took only seconds and the first reply came from Reno. Then he called. Ruin called right away. Chains texted Monroe and called twice. Axel tried texting Scarlett. Tomb called several times. Devil hit up Kelly's phone.

Bash didn't call or text.

Shoot. He was probably away from his phone.

The first Harley Davidson pipes arrived some twenty minutes later, about the time it would take between the MC and Rory's house.

They crowded against the window, and Rory squealed with victory.

Ruin was the first.

But then they heard more motorcycles, and within seconds, Axel, Tomb, Devil, Reno, and Chains were pulling up next to Ruin, who had already de-biked.

And oh, god. Lottie's heart jumped out of her chest when Bash was behind Chains.

As they marched up the steps, they exuded an intimidating aura with their tall frames, fierce expressions, and badass soldier-like appearance in leather garments.

The girls shrieked and dispersed away from the window so they weren't caught ogling.

"Act natural." whispered Nina.

Lottie's heart clattered, and her panties grew damp.

"My beauty, wrap up girl's night." Growled Ruin from the doorway, and he came for his wife.

"Mama, you're in so much trouble," Reno told Kylie, lassoing an arm around her waist.

"Time to go, Lucky." Chains informed Monroe and roped her in for a kiss by the neck. Oh, swoon, that was romantic.

Devil didn't even use words, he just grunted and hooked Kelly up and strode out.

Scarlett's excitement was palpable when she saw her guy. "Get over here, wildcat." Axel palmed her ass and bent his head to whisper something only she heard. When she raised her face, Scarlett was as red as her hair. And she was grinning.

"You know my answer is yes, *wife*." Growled Tomb. "Let's go." He tucked Nina under his arm and barely gave her the time to shout bye before he whisked her away, laughing.

Whoa. The pheromones in the room drowned Lottie, but her heart stopped as she saw Bash enter the scene.

He looked predatory.

Feral.

And all hers.

When their eyes met, she felt an undeniable connection and knew he was hers, filling her with love.

She was in love with Bash. *So* in love.

He stole the breath out of her lungs with the unmasked lust burning in his eyes. She didn't see him moving, but he was suddenly in front of her. Lottie tipped her head back and exposed her throat. He instantly made a necklace with his hand and grasped her gently. There was no fear, no doubts.

Only love.

And want.

She needed him. All the time. But especially now.

"Little darling, you've got another appointment to get to."

She spluttered a laugh, but Bash didn't give her time to say much as he directed her out the door.

"Are... are we on the kitchen floor... *again*? How does this keep happening?" Lottie was out of breath a little while later.

It might have been an hour. It could have been a week.

Once Bash got her home, clothes were torn off. He barked filthy orders, and she was so wet that she dripped down her thighs and onto his fingers, when he pushed her over the table and fucked her with vigorous abandon.

His hand was between her legs, cupping her possessively. "You told me you wanted my big, fantastic cock. That's what happened, *my good girl*."

Only Bash would praise her for teasing him. The aches would come later, but worth it. His fantastic cock had demolished her in the best way.

An hour later, or it could have been a minute, Bash said. "The cat is looking at us."

"You defiled his mommy. He's pissed at you," Lottie murmured into his shoulder without looking at Prince.

"He's figuring out how to get his food if we're dead."

Lottie complained. "I can't move, Ben."

"Christ, woman, my balls are empty for the next hour. Quit trying to seduce me." He groaned, and with an athletic move, got to his feet. Lottie was checking out her man as he pulled up his jeans and left the shirt on the table. "Come on, up you get." He held out a hand, and Lottie whimpered, staggering to her feet. "I can't walk. Will you carry me?"

"Anything for my dirty little darling, who summoned me home because she needed a fucking." He swept her into his arms bride-style, her head rested on his shoulder, and he started the stroll through his house.

"I didn't know if it would work."

He looked at her like he thought she was mad and then smirked, dropping a small, lovely kiss on the tip of her nose. "Always will, Charlotte."

And wasn't that just perfect?

Bash

Bash

No one ever thinks they'll murder someone.

Serial killers, maybe.

Bash, not so much.

But he was with his brothers all the way. Regardless of how the night unfolded.

This had been years in the making. A long wait for Denver and his family.

Since Denver's attack, his friend had been spending hours a day, using every resource, to search for Albie. Years back, Albie was obsessed with Casey and would put her in sketchy situations for his gain. But then she left that life behind and met Denver. Albie lost his mind trying to find her, but he quit when he learned she was with the Diablos. Until recently.

Bash and Denver were behind several establishments in an alley off Main Street. The alley reeked of decaying garbage, and likely had been used by hookers for quick jobs.

"You tight, man?"

Denver wore all black, like Bash, with no club colors.

"I want this to be over so my wife and girls can have a normal life again. Casey might stab me if I continue to confine her in the house."

He said it with a grimace, but Bash chuckled. Casey was an unstoppable force in stilettos, and so damn smart it scared the shit out of everyone. Using her intelligence, she'd helped the club multiple times by gathering information in plain sight. She was adept at negotiating. The guys teased Denver, claiming his wife was like Helen of Troy.

Bash wouldn't start a war over Denver's woman, but he would for his own.

"We'll get it done." He promised.

Bash smoked two more cigarettes before their comms sounded. Phones were left at home tonight, so their whereabouts couldn't be traced.

"We got him. On the way." Axel said in a few words.

Denver went from a relaxed state to having his game face on.

There was obvious tension as the pair took a few more back alleys, avoiding any known CCTV as Bash and Denver walked to Kylie's funeral home.

Only a few patched brothers knew Reno's old lady was the infamous cleaner. She'd been operating a double life for years. By day, she was the town's respectable funeral director. And by night, she made crime scenes disappear. She'd worked with the Diablos for years, even before she got with Reno.

Tonight, her crematorium was going to play a vital role.

Although Bash and Denver had been waiting for hours, everything sped up once they reached the blacked-out SUV at the rear of the funeral home.

The adrenaline was high.

They were all here to support their brother.

Anyone of them could have killed Albie, or made that whole mess go away, but Denver wanted—needed—to be the one.

Bash pulled open the back door, and Reno jumped out, followed by Ruin. Diamond, as always, was with Axel as his protection. The president had control over the man, who was bound, blindfolded, and his mouth taped shut. Axel forcefully yanked him out of the vehicle, letting him land at Denver's feet.

"He was right where you said, D. Offer a man an all you can fuck buffet with a busty hooker, and he came out of the woodwork with his dick in his hand."

The Diablos played Albie like a fiddle, and he bought it completely.

There were no free hookers, no free blow.

Just Albie's imminent death.

"Get it done, brother," Axel said gravely. "We'll wait here; don't take long. We all need to be tucked up at home with our old ladies."

Reno gave Bash the key fob for the back door of the funeral home, and together with Denver, they dragged a groaning Albie inside, into the darkened funeral home and to the tiled room they had scoped out earlier.

The whole thing felt anticlimactic.

There was no big Marvel battle scene.

But not every violent act needed a concerto soundtrack and a sweeping crescendo finish.

This fight had been a long time coming for Denver, and the Diablo brotherhood wanted it to have the right finale.

Bash noticed a huge steel table, the kind they used to slice up dead bodies in autopsies. The tray was slanted so body fluids could drain out. Pretty fucking creepy, Bash thought. Every murderer should have one, and he bet Ruin had it on his Christmas wish list.

Though he was here with his boy, and would assist in whatever Denver needed, to give him peace again, Bash's head and heart were elsewhere.

They were at home with his woman.

Charlotte wasn't becoming his obsession.

She'd been that for a long while now.

She was so twisted around his every molecule, he couldn't separate her, even if he wanted to.

He was fully present tonight, but he longed to be with his little darling, earning one of her smiles and fucking cries out of her.

Easing the thought of Charlotte aside for the time being, he looked at the pitiful bag of shite on the floor as Albie struggled, and attempted to get to his feet, only for Denver to kick him over again.

The guy mumbled in pain as Denver kicked him repeatedly. He searched Albie's pockets and found a phone and a wallet. Bash caught both when he threw them.

Finding a teen picture of Denver's wife in one of the wallet slots was creepy. Bash flashed it to Denver, who became enraged and stomped on Albie's ribs, then yanked him up from the floor, and ripped off the blindfold and mouth tape.

"Surprise, motherfucker. I swore you'd see me again one day, didn't I?"

He let the brothers-in-law have a moment, Denver beating the shit out of him while Bash went through the phone. He whistled through his teeth, scrolling through the photos. It was like he'd started a scrapbook of everything Diablos related. It was stuffed with property info. There were also a few hundred of Denver's house, from all angles, but the surveillance pics of Casey made Bash's eyebrows jump into his hairline.

The scrolling went on forever, going back years.

Thousands of pictures.

Holy fuck, the guy was a straight-up stalker.

Based on the dates, he probably spied on Casey every few months.

Sicko. "This creepy little bastard has a museum's worth of spy pics of your old lady, Denver."

"That's mine!" screeched a bloodied Albie.

"Not anymore." Bash pocketed it.

Denver neutralized Albie's madness with a throat punch. "You *stalked* my fucking wife? You demented fuck."

"*She's mine.*" Anger oozed from the enemy, spittle flying out of his mouth. "She was always - to be mine."

"Not even in a parallel universe, you sick cunt." Denver forcefully pulled Albie's hair, causing his head to jerk back, and confronted him up close. "You'll never know how good her life is, how fucking happy she is. She'll be happier still when I go home and tell her I've burned your mangy bones to dust."

There was a spurt of rage in Albie's eyes, but Denver didn't give the other man a chance to react. He didn't toy with his food. Denver snatched the hunting knife from his pocket, and stabbed Albie in the throat repeatedly, before releasing him. He dropped like a sack of bricks, and he was dead before he hit the floor.

Wearing gloves, the pair silently placed the body into the cremation oven.

"Knife," Bash said and took it from Denver. It would be melted down and disposed with their clothes. Harvey wouldn't give a damn if one of his men didn't make it back, but if he was reported missing, the Diablos wouldn't get into trouble.

"Thanks for being here, brother."

Suddenly, the room lit up as the tube lights flickered on, and there she was, the funeral director, standing in the doorway. Behind her was Reno.

"I'll take over." She informed business-like. Then turned to Denver. "Are you okay?" He nodded. "Go home to Casey. I have it in hand here."

The pack took less than twenty minutes to drive to the clubhouse, shower, burn the clothes, and then separate to their own homes.

It was dark, but Bash wasn't worried when he let himself in and traced through Charlotte's house.

His heart was on fire to see her.

In her bedroom, the one he'd shared with her for weeks, fucking her, making love to her, teaching her every dirty act he knew, and reveling in how she became pliable and loving under his hands, Bash slipped out of his clothes. All that was left to take off was the watch on his wrist and the rings.

Then the lump in the bed suddenly sprang up to a seated position, with his girl holding onto the blankets, her hair in a gorgeous disarray. "Oh, my god, Bash, it's you."

"Who else would be in your bedroom?" he twitched a smile.

"I don't know. Aliens? How did you get in?"

"The usual way." He casually replied, as she was unaware he had a key made long ago.

"You kicked the door in?"

His woman slept like a corpse but was eerily alert the second her eyes were open. Bash found it adorable. He found everything she did sweet as fuck.

"Drop the sheet, baby." He ordered, approaching the bed. She had a feminine bedroom, white and pink. It didn't deserve his filth all over it, but it was about to get it, anyway.

"Oh," she whispered, catching his drift, and his saucy little woman let the sheet go, pooling around her waist. She only slept naked when she was with him. The nightgown cupped her tits and was like silk in his hands. As he pulled the blankets entirely off her, Bash was already fully erect, and his Charlotte dropped her eyes down and then licked her lips.

He hadn't tried fucking her mouth yet. He wouldn't force something she might not like, but it wasn't her mouth he needed.

And he needed so much right now. He was coming out of his skin.

"I need to fuck my little darling," he confessed. "Roll over onto your stomach."

It was the last vestige of niceness he had in him.

When Charlotte gave him her innocent, yet good girl look, and then did what he wanted, her nightgown rode up, revealing her smooth thighs and bare ass.

There was an instant change in Bash.

From man to feral beast.

And then he was all over her, covering Charlotte's softer body with his weight. His hard cock nestled in her ass crack, and he looked forward to the day he taught her how anal sex would make her howl with pleasure. There wouldn't be an inch of Charlotte's body he didn't own.

"I wanted to be home with you all night." He rasped, kissing the back of her neck as he snuck a hand between her and the bed, and found her welcoming slit, so warm and getting wetter as he played with her.

"I'm going to fuck you."

"Yessss." she said with her face turned to the side.

He never missed a chance to appreciate how incredibly fortunate he was to have her. There were no doubts in his mind that Charlotte was the love of his life.

And as much as he worshipped her, he needed to fuck like he didn't.

He was filled with endorphins, and there was only one place where he wanted to work them off.

"I smell your arousal, Charlotte. Do you need a good fuck?" his words stroked her ear, while his hand played with her now-drenched pussy. As he put his cock in place, she moaned, bumping him with her ass. Little tease.

He pushed inside even before she answered, "Ben, yes."

"Ah, fuck. My soaked girl." It was heaven.

And then Bash realized why. He'd gone in bare for the first time. He nearly saw stars when Charlotte's grabbing little pussy clasped him as he tried to pull out. And then all rational thought vanished.

He fucked her in her pretty bed with his girl pleading to come. Hard, forceful shoves from his cock. Each time she cried for more, the deeper he became addicted to her sounds.

There was just a pinch of sense left, so Bash didn't come inside her, not without her knowing about it. But now he wanted that more than he needed his next heartbeat.

His next thrust was hard, and she shot out a hand. He laced their fingers by her head, his mouth on her neck. She was getting tighter with each slam, making him work to get inside her. His girl was close to detonating.

"You don't know how I want to fuck all my come into you, baby, keep you drenched all night, sleep with my cock buried inside you."

He went on with his crazy thoughts and shared all the dirty ones with her until she was a total mess of gibberish.

When his Charlotte came, it was screaming his name.

With the devil of pleasure riding his back, Bash gave a last slam of his cock and pulled free, pressing the throbbing head to her ass and spurted out his orgasm. His breaths stuttered until he was done.

"You made a mess on me," she exhaled into the pillow, and Bash collapsed next to Charlotte, pulling her over his chest. Her ass fucking glistened like frosting, and he grinned like a dirty bastard to see her basted in his seed. His fingers had the urge to gather it up and put it where it should be, deep in her cunt.

The room was silent as Bash kissed Charlotte softly. The moment he entered her house, he had one thought.

To rut his woman until her orgasm shook the bed.

She tasted of sleepy sweetness. He tried to feel an ounce of guilt for waking her, but he couldn't. Smiling into the darkness, Bash kept her snuggled in his arms, assuming she'd fallen asleep, but she suddenly reared up to her knees and straddled his thighs.

"You've had a few minutes' break, old man. Now I get to be on top." She whipped the nightgown over her head, and her happy nipples were right there in his face, begging for his tongue.

"My perfect woman." He praised, and she beamed as she fixed herself in place, grappling with her hands around his growing length. He loved watching her handling him.

"You better believe it." She went for his mouth. "Now get ready for the ride of your life, my biker boyfriend." She looked so damn sexy on top of him that his satisfied shaft was throbbing once more. Then it got better when she stood it up and sat on it.

They groaned together when she fought to get all his inches inside. It took a few persuasive circles from her hips, but his girl was no quitter, and she took him down to the root with a pleased grin, so proud of herself.

"Gotcha." she announced proudly.

She had all of him.

Every inch of his heart was hers.

And then she went to town, screwing him wildly. There was no sight more beautiful than his girl taking all of her lust out on his body. Only after a minute, she grasped his face and looked down between them. Her fingers spanned the base of his dick while she rose and fell on it and then exclaimed. "Oh, shit. No condom, Ben!"

Bash laughed, pulling her down onto him before he smacked her ass. He forcefully kissed her. "Fuck your man *now*, Charlotte."

And that's what she did.

Bash

Death came to everyone eventually.

It was the one thing no one could avoid.

Death, when it arrived, was never easy, even if it was expected or orchestrated.

Bash's biggest regret was not being able to do anything for Charlotte.

His girl, the love of his whole life, trembling and crying in his arms, and he could see the surrender in her beautiful, teary eyes.

She was giving up.

She was accepting what was coming.

And there was not a thing he could do about it.

He didn't give a shit about what happened to him. Death could claim him as its prize, and he'd happily go instead of her.

He regretted pursuing Charlotte and allowing her into his chaotic life. It was a mistake driven by selfishness and love.

With his lifestyle, it was bound to hurt people.

And what made it even worse was that it was always their women who got hurt.

It was way too late to turn back.

Death had already opened the door and was coming inside.

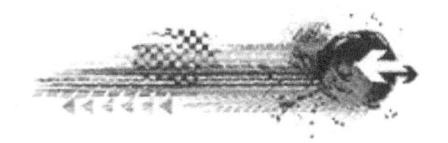

TEN HOURS EARLIER

"You are an absolute menace, Benjamin Laurent!" she squealed, dodging before he could shoot her with water again. "I'm gonna get you."

Across Denver's yard, his twin daughters were hooting with laughter.

Bash didn't know he'd be roped into an epic water battle with his woman.

Charlotte was currently hiding behind a Lacebark Pine tree in the backyard. Like she thought a tree would keep him away from her.

Bash smirked and waited until she peeked out, as he knew she would. She laughed as they fired together.

When he collapsed on the grass sometime later, soaked to the skin, she fell into his lap, and he eased the hair away from her face.

"This was fun," she smiled as they watched the girls scampering around the yard. "We should babysit more often."

Denver hadn't felt safe taking Casey out on a date in a while. Now that his wife wasn't being dogged by her demented stepbrother, he'd asked Bash to watch the girls so he could take her out for a few hours.

"Don't think I've overlooked what you did, little darling."

"What did I do?" she asked, toying with the silver necklace around his throat. She then traced over the four silver rings, all connected by one chain.

"You used my name. And you know what happens when you do that."

Charlotte's eyes lit up. "You can't do *that* here, so I felt confident using it."

His teasing girl thought she was safe, did she?

"Can't I? I can give the kids a plate of cookies and soda and carry you into the house to the downstairs bathroom, where I'll make you hold the sink while I peel those sinful shorts down your legs and then bury my mouth between them from behind. And you won't be able to scream, Charlotte. Then I'd push in behind you, getting in nice and tight to that ass I love. I'll have to cover your mouth with a hand before I shove in, because my sweetest darling can't take me all at once and it hurts at first, doesn't it? But then the pussy I own softens and takes every inch."

"Bash," she groaned, pressing her face into his shoulder. Her fingers went tight on his shirt. Lust shook her voice. "You don't play fair."

Bash kissed the top of her head.

It was only fitting since she had him in tangled knots over how much he loved her.

"Later," he promised.

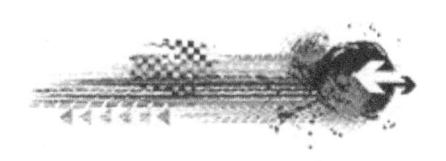

SEVEN HOURS EARLIER

"Hey, hotness, I have something that needs fixing."

Because he recognized the sultry voice catcalling him from the open garage door, Bash was grinning when he saw Charlotte leaning against the wall, trying to go for a bad girl look. But she was every inch the good girl, and he fucking loved it.

He'd put his overalls on to change the oil in her car while Charlotte was inside the club. He peeled them off his legs and tossed them aside.

"I got the right tool for that, darling."

"I bet you do," she squealed when Bash tried reaching for her.

"You're all dirty! Don't touch my shorts with your dirty mitts, mister."

"You usually like me making you dirty."

"In bed only. Not on my clothes."

"Is your girl's meeting over?"

"Yes." She flashed a secret smile.

"And what trouble do the old ladies have planned?" He remembered the night he played cards with his brothers when they all started receiving dirty texts from their women. They couldn't get out of the door fast enough.

"Nina is hosting an after hours' night in her salon. I might come home with blue hair. What do you think about that?"

Bash shrugged, walking to her after washing his hands. "You could have no hair, and you're still the most beautiful thing I ever saw." He bent at the waist to tap a kiss on her waiting lips.

She melted against him and wound her arms around his waist.

"Aww, you're so cute."

He'd show her cute. Smacking her ass, he urged her toward her car. "Let's go get food."

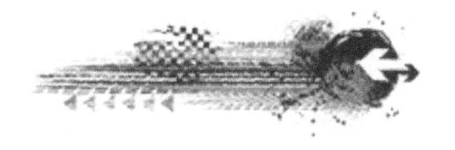

FOUR HOURS EARLIER

"Is it too early in our relationship to go on vacation together?" she asked from the floor. She was currently grooming the most pampered cat in all of America. Bash was equally responsible for spoiling Prince. The other night, he brought home a bell toy he had seen while paying for gas.

He was sitting on the couch doing his favorite thing. Watching Charlotte.

Nothing was too early for them. He was going to race them to the end zone soon.

"Where do you wanna go?"

"Somewhere tropical, with golden beaches and endless carbs."

"I'll make it happen, baby."

"Noooo. I didn't mean you pay for it, Bash. We can go halves. I wasn't sure if I was moving too fast for a couple's vacation."

"You're my woman. I pay for what you want." That's all he had to say about it. "And move faster, baby, catch up to me." he winked when she smiled shyly. "I'm gonna talk about moving you and Prince into my house soon. Like in days, maybe a week. So let your mind work around that."

Look at him being a compromising prick by giving his girl some time to mull over his decision. Maybe he was one of those modern men he'd read about. Bash watched all the emotions rush across Charlotte's face.

She was an overthinker, and he was a doer. They matched fucking perfectly.

"Well." she finally said, returning to brushing the cat. "I guess I better think about that. I do like your bed better than mine." Bash's heart boomed in his chest.

"When you're done with Prince, get over here and give me some attention." He rasped, and his heart went again when she looked at him with undiluted love in her eyes.

They might not have shared the words yet, but he knew Charlotte loved him.

Bash was the luckiest sonuvabitch.

He silently vowed to give her the best life together.

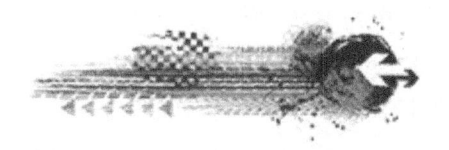

THREE HOURS EARLIER

While Bash showered, Charlotte couldn't wait for him to do it and had snuck out to collect a pizza and popcorn for their movie night. He'd spank her little ass for that trick when she got back.

He waited by the open garage door, eager to get his hands on her. He'd made specific promises to her today and would keep to them.

Bash grew increasingly worried as time passed.

He only got her voicemail when he tried calling several times.

"Where the fuck are you, Charlotte?" he murmured.

BASH: Little darling, are you munching the pizza in the car?

The message was read, and his heart rate decreased with relief.

There were no three bouncing dots showing that she was replying. She was likely driving, and his good girl wouldn't text behind the wheel.

He held his phone like a teenager, fixated on the screen. Another ten minutes went by. The pizza place was only fifteen minutes away. She should have reached home by now.

His concern skyrocketed.

Another call, and after a few rings, it dropped to voicemail like she'd cut it off prematurely. *The fuck*?

BASH: Charlotte, where the hell are you, woman?

Again, the message was instantly read, but no reply came.

Right then, Bash leapt into action. He grabbed his keys and quickly got on the bike. His imagination was going off the rails. She'd been in an accident and couldn't reply. Or she had phone trouble and ended up stranded on the road. He checked the pizza place twice, but no sign of Charlotte's red Blazer. He stopped by her place, and it was dead silent.

He left his bike and paced to the door of his house.

No amount of calling made Charlotte pick up.

He knew *she* wasn't cutting his calls off. She wasn't like that. They'd had a good day together, no cause for her to throw a fit.

He had to think rationally and not with his racing emotions.

In case of an accident, the hospital would have called or answered her phone. She had already shared with him the procedures they follow to inform families.

He called the clubhouse in case his girl was there. He was grasping at thin fucking air, looking for a rational explanation. But the prospect on duty said she hadn't been by.

If Primo wasn't in jail, he'd ask his buddy to hack into Charlotte's phone and see her last texts.

Something had happened, but Bash couldn't figure out what.

Then he remembered someone else who could lend a hand.

The Apollo Kingsmen were allies to the Diablos. Axel had worked with Jamie Steele, their prez, several times. But he didn't need Steele. Since he didn't have their numbers, he called their clubhouse.

"This is Bash from the Diablo Disciples MC. I need to speak to Amos. Is he around?" he told the woman who answered.

Amos was their VP. He had a hacking skill, and the Diablos had previously used him for background checks.

"Hey, Bash from the Diablo Disciples MC." She had a smile in her voice. "Hang on a second, and I'll see if his snarkiness is around." She must have used a sound system because Bash heard her call out for Amos. A minute went by, and then he heard.

"Bash?"

"Amos, how quick would it take to hack into someone's phone records?"

"You need a service?"

"Yes, like yesterday. My old lady has disappeared into thin fucking air. She's getting my messages, and my calls are being cut off. I'm probably jumping to conclusions that some shit has happened to her. But I'd rather that than sit on my ass and wait."

Being in MCs meant Amos got the urgency. To pay attention to intuitions that are unfathomable to a regular person. After a few hours, civilians would contact friends, family, and the police, following the right protocol.

Deep in his gut, Bash felt a sinking sensation, a sure sign that something had happened to Charlotte. She wouldn't ignore his calls unless she had no choice; a clear indicator that something was amiss.

"Let me grab a pen to get the deets."

"Whatever you charge, I'll pay it," he assured.

"We'll see what I unearth about your old lady before discussing the price. This isn't a DV sitch, is it? I'm not getting in the mix of a domestic if she's run away."

"I'd never lay a finger on my old lady, and she hasn't run the fuck away. She only went out to pick up pizza." Trying to hold his shit together, Bash was close to losing it.

"Maybe she met with a girlfriend. They do that shit, chicks, man. They have like fifteen side quests a day."

He knew that. But his Charlotte was level-fucking-headed more than most. She was punctual as fuck and reliable. This was out of character for her. He was scared for her, and his stomach churned.

"Charlotte isn't like that."

"Okay, I'll tell you what I find shortly. You wanna hang on the line?"

"Yes."

It was a long wait, feeling like decades, as he listened to Amos typing on the other end.

While he waited, he sent a text to Axel.

BASH: Charlotte is missing. Can you ask the old ladies if they've heard from her in the last hour?

If he had to mobilize the brotherhood, he needed them on standby.

They were powerful individuals with discerning skills, but the Diablos were a force to be reckoned with as a group. If Bash needed a force, there were no other men he'd want at his back.

He just hoped assembling the MC was not needed.

When Axel's text popped up on his screen, he was grateful the prez didn't ask unnecessary questions. He was a no-fuss leader, who quickly cut through the bullshit.

AXEL: I'll put Scarlett on it and call Fielding to check local CCTV. Keep me informed.

"Okay, I got something. You ready?" Amos finally said.

"Tell me."

"I got into her messages. Your girl likes to keep everything. The messages she's had today are yours, asking where the fuck she is. And another text thread with someone who isn't in her contacts. The first text is signed by Nora. You know her?"

Bash frowned. "It's her estranged sister."

"Do you want me to read 'em out or forward this to you?"

"Both."

"Gotcha. Right, the messages go as this: Lottie, it's Nora. I'm in big trouble, sis. I need help. I think I've killed someone. What do I do? Then your old lady replies: What? Are you joking? Nora says no. She explains someone was attacking her, and she stabbed him. She's scared, yadda, blah blah, and doesn't know what to do. She asks your old lady for help and tells her not to call the cops. She says again how scared she is and needs her sister."

"Fucking hell." Bash punched the wall.

"There's more. Nora gives your old lady an address. She tells Nora she's on her way. That's the last message, Bash. I've forwarded it all to this number."

"Did she have any incoming calls in that timeframe?"

"Only yours."

Why the fuck hadn't she called him? He was *her* goddamn attack dog and would have sorted it out for her.

Because Nora is her sister and Charlotte is a bleeding heart for that woman. Of course, she'd charge into the fire without protecting herself first. It was so Charlotte-coded.

For Christ's sake, they would talk about that later.

Bash dragged a hand over his hair. "Thanks, man. Let me know what I owe, and I'll transfer it."

"Nah, we're good. It was hardly anything. Call it a favor."

Bash was surprised. Amos wasn't known for his generosity. "You sure?"

"Yep. One day, I'll call it in. Good luck with your wayward old lady." He chuckled, and they hung up.

When he looked up the address, Bash frowned. It was an out-of-business aquarium. Weird fucking place to kill someone. He could only assume that bitch and her man were using the dump for their base.

He refused to stand idly by and analyze the situation; his focus was on ensuring his woman's safety. Based on what he had heard about Nora, she had a reputation for exaggerating shit. Charlotte may have unknowingly walked into a trap set by Nora to win her sister around again.

BASH: I got some info. It's some bullshit with Charlotte's sister. She claims she offed someone in self-defense and needs Charlotte's help. <includes address> If I don't contact you in an hour, you know what to do.

AXEL: I can be on my bike in 5.

BASH: I'll check it out first.

AXEL: One hour.

Before Bash even left the garage, his phone chimed. He expected Axel or one of the other brothers to offer to ride with him, but he was shocked when he saw Charlotte's name.

The relief hit him like a train.

She was okay. Thank fuck.

Yet, the relief was short-lived, and his blood became icy cold.

CHARLOTTE: Lottie isn't coming home, and if you want to see her alive again, you'll follow the instructions to the letter.

CHARLOTTE: DO NOT CALL ANYONE. YOUR CLUB OR THE COPS. NOONE. WE'LL KNOW IF YOU DO.

CHARLOTTE: We hear one siren, and I'll slit her fucking throat. Got it?

CHARLOTTE: Lottie said you're good for readies. Bring 40k in an hour to this address.

CHARLOTTE: It's a simple exchange. Money for Lottie.

CHARLOTTE: if you think you can be the big hero, think again. IF YOU BRING YOUR MC OR THE COPS SHE DIES. NO BARGAINING.

CHARLOTTE: 1 hr from now.

CHARLOTTE: <Picture> PROOF SHE IS ALIVE RIGHT NOW.

His girl was sitting on a chair; her hands clasped together in her lap. She wore the outfit she'd left the house in. It wasn't clear if she was injured, but a man was standing over her, holding a hunting knife to her throat.

Bash's world fucking shattered. His rage was colossal.

He didn't know Nora well enough to know if she'd hurt her sister. He only had Charlotte's opinion of Nora. And he trusted her judgment—to know the other woman was as sly as a fucking rattlesnake and unhinged to attempt something this crazy.

That bitch thought she could shake him down for cash and threaten her goddamn sister like that? Was Harvey responsible for it? Or was Nora working independently?

Whoever was aiding Nora, mostly likely that simpleton of a boyfriend, those cocksuckers were going to die.

Charlotte

There were no limits to her stupidity.

One pleading text from Nora, and she was right back in that frame of mind, wanting to save her sister.

Who said the definition of insanity was doing the same action and expecting different results? They had it on the nose, and Charlotte hated herself a little more for being fooled so easily.

She knew better. That was the sting. She knew Nora so well that falling for a stupid ruse was on *her* toes, no one else's.

There had been choices in front of her. Why didn't she pick any of them?

Pulling up outside an out-of-business store should have been Charlotte's first clue to turn around.

There was no dead body. Nora wasn't in trouble.

Charlotte was the one in trouble.

Seeing Thorn's smirk, she realized it was an ambush and attempted to flee, but he yanked her back by the hair. "Got you now, big sis, don't I?" he'd sneered.

Her sister, the family she should have been able to trust, turned into her enemy. The one extorting and holding her captive. It was disgustingly ironic that *Nora* meant honorable one. There was no honor in her sister.

"Lottie, it's fine, I promise." Nothing was fine. And like always, Nora was under a delusion that she wasn't the bad guy in this scenario.

The realization felt like acid all over Lottie's heart.

"How is being held at knifepoint fine, Nora?"

There was no answer. She was too busy playing with her phone.

Nora was a lost cause. It hurt to realize it. Lottie stared at her glamorous yet despicable sister and shook her head in disbelief.

"All this time," Thorn smirked, standing with his crotch almost in her face. Lottie tried not to grimace and tilted her head to look up. "All this time, you acted innocent, looking at us like we were dirt underneath your feet, and you were giving up the pussy to a biker. I'm thinking I chose the wrong sister." He licked his lip like he was trying to be sexy. From Bash, yeah. From Thorn, her stomach curdled.

Nora threw her head up. "Shut up, Thorny."

"Woman, I told you to stay the fuck out of this. I'm dealing with it now."

"Was this your idea, Nora?" Lottie asked. This guy couldn't think his way out of a paper bag, much less pull off a money scam. He was the hired village idiot at best.

"We only need cash so we can move to Boston, okay? Nothing to get worked up over." So yes, it was Nora's doing. That hurt even more. "The Diablo bikers are loaded. Your man isn't going to miss a few bucks."

"That's if he wants you back," Smirked Thorn, roving his eyes over her body in a way that made her feel sick. "Did he reply to the texts?"

"Nope." Nora answered.

"He doesn't care. Maybe we get to keep you." He pressed his mouth to her ear. "You'll like that, won't you? Now you've had a taste of the wild side. I can give you more of that, baby. Show you what a real man can do."

Lottie bit back her disgust.

Guilt made her chest heavy.

She could only imagine what Bash was thinking.

How disappointed in her he'd be for falling for something so reckless.

The money they wanted was ridiculous. Nora must've thought she had a money tree in her backyard. But when Thorn boasted about getting the money from Bash, Lottie was horrified.

She'd done everything to make Nora stop. Take her savings. Take her car. Anything was better than getting Bash involved.

But Bash wasn't one man. He was a whole MC of men that would raise hell for one of their own. She didn't want to bring her family shit to their door.

She knew Bash would come.

But not as quickly as he did.

When he arrived, it wasn't in a blaze of fury. But the energy shifted.

With confident strides, he entered through the back door as if he owned the place and had all the power.

Lottie's eyes searched his face. *Please don't hate me.*

His face showed no trace of hatred as he glanced at her. With a gun in hand, Thorn instructed Nora to frisk Bash. It was unbelievable that the man she adored didn't even think of bringing a gun for his protection. What she hated most was the way Nora touched him.

He showed no emotion. A tick worked his jawline before he turned his hardened eyes on Thorn. "You have something that belongs to me. I want it back."

She felt her heart plunge into free fall.

Despite the overwhelming panic, Bash's presence provided some relief.

Lottie was no action figure.

She wasn't built for this kind of trouble. But she'd turn into the world's worst rabid rodent to keep Bash safe.

"I don't see any cash." Thorn hissed.

"You think I can lay my hands on forty grand in an hour? I'm not a Swiss banker, you gormless prick. It needs to be electronically wired." Bash threw shade at Thorn in a snap, then turned to check on her. Thorn held a gun on Bash and a nameless guy had a knife to her throat. Yet the fear was minimal when she couldn't tear her gaze away from him.

"You draw one drop of her blood, and I'll crush your fucking skull," he warned the knife holder. "Are you hurt, Charlotte?" His voice was grave.

She shook her head, her bottom lip wobbling. "No, I'm fine. I'm sorry, Bash."

"There's no need to be sorry, darling. Your money-grabbing cunt of a sister is to blame."

Even with her history of questionable actions, this was the most egregious thing Nora had ever done.

"Nora, please stop." She begged. "You've gone too far with this."

Her sister only gave a shoulder shrug.

The familial bond between them bled out.

"Don't be so fucking dumb, Lottie." Thorn snarled. "Nora saw you sucking face with the biker, and she made this happen."

"Does Harvey know what you're doing?" asked Bash.

"Who fucking cares what he thinks? He ain't the boss of me. We'll be out of here as soon as we get that cash. Enough fucking chit-chatting. Or the bitch gets it."

Or the bitch gets it. It was such a movie cliché that she wondered if Thorn had been studying the handbook about being a bad guy.

The punch was sudden. Bash was calm until his fist cracked against Thorn's face.

"Never call her a bitch."

In the movies, Bash would have gotten the gun from Thorn, and the situation would have de-escalated.

But this wasn't the movies.

The man holding the knife ran and struck Bash on the back of his head with the handle. Time seemed to slow down as the person who held her heart dropped heavily to the ground.

Lottie didn't realize she was screaming until Thorn threatened to shoot her if she didn't shut her mouth.

He was dead. *He was dead.*

"Let me go to him. He's hurt." Worse. Her heart nearly stopped when she saw how still Bash was. Despite her desperate begging, the monsters showed no emotion.

"Nora, please! I need to check on Bash."

"He's fine," she tutted, but she looked at Thorn as though needing his approval to breathe.

"Help!" she started shouting at the top of her lungs. "HELP!"

Lottie hadn't even thought of a single idea, let alone a good one, but she had to get to Bash. "HELP!" She kept screaming until the knife guy pulled her hair so hard that she felt her neck snap.

The punch to her temple was a surprise.

The pain came suddenly, but the darkness came faster and pulled her under as she heard her sister's distant voice. "What the fuck did you do?"

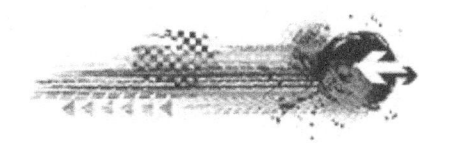

Bash

When Bash was seven or eight, his family lived next to his then-best friend, Bran.

They were always up to no good.

Bran's family was wealthy, while Bash's family was not. Bran had all the latest games, and his room had a huge aquarium wall. He remembered being super fascinated by all the fish in the lit tank, totally memorized by their cool colors. They were obsessed with tropical fish for weeks, learning everything they could, until something else caught the boys' attention.

Bash hadn't thought about Bran in ages and had no clue where he was now, but he remembered how sturdy that fish tank was. They'd accidentally chucked a baseball at it, smacking the glass with some force, but without leaving a scratch.

He came out of unconsciousness with his skull in agony and instantly felt like one of those trapped tropical fish. While he was knocked out, those twats had confined him and Charlotte within a glass container.

Fuck. *Fuck*!

Because they were laid on their sides, he knew it exceeded his height by a small margin and was too narrow for him to extend his arms fully. The lid above them was tightly sealed and impossible to remove, no matter how many times he tried to push at it.

What was more concerning, however, was why the hell Charlotte was lifeless. A soon-to-be dead motherfucker had hit her, clear from the noticeable red mark on her temple.

Bash quickly analyzed the situation. The room was now pitch black.

He heard footsteps. Then there was a thud on top of the tank. "You've got fifteen minutes to decide about the money, biker scum. Or you explain to your pretty little prude why she's about to die in there."

Thorn's retreating laugh was nothing compared to the sound of a sudden trickle of water. It took Bash a second to realize it was coming into the tank near their feet.

Bash attempted once more to open the lid. Then, with the minimal space, he endeavored to rock back and forth to force the tank to tip over and hopefully smash. Better to be cut to shreds by glass than drowning, but it felt like it was anchored to the wall.

Suddenly, Charlotte groaned and moved. He wrapped his arm around her, wanting more than anything for her to be safe and sound at home.

"B-ash?"

"I'm here, darling. Don't be frightened, okay? I'm gonna get us out of here."

Since being knocked out, he had no way of knowing the time, or if the others were on their way yet. His phone was cracked and fucking useless.

He would make those bastards pay for this.

"Where are we?" She sounded eerily calm. "I can hardly move. Oh, my god, are we in a coffin?"

He told her what he knew.

"Is that water? Is water coming into this tank?" The pitch of her voice went up by one octave.

He was her man, he should be able to protect her, and he couldn't do a fucking thing.

Seconds felt like hours.

More and more water flooded in.

He estimated it would be full in fifteen minutes.

There was hardly any room to move, even though he tried blocking the pipe with his boots, hoping to slow it down.

Dread made his limbs heavy as he cuddled Charlotte into his chest.

"I'm so sorry, Bash." She whispered.

"Told you, baby, nothing to be sorry for."

"I shouldn't have come. I was stupid. I thought…"

"You thought your sister was in trouble. We'll be out of here soon. The boys are on their way." He hoped.

"They are? Why is it so dark? Where did Nora and Thorn go? I can't believe she did this, Bash. She's never been this cruel—this heartless." His girl was panicking. Her teeth chattering as the water level increased. "NORA!" she screeched. "Nora! You can't do this!"

"Baby, they're not here." He knew they'd left. He comforted her with a hand on her hair, but she cried out for her sister until she finally gave in and rested against his chest.

"This is my fault. I'm so sorry."

"Stop, Charlotte." He kissed her head.

They collaborated to move the lid with their feet and tested if it would topple. Nothing worked. *Goddammit.*

His brothers needed to get here ASAP.

The water was in the middle of the tank now.

Her voice quivered. "What did I do to her to make her do this? And that asshole hit you, Ben. *He hit you.* I want to smack his smug face."

Despite the impending doom, Bash chuckled and kissed her head again. "My little Rottweiler. Do you have anything sharp in your pockets? Keys?"

"Nora took everything off me. *That bitch.* The glass feels too thick. What if we run out of oxygen?"

They were likely to drown first, but Bash kept that to himself.

The boys would come in time.

They had to.

There's no way that he just found the woman he was meant to be with, only for them to die now.

"We'll be fine, darling. Kiss your man."

Her lips pressed to his, and he kissed her like it would be the last time. Slipping his tongue into Charlotte's mouth, he poured his love into her until her sob rippled against his lips.

"Are we going to die? Oh, god, please don't die, Ben. I couldn't stand it."

He soothed kisses all over her face, using his wet hand to hold her hair back, trying to ignore the water rising as it reached their shoulders. Bash placed his hand beneath Charlotte's chin, holding her up to create as much space as possible.

"Do you think you can get rid of me now, baby? After hunting you down for a year?"

She gave a watery chuckle. "You were steadfast, even when I wasn't nice to you."

"I always knew my little darling was underneath that scowl. That first day, you cast a spell on me."

She half-laughed, half-cried. "I don't know why. I'm very ordinary."

"Baby, you are fucking *extraordinary.* I'm in awe of you every single day, and I'm the lucky bastard who gets to love you."

"Don't say that." She gripped his shirt. "Not now, not here. Not because of this. I wanted to say it first."

"Then tell me you love me, Charlotte, so I can tell you I'm so fucking in love with you. I'm crazy with it."

"You are crazy," she chuckled, followed by a tearful hiccup. "I wish I hadn't been so stubborn. We could have been in love so much sooner."

"We are now, baby."

"You've made my life so different, *good different*. I've loved spending all this time with you, Ben."

Fuck, it sounded like a goodbye, and he couldn't handle that, but the water lapped around his chin, and they were barely keeping their heads against the top of the tank, grabbing at the last inches of air.

"Do you believe in heaven, Ben?"

"I don't know. Do you?"

"I don't know either. But if there is one," Charlotte's voice cracked, and he knew there would be tears streaming down her perfect face. "If there is one, will you find me? I don't want to be without you." She cried now. All Bash could do was squeeze his arms around her. "This can't be happening. I only just got you, and now I'm going to lose you."

"You could never lose me, little darling. I'm yours all the way, every inch of me. Body and heart, and if I have a soul, your name is tattooed all over it."

Their lips met, and he said the words right into her mouth.

"I love you, my Charlotte, in this life. And if there are others, I will find you. No worries about that. I'll be a fucking bloodhound until I have you in my arms again, you get that? Nothing can keep me away from you. You're mine, and I'm yours."

She sobbed as the gap between the tank's roof and the water grew shorter. They were about to take their last breaths.

"I love you so much, Ben. You're my everything. The best man I've ever known."

She fucking flayed his heart open.

"I was going to get you to quit smoking."

"I'll start as soon as we're at home."

The water was lapping at his ears. Was that banging he heard?

Please fucking god.

"Don't fall in love with someone else in the next life, Ben. You're mine. I will find you, I promise. I'm a biker's old lady."

"Damn right you are." He choked water, holding Charlotte's head back as high as he could to keep her breathing. "Baby, I need you to do something for me."

"Anything."

His good girl to the last. He fucking loved her.

"When I tell you to, I need you to take the biggest breath you can, okay? And hold it for as long as you can."

"You too. Please don't die, Ben. I don't care about what happens to me, but don't die."

He felt the same about her.

His life was nothing without her. He'd been empty until he found her, so if Charlotte was dying, he was going with her.

There it was again! As he caught the sound of heavy feet and crashing sounds, Bash felt hope fill his brain. Was someone calling his name?

But Bash and Charlotte only had seconds.

"Baby, take that breath now."

"Ben..." she said, scared.

"Now, baby."

There were only seconds before they were completely submerged. Bash kept hold of Charlotte's face, their foreheads together.

His head roared. This wasn't how their lives were supposed to go.

He had so many plans.

The outside sounds were muffled, but he was sure he heard something. Then, dark shadows were outside the tank before light suddenly illuminated the room, and he saw his brothers.

He pounded on the glass, and even though he couldn't hear their voices, he could anticipate their conversation as they searched for a method to remove the lid.

His gaze returned to Charlotte.

She was so fucking pretty. His heart hurt.

I love you. Bash silently told Charlotte.

I love you. Her eyes replied.

It wasn't the end for them.

It couldn't be.

Hold on, little darling. Hold on for me.

Bash's lungs burned, and then Charlotte's eyes started flickering, and the hold she had on him loosened.

No. No. No.

Hold on, baby.

He felt when unconsciousness dragged her down as her lips fell open and bubbles came out of her nose.

Fucking no!

He slammed his lips to hers, pushing them open, and pinched her nose to exhale the air he'd been holding, until his lungs felt like they'd caught fire, and still Bash blew the last of his oxygen into his entire world.

Needing her to live more than anything.

Hold on, baby.

Suddenly the tank was opened, and Bash surfaced like a gasping fish, dragging Charlotte with him, but she was so fucking still.

"Take her. *Fucking take her!*" Bash coughed and fought a pending blackout, even as his vision blurred with dots.

His girl was pulled from the water. Axel was yelling commands, and other voices were speaking, but all Bash heard was his roaring fear as someone helped him out. He landed on the floor with a sopping thud, half crawling to where Denver was breathing into Charlotte's mouth.

"*Breathe, baby.*" He prayed. "Fucking breathe."

It was a life-changing sound when she suddenly inhaled. Denver put Charlotte in the recovery position, and she immediately started coughing up water.

Thank fucking god. The relief blasted through Bash like heat.

"Mouse! Bring the cage around ASAP," Axel said into his phone.

"Place is empty." Chains said, stalking into the room, followed by Ruin, both seeing the carnage. "What the fuck happened here?"

"The bastards tried drowning them in a tank."

Charlotte was alive. She was breathing and clinging to his hand. "B-ben." Her attempts to speak came out as a wet, wheezing sound.

"Right here, little darling. I got you. She needs the hospital."

"On it, brother." Said the calm prez. In no time, they were in the SUV, speeding to their destination with his frozen girl on his lap.

They cut through red lights and stop signs.

Bash didn't fucking care. He would have sprouted wings to get Charlotte to a hospital as he listened to her gurgle-like breathing. Her eyes never left his. He bent closer and put their foreheads together.

"I love you, baby. You're gonna be fine." He promised.

"Love you." She mouthed.

She's going to be okay.

She's going to be okay.

He held Charlotte a little tighter, willing his life force into her little body.

She's going to be okay.

At the hospital, when they took Charlotte from him, Bash heard things like vitals dropping, dry drowning, chest X-ray, and pulmonary specialist.

Surrounded by his club brothers, they refused to move out of the waiting area until Bash heard something.

The hour felt like an eternity for him.

Holding on with all he had. If they told him bad news, he'd wreck the fucking place with his grief. He felt a sense of spinning without motion.

His heart rate was elevated when the doctor emerged. The smile told Bash all he needed to know.

Only then did Bash surrender his strength; his knees gave way, and he would have landed on the floor, if not for his boys holding him up.

She was okay.

She was okay.

His old lady was going to live.

Bash

Charlotte was pretending to be asleep again.

Bash stood motionless, waiting for her to roll over and let him know she was awake. But she kept her back to him and her hands tucked beneath her chin.

After two days of observation in the hospital, she'd only been home for four days. Bash understood he had to give her gentle gloves for her recovery. She might be okay physically now, but was deeply hurt by her sister's betrayal.

Prince sensed her sadness and stayed by Charlotte's side, sleeping next to her every night. As the sound of motorcycles grew closer, he hurriedly made his way back through the house. To avoid disturbing her, he shut the door and joined Axel and Chains outside by the garage.

"Give me good news." He said as a way of greeting.

The club had been working non-stop, and he needed something good to tell Charlotte so she wouldn't be afraid to step out of the house again.

"They're gone," Axel announced.

"Dead?"

"Not yet. We found where they were hiding, but the place was empty. Harvey says he had no clue about Thorn's plans, and it wasn't his call. Not sure I believe anything that old coot says."

Anger burned in the back of Bash's throat. He needed to be there to take down that asshole Thorn, but he couldn't leave Charlotte alone.

"So that's it? We let them off Scot-fucking-free? He nearly drowned Charlotte! Another goddamn minute and she would be dead."

"You too, my brother." Added Chains.

"I don't matter. But that bitch of a sister and the prick tried to shake my woman down for money. They left her to die. This won't be brushed aside and forgotten. I want him fucking *dead*."

"And you know that's what's gonna happen, Bash. We aren't letting this go. He fucked with one of ours. He fucked with your old lady. You know we don't forgive and forget." Axel said grimly. "There's a network of sources at our disposal. We're tapped into CCTV along the freeway. The airport, train and bus stations. And we've hacked Thorn's phone and bank account. We're closing in. Chances are, he scuttled back to Alabama. Halfwits always think they're safest on home turf. Ruin will travel wherever we need him to go. I've already spoken with Drifter, Atom, and Silver. They're ready to finish the job. "

"Hack Nora's phone."

"You want her dead, too?"

He thought about it. Bash wanted her gone. "Charlotte wouldn't want that," he decided. "But if she steps one toe back in Utah, my promise not to hurt her is off."

His soft-hearted girl had forgiveness. Bash didn't.

"How's your woman?" asked Chains. "The old ladies wanted to come over. We put them off for now."

"Let them come. She's withdrawn right now."

They spoke for a minute more when he heard.

"Bash?"

He spun around and saw her in the doorway. He was beside her in no time, and she practically glued herself to him. Trembling.

"I thought you'd left."

Bash hugged her tight. "I'm right here, baby. Just talking to the boys out here so I didn't wake you. You okay?"

"Yeah. I didn't know where you were."

"I'm going nowhere, darling," he promised.

"How about you move your enormous head so I can hug your girl." Said Chains, and Bash heard Charlotte chuckle. The first one he'd heard all week.

"Hey, guys."

"Hi, babe. You feeling okay?" asked Axel. And she nodded. It was Chains who pulled her into a gentle hug. "You might not know it yet, babe, but since you're hooked up to this guy, you're one of us. Whatever you need, if Bash can't get it for you, one of us will."

"Thank you. Both of you. I know I haven't said it yet, but you came for us, and I'm so grateful."

Bash pulled her into his arms.

"It's what we do." Winked Axel.

"How about I grill burgers for dinner?" he asked her once they were alone.

"That sounds good. I could eat." Thank fuck for that. If he had to force her to eat again, that would be unpleasant for them both.

They worked together in the kitchen. Charlotte was mixing the dressing for homemade coleslaw, and Bash made the burger patties for grilling out on the deck.

Bash kept sneaking looks at her to make sure Charlotte was okay. Every time she walked by him to grab something from the fridge, she playfully traced her fingers on his back.

Food prep was done, hands were washed, and just as Bash was about to grab some beers, Charlotte pressed against his back.

He smiled and turned his head. "Everything okay, baby?"

"I miss you," she spoke into his back.

Bash's lips turned up. "I'm right here."

"No. *I miss you*, Benjamin." Her hands slid under his shirt when he turned, caressing the ridges of his stomach.

"What do you miss, baby? My mouth?" he stroked it over her lips. "It's yours. Do you miss my hands?" he found her braless breasts beneath her shirt, holding the tiny but perfect treasures in both hands. "They're yours." Bash raised Charlotte's hand and pressed it against his firm shaft. "Or is it my cock you miss? Because you know who that belongs to, don't you?"

She nodded, all shy.

"Tell me who this cock belongs to, Charlotte."

If she kept squeezing what she owned, he was going to blow all over her fingers.

"It belongs to me."

"What does?" He smirked, and her fingers shaped him in the best way.

She wasn't a filthy-tongued bastard like he was, so when she gave him dirty words, Bash got off on it.

"This cock belongs to me, Ben. Will you please use it on me?"

"Because you asked so fucking sweetly." He husked and nipped her lower lip with his teeth before he swept her up and deposited her on top of the table. Her shorts were ripped down her legs, revealing his gloriously bare girl. The rest of their clothes followed, and Bash was ready to fucking devour his woman, to reaffirm they were alive, with endless years together in front of them.

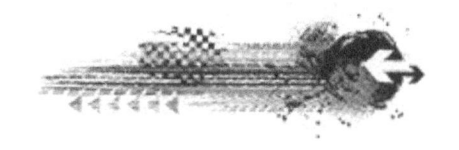

Charlotte

A vital spark ignited between them.

The air crackled with love, with lust, with their constant connection. Bash's touch awakened her. In more ways than one. He'd been her catalyst to a better, more fulfilling life with the greatest love she could have ever imagined for herself.

Her knees grew weak as she wrapped both legs around Bash's trim waist, and a shaky feeling spread throughout her entire body.

He'd been so patient and caring with her for days, making her tumble deeper into love with him.

He was sweet.

And so tender.

Comforting her every night, easing her troubled mind and soothing her from the nightmares of losing him.

Bash's touch between her thighs made her breathless as she braced herself on the table.

He played with her, and Charlotte moaned, begging him.

She had it bad for Bash. So bad. There was no life without him.

How did people cope with overwhelming feelings?

Every breath, thought, and heartbeat was all Bash.

Her man.

Her savior.

Her everything.

"Ben, please. I ache all over."

It was his catalyst, like she'd tossed gasoline onto his fire as he growled against her pussy and started devouring her like he was sitting at the last supper table. Slurping her with precision, flicking viciously over her clit, until the bud grew hard and needy, and her fingers fisted into Bash's hair, hoping she didn't rip it out at the roots. But oh, well, there were always casualties in a heat this sexual. His hair would grow back.

Lottie loved it when Bash took control of her body.

He was an expert on what she enjoyed. Her hands worked over his skin, touching, owning, leaving her scratches behind so Bash would never forget her.

Lottie's pulse pattered to an uneven beat.

Bash pulled her backside to the edge of the table, splitting her legs for him to fit between.

Their love drummed a sound through her ears.

A relentless attraction.

He tasted like he smelled, like sin and dreamy affection. And she couldn't get enough.

The fear of losing him haunted her every waking moment, and she doubted she would ever recover from it.

Bash's gentle mouth calmed her frantic actions as she grabbed, took, and ate his kiss.

"We have all the time in the world, little darling," he assured. Kiss after kiss.

She was all over him, reassuring herself with a touch that her man was real and he was okay. Running her greedy hands over his long torso, he grunted her name.

"Enough now. I can't take more teasing," he groaned at the end of his patience and fisted Lottie's ponytail to reel her in.

Her eyes were half-lidded. She was mindlessly panting. A fever burned under her skin. One that could only be sated by one man with addictive eyes.

Bash's gaze stayed focused between her legs while he toyed with her. She knew she was wet. She could hear it when he thrust two fingers inside and then stroked that wetness over his long cock, grunting while he did.

He was a dream.

A dirty, delicious, all hers dream.

"What are you waiting for, Benjamin?"

He was treating her softly like he expected her to break. They've had rougher sex than this, and that's exactly what she needed right now. The out-of-control boyfriend who used her body like his own toy.

She felt the tip of him anchor to her entrance, and she nearly wept with relief.

"I'm waiting for my little darling to ask nicely to be fucked by the man who adores her."

Boom went her heart.

And Lottie had no hesitation as she wrapped one arm around Bash's shoulders.

"Please, will my gorgeous boyfriend, who I love so much, fuck me so deep, and so hard?"

His smirk was so damn corrupt, it turned her on and made her even wetter.

One shunt of his hips and Bash found his way inside her, his marking heat so thick that Lottie almost choked on her arousal. Slowly, he started to thrust.

The force of Bash's pelvic shifts made her muscles jolt. Lottie was on fire with his look of unguarded love, and she arched her hips into him.

Their lovemaking was frantic and perfect. She touched him all over, encouraging her man to take what he needed from her body as she rimmed the base of his cock, to feel how desperately he fucked her.

He was bare inside her, skin-to-skin, and she loved it.

She knew that this was a novel experience for both of them. Bash never had sex without using a condom. And something they only did once together.

The risks were minimal.

The pleasure was indescribable.

The desire was hard to ignore when they generated this much passion between them.

Despite his smooth, whiskey voice, his teeth remained tightly clenched. "You've created a monster letting me fuck you bare, Charlotte."

He was all up in her ear, talking and screwing, making the table groan under the strain. Making Lottie go wild and leaving nail marks all over his torso. "You take my bare fuck *so good*," he praised. Her climax climbed. "So fucking *tight*. You're making such a sexy wet mess, Charlotte."

Skin against skin.

A scrape of teeth.

The heavy pressure of him was all over her. *Relentless*. Gasping for air, she fought through the intensity of what Bash was giving her.

His body worshipped.

His hoarse, dirty words exploded her passion.

Every thrust kindled a spark that only the next thrust could satisfy. If Lottie had needed an affirmation of life, this was it.

She had no inhibitions in his kitchen, possibly never again.

What they shared was pure magic, born from a love she'd never envisioned existed in her lifetime.

"Take it," he growled. A slight shudder rolled under his skin when Lottie sank her teeth into his pec muscle.

When she came, her vision blurred. She only remembered crying his name, telling Bash how much she loved him. Only losing the thickness inside her made her open her eyes to see his glorious shaft in his hand, stroking out the last of his climax on her pussy and lower abdomen.

When he was finished, their breaths gasping, he grabbed her close, and Lottie latched on with arms and legs like a spider monkey.

"Christ. Thought my heart was gonna burst. You take me so perfectly."

"I love you. I love you so much, Ben."

"Ah, little darling. I fucking love you, too."

Only the gurgling hunger of her stomach broke into their love-filled bubble, and Bash chuckled, pulling away to look at her. "I better clean my girl up so I can feed her. Stay there." He instructed in the dominant voice she loved him using. Since Lottie's legs wouldn't work, she was happy to obey and watched him walk around the kitchen.

Naked. Gorgeous. All hers.

"We need to clean this table. Like a lot." Her face burned.

Bash only laughed and grabbed for the paper towels.

Bash

It had been a mellow couple of weeks, but Bash couldn't unwind knowing that scumbag was still out there, living his life after trying to harm his old lady.

He had been contemplating something for a while now.

It wasn't something he could spontaneously surprise Charlotte with.

A vote had to be taken. He'd brought it up at the latest meeting, and it was unanimous.

Then, he had to put in a special order. It came in this morning.

What felt like fate was Ruin striding through the club entryway, and his eyes sought Bash, who was meeting with Axel about next week's appointments.

"You're back." Greeted Axel.

Ruin had been gone several days. The last they heard, he was in Arizona on Thorn's trail. He wore his traveling leather jacket and slipped off the shades to pocket them. Reno must have had a twin sense that his brother was around because he came in from the garage. The pair were like bookends in looks and solar systems apart in personalities, but they were closer than blood brothers could be.

Ruin's soulless eyes met Bash's. "Tell your old lady she doesn't have to worry now."

"Thorn?" Bash jumped to his feet. "You found him?"

"Found and eliminated him."

"Fucking A." crowed a grinning Reno, smacking his brother on the back.

"Well done, Ruin," half smirked Axel. "Did you have any trouble?"

"None. It wasn't like Thorn was smart. I caught him so easily, even I was bored. I met up with Atom halfway. He's a demonic motherfucker, cold as ice."

"Coming from you, I don't know how to gauge that." laughed Axel.

"Did you know he makes this homemade solution that melts human remains? Nothing is left behind. Fucking wild." Remarked Ruin, looking impressed by another murderer's tactics. "You should ask him to quit being a nomad and make his base here."

Everyone gaped at Ruin.

In all the years they'd known the quiet enforcer, he could go months without grunting at someone. And it was unheard of that he'd ever be proactive by inviting someone to the club.

It was Reno who spoke. "You *want* Atom to become a full-time member? Here?" he spoke slowly, like they'd all collectively heard Ruin wrong.

"If there's someone else to share the enforcer mantle so I can spend more time building my furniture and being with my old lady." He shrugged. "I'm open to it."

Whenever Ruin said over two monosyllabic words at once, everyone listened.

"Well, fuck me," chuffed Chains.

Ruin wasn't one for standing around gossiping, and he turned on his heels to leave by the way he came in. Bash quickly shouted Ruin's name. He looked back.

"Thanks, brother."

It wasn't quite a smile, but Ruin did something with his face to reply. As he walked off, he called back. "Put me as absent for a few days, secretary. I'm spending it with my old lady."

"Was that Ruin saying whole sentences?" Asked Devil, coming from the kitchen, holding a sandwich.

"You should have heard him." Chains said, brushing an imaginary tear from his eye. "Our puppet is becoming a real boy."

Bash laughed along with the others, but his mind was whirling. Thorn was dealt with. He hoped he felt unspeakable pain at the end.

Today felt like destiny, more so than ever before.

When one bad chapter ended, a better one began.

Bash made the call, and he did it smiling.

He was at the entryway, waiting like a loyal fucking puppy, when Charlotte's car pulled in next to his bike. Bash was already at her door before she even turned off the engine. He quickly unbuckled her seatbelt.

"Hello to you, too," she chuckled and stepped straight into his arms. "Your call sounded ominous. Is something wrong?"

"Nothing, baby. Happy to see you."

She had confessed to him she had never been in a relationship, nor felt this obsessed chemistry with anyone except him. She was unsure about her skills at being a girlfriend and if she could handle the emotional side of it.

Bash wished she could see herself through his eyes.

How easily she walked into his arms for affection without being prompted. Or how she sought him out in bed while she was sleeping. How many times a day she texted him with simple things or to say hi, and she missed him. She was the backbone and beating heart for a biker like him.

There was no other girlfriend better than Charlotte.

And he revered the woman.

Right down to the soul, he adored her.

Every smile and piece of her heart he got from Charlotte, he held on like she'd given him treasure.

"Come inside, baby. I'll get you a drink."

"Oh, a big one, please. It's been a day."

She meant a full-sugar soda. She'd sworn off alcohol for right now.

"Did you kill anyone?" he joked, and she jabbed him before winding her arm around his waist. Bliss followed.

"It came close. Someone came in with a chest infection and threw up on my Crocs! I'm lucky to have five spare pairs." His girl was addicted to buying Crocs in all colors and patterns.

It was a relaxed night. Most of his brothers were around with their old ladies. More arrived after they found out what Bash was planning.

If Charlotte noticed the old ladies wearing their property cuts, she said nothing. Partway through the next hour, Charlotte skipped to the bar where Scarlett had set up her iPad with Rory on a Facetime call. When Rory didn't feel up to leaving the house, she still joined club events through technology.

While she was away from his lap, he had a prospect bring over his surprise.

Bash felt oddly nervous.

He knew Charlotte loved him.

It was something she didn't hide now, and he felt it every day.

They were a partnership and were creating the foundations of something long-lasting.

"I need to talk to you, baby."

"Oh?" an eyebrow climbed.

"You know already I'm fucking wild about you. You're my world, Charlotte."

Her face beamed.

"You're someone I want to share my secrets with, confide in, and have you be a sounding board. And I want to be that for you, too. I'm the person who will shield you or stand at your side when you need it. I'll fight any demons to keep you, Charlotte. You're it for me. One day soon, I will put a ring on your finger—make us legal." She had so much emotion in her eyes. People laughed as he confidently declared that marriage was on the horizon.

"The first thing I want to give you will make you mine in the Diablo law, Charlotte."

She exclaimed, wide-eyed. "Do I have to get a tattoo? I don't want those big skulls you guys have, Bash."

Something loosened in his chest, and he chuckled, tagging a hand around her neck and drawing her closer so he could rub her nose with his.

"If you get some ink, you'll be sitting on my lap while you do. But that's for another day. Tonight, I wanna give you this." He brought out the cut. "Will you wear my property cut, little darling?"

The time seemed to go on forever.

It was a big moment for Bash.

It meant something to every biker in the clubhouse. No man gave his property patch to just anyone.

This was a forever kind of declaration. He was telling Charlotte and his patched brotherhood that this was his woman. And he was hers.

Bash watched her fingering the white leather, custom-made for her body frame. The old ladies' property cuts weren't boxy like the men's. They were tailored to a female frame and looked sexy as fuck. He couldn't wait to see Charlotte in hers.

If only she'd answer.

But he knew to have patience.

It had taken him a long time to get his girl to look at him as something other than a dangerous biker and a friend.

And then his Charlotte smiled.

"I get to be an old lady?" she smiled bigger. "I'm an old lady now?" her voice soared, and everyone around them laughed at her excitement. She glanced at the iPad on the bar and shouted. "Oh, my god, Rory Kidd, look!" Bash's arms were full seconds later as she leaped into them, kissing him all over his face, half crying and laughing.

"I'm Bash's old lady. Put it on, put it on me, please." She slid down his body and whipped around. Her grin was infectious.

Bash couldn't take his eyes off her when the white leather was on her back.

White for his pure little darling.

The woman with her big empathetic heart.

His innocent light in this world.

"Fucking beautiful." He remarked and ran his fingers over the markings, declaring her his woman. "Now you're mine." He said with emotion.

She turned the sweetest eyes on him and stroked a finger over his goatee. "I was yours even before I knew it."

Damn straight.

Everyone started hollering and congratulating them as he lifted her into his arms and took the kiss he was craving.

Something occurred to Bash when a pair of perfect lips were on his.

He might have been the architect of their relationship. He built the foundations, but those walls were just that, until his Charlotte brought the color and the joy. She brought a reason to his life he hadn't honestly had before.

If he were the architect, Charlotte was the light source. The beating heart. The very soul of the foundations.

"My old lady." He murmured against her sweet lips.

"Does that make you my old man? Because…" she poked her tongue into the side of her cheek, teasing about their age difference that neither of them gave a fuck about.

"I'm anything you want me to be."

Once the onlookers dispersed and Bash was alone with Charlotte, he told her in a ragged whisper. "I'm gonna fuck you in only your property cut later."

"Okay." she gasped, her eyes already filled with lust. He loved that look.

Charlotte was aware of some of the Diablos' regime now, but if she needed an up-close look, something unpredictable came not long later while sitting on his lap.

"What the fuck?" They heard, and everyone turned to see Diamond shooting forward in his chair. His stare was like a bomb had gone off on the TV.

The local news report showed amateur footage of someone being arrested. The woman was fuller figured and dressed in every rainbow color, but her purple hair was the standout feature. She was being handcuffed, and Diamond cursed.

"Fucking hell, Joelle, what have you done?"

Everyone shared confused glances, and Diamond wasn't answering how he knew the purple-haired bohemian.

It got weirder.

The reporter announced the woman was Joelle Snow, and her father was the renowned Judge Snow.

That guy was not renowned for anything but being a shady motherfucker whose prestige could be bought. The Diablos knew this well. He'd been on their payroll for a while.

Diamond quickly stood up as the news shifted to another story, grabbing his jacket. "*Where the fuck is my son, Joelle?*" he growled. And then he took off at a fast run, out of the door.

"Does Diamond have a son?" asked his girl.

"Not that we know of."

"What the fuck is going on? Did he say a son? Since when?" asked Devil.

All fine questions no one had the answers to.

Diamond wasn't a closed book, nor was he secretive.

But maybe he was.

Bash nuzzled Charlotte's neck, kissing over her pulse.

"Don't let this scare you off, darling. We don't all have secret babies."

She turned her head, her lips brushed his beard. "If a woman came in here now and claimed she had your baby, I'd have to punch her in the nose." God, she was spectacular. "Then, with my nurse's oath, I'd probably have to hand her a tissue, but she'd get the message, Bash. You belong to me. And all your future babies belong to me. I'll be the baby mama."

It was like she set a rocket underneath him.

His heart burst out of his chest.

She was giving him something Bash didn't even know he'd wanted.

"Nothing will scare me away. I'm a Diablos old lady now. That means something." She whispered the last part against his cheek and then nuzzled around to find his waiting mouth. "I love you to infinity, Ben."

Falling in love hadn't changed Bash's life.

But meeting Charlotte had.

She'd turned what he'd always known on its head.

Focused him.

Gave him a greater purpose.

Love served as a powerful driving force.

But Charlotte was the whole reason.

For everything.

"Ah, my little darling." he grinned, kissing the tip of her nose. "I got you in the end, didn't I?"

She laughed, pushing her face into his chest.

Yeah, he'd gotten his perfect old lady into his property patch.

But it was far from the end for them.

Charlotte
HALF A YEAR AFTER THEIR WEDDING

Every decision they've made together as a couple so far has felt right.

Bash was so romantic when he proposed.

He'd told her the truth that he would ask. It came only days after he'd given her his property patch. Her man was so impatient. And gorgeous with it.

It was the easiest yes of her life.

She couldn't picture a day without Bash. Of course, she wanted to tie him to her forever.

They decided on a simple ceremony with only their closest family and friends attending. Afterward, they held a massive party for everyone to celebrate with them.

She'd married a biker, and certain people now looked at Lottie differently. Like she'd lost her common sense, and they were wondering why she'd chosen to be around bikers, of all people.

They didn't get it.

How inclusive the MC world was.

This was her world now. She'd gladly left the old one behind. That world didn't have color and joy. It didn't have Bash. Lottie also said her last goodbye to Nora. A letter arrived in the mail, four months after her near-death experience. The handwriting belonged to Nora, and the postage mark showed it was from Cancun. Lottie didn't even have to think about opening it. She knew it would only be a bunch of fake apologies. And she wasn't that woman anymore. Nora made her choices, and Lottie did, too. She ripped it up and chucked it in the trash without even looking at it.

Her life was here now.

Her heart gave a little bump, and her bloodstream became red hot when muscular arms came around her waist from behind.

"Are you thinking about me putting a baby in you, darling?" the rough-sounding man said in her ear.

Lottie got an all-over body shudder.

He was so mean for turning her on in public.

It wasn't like people were saints at the Diablos' parties.

If she looked across to the bonfire, she'd see Kelly straddled over Devil's lap while they made out. Mouse was getting attention from a club girl, and Scarlett had her hand up Axel's shirt while he played poker with the older members.

Personal displays of affection were a given, but Lottie wasn't that far advanced yet that she'd start going at Bash with abandonment.

"I need to teach my husband how to use his big boy manners and not say things he can't back up with action."

It was the wrong thing to taunt Bash with because a rawness entered his eyes when he whirled her around, clasping onto her hips, bringing them groin to groin.

Her husband, of several months now, was a man of action.

That was why she never stressed the big or small stuff anymore.

It was like he'd charged into her life and given Lottie this relief that she was no longer alone and didn't have to rely on only her.

Bash took care of her like no one else had.

Every day, he expressed his love for her in numerous ways.

Not only with words.

His acts of service were dizzying and so lovely.

She was, beyond a doubt, a spoiled wife.

Bash had built them a fantastic marriage. There was nothing she couldn't ask for.

But it was his love she craved most of all.

It was all the little things she loved the best. The trivial workings of a marital relationship.

It took little to no effort to make her husband happy, but it was what she strived for each morning when she woke up.

"How much action did I bring last night, wife? And this morning. You wanna keep running your sweet mouth at me?" He nuzzled behind her ear.

"Eh, you brought enough. As my English Lit teacher would tell me, could do better." She teased, barely holding her smile as she watched Bash's eyes flare.

"Woman, you know I'll sit your pretty ass on that bar, open your pants right here and show you what a gorgeous liar you are."

He was so easy to tease.

Bash wouldn't go through with his threat. He respected her boundaries.

Sure, he'd push her into a private bathroom and fuck her there, making her scream, and then hold her hand while she did the walk of shame as he smirked, pleased with himself.

"It's a good thing I'm the medical professional in this family because oral sex isn't how babies are made."

When his eyes twinkled, a vise grabbed her heart.

Lottie was so stupidly in love with this man that it was sometimes hard to breathe or think without Bash at the center. Only when she was in his arms did the world melt away and all the noises it brought.

They'd spoken about babies. He wanted them more than she did, but that was because she was still experiencing all these emotions for the first time, and she'd never given children a thought before Bash.

She'd agreed to start with one baby.

They already had Prince, who was as good as a baby. Being cat parents took a lot of work.

"I thought, if you weren't knee-deep in club stuff next weekend, you could whisk me away for a dirty, wicked time." She proposed.

"And putting a baby in my wife." He growled low, so hot she shivered and grabbed his wrist to keep steady.

The thought of Bash giving a piece of himself to her drove her husband feral. They weren't freaking out about getting pregnant. If it happened, it would be great. If not, they were having a gorgeous time making love.

"You better bring your A-game, Benjamin. I'm expecting spectacular fireworks all weekend." His chest practically vibrated. "I'm talking about acrobatics and longevity, and I expect to be scandalized the next day."

"*Wife*," Bash growled again, all heat and predatory intent. She loved it when Bash became savage. He climbed to his feet, and she was over his shoulder before she knew it. "I'll show you longevity right fucking now."

It was probably the wrong time to tease him since she was still a little tender from the shower sex this morning, and Bash never backed down from a challenge, but she loved him like this. All feral and without bounds to claim her. Like he thought he didn't already own her.

The crowd gave them a raucous send-off, and Lottie giggled on the way to his office.

Six months later, right around their first wedding anniversary, Lottie was pregnant.

Eight months and two weeks after that, like he couldn't wait a day longer, their son was born.

If Lottie had thought Bash was the sexiest man on the planet before, seeing him in dad mode tipped her over the edge. They didn't even wait for the full recovery time before she attacked him one night, after seeing him bathing Levi and telling him a story about how he wooed his mom sitting on a hospital bench.

That husband of hers, that wonderfully patient man, might be an officer of a one percent MC, but to Lottie, he was one hundred percent perfect for her.

And she knew he always would be.

Bash claimed her first. But Lottie claimed him forever.

He'd loved her longer, but she would love him harder.

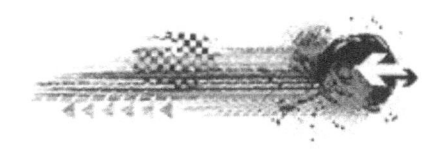

Levi Laurent
SOME YEARS LATER

With the bat-out-of-hell way Levi was riding his bike, it was fortunate he didn't give a shit about the amount of speeding laws he was breaking.

A four-hour trip was cut in half, and he stepped off his Harley, leaving the half-bucket helmet swinging on the handlebar.

Gun? He felt around the back of his waist and found his weapon holstered. Check.

A raging temper that would blow the whole fucking universe apart? Check.

He carried both like they were extensions of his body.

No one stopped him when he entered the skyscraper. They wouldn't dare. Security probably took one look at his dark scowl and let hell itself wander about the building.

Levi was here for one reason only.

The building was built on status and stank of wealth and privilege.

He wasn't without both. He hadn't known a deprived day, and being part of the Diablos Disciples MC provided enough status to swell his nefarious ego.

But this was old money that went back generations, steeped in outdated traditions, upheld by men who should have been in their coffins already.

She was inside him.

Burning in his veins.

Dominating his mind.

Tracking every inch of her existence all over his, until Levi was no longer himself.

He was something else.

Someone that belonged to another.

His body was a weapon: hers.

And that's who stepped into the fifteenth-floor corner office and was hit directly with green eyes as she lifted her pale face and clocked him in the doorway.

Levi ignored the bigwigs. Fucking halfwits with their fancy suits, shuffling papers like they thought that made them important.

"Kara. Come." That's all he had to say, and she came off the chair and flew across the room, taking the hand he held out to her.

Only the bark of another voice stopped Levi, and he cocked an arrogant eyebrow at the old dude who'd dared shout Kara's name in that condescending tone.

Levi should cut his fucking tongue out of his head.

"Where do you think you're going, Kara? And who the hell is this?"

Levi couldn't describe the peace he felt when she was near.

Or how outrageously psychotic he became if they were apart for too long.

It felt like a disease ripping him apart from the inside, and he knew it wasn't good for him, knew it was all wrong in so many ways, but he'd never been able to quit.

Without even trying, Kara tormented his darkest needs.

Inside his palm, her fingers shook. Like she was frightened of this rotund motherfucker stretching his navy suit. The surrounding men were no better. Sniveling Yes Men, Levi bet. Wouldn't know how to wipe their asses without the Bossman ordering them to.

Levi kept his eyebrow arched, moving his warning gaze from person to person.

They didn't know who he was, but could see the DDMC logo on his jacket.

His appearance might be young, but his dad called him an old soul. And he'd always been able to put the fear of god into any man, no matter his age.

"Me? None of your fucking business."

"Kara, get your ass back here right now." The old man ordered, slapping a hand on the table to exert his authority.

"I'm not staying." She finally spoke, her voice going through him like a poison dipped arrow.

Two weeks had been the longest he'd gone without talking to her.

After two of the longest weeks of his life, he'd been close to going on a rampage until she sent out her SOS call.

"I'm leaving, father." She said, bolder now as she squeezed his hand.

Ah, so this old twat was the bio dad, huh? Not what he imagined.

Foxie had so many secrets he was going to punish her for.

A preppy guy appeared among the older men. He was younger and projected such an attitude that Levi might have been impressed if he hadn't already been bored.

"Sweetheart, you can't leave right now. We have important things to discuss."

Sweetheart? Really?

Was Foxie hoping to see blood splattered on the walls today? He saw her face twitch with heat and guilt. She had fiery red hair and a face covered in freckles, making her reactions impossible to hide.

She squeezed his hand again, and Levi's inner rage went down a few notches.

Only a few.

She would face consequences for allowing a man to call her sweetheart.

"I already told you, Heath, like I told Father, this isn't my fucking mess to fix. If you want the merger, do the deal like normal people. Don't make me a part of it."

Foxie was always excessively talkative. He loved it. Levi had a devilish grin on his face. Proud like a papa. He'd properly educated her on how to use profanity.

When he'd met her, she'd used words like darn and shucks. He doubted she'd ever said a fuck in her life until she met him.

"You'll watch your mouth, young lady," dearest sperm donor spouted. "And remember where you are."

"Kara, sweetheart, let's talk." The smooth dipshit coaxed as he snapped warning glances toward Levi. "You know I'll be a good husband. It makes sense to unite our families after all this time. Your father just got you back. Don't walk away now."

You know I'll be a good husband.

Oh, there was so fucking much to unpack from that. Levi about vibrated out of his skeleton.

His head buzzed with static radio waves.

Murder radiated out of his pores like poison.

He could already see ten seconds into the future and how the shit would hit the fan. He wanted to revel in their suffering, using their guts as a damn necklace.

He didn't know he'd started growling until Kara yanked on his arm. "Lev, let's go, please." She looked up at him with her green-green expressive eyes, and his soul settled down, doused by her calmness.

She tugged at his hand, and they moved.

"Kara! Don't you dare leave. You know the consequences if you do. You will tell me who this man is at once."

Levi smirked, looking at the head clown and his entire circus surrounding him in their ridiculously affluent suits.

Apparently, this asshole had given Kara life.

But he wasn't *her* life.

That guy was nothing to Foxie.

Levi was sure of that because he knew the people who were her actual family.

"I'm her fucking brother," he announced, ignoring her shocked gasp, "and if she marries anyone, it'll be me. Adios, motherfuckers."

As parting words, he shut the room down like a mushroom cloud.

Technically, Kara Fox was his foster sister and had been since they were twelve years old. It was a long story, but she'd been with his parents ever since, raised together, and never once had Levi felt one ounce of brotherly affection for her.

No, Foxie was something else.

Something big. *Colossal.*

But she was a line that couldn't be crossed.

Kara was a pulse he had to ignore.

"Lev…"

"Not one damn word, Foxie." He warned, on the fringe of his sanity splintering.

She kept quiet even when he put her on his bike and latched the helmet underneath her chin. She watched him, tears pooling in her lovely, witchy eyes.

Climbing on in front of her, she grabbed on immediately, and his peace brought a roar to his ears.

It was funny. For as long as he could remember, Levi had to wear earbuds with a low noise playing. Either music or white noise, low enough so he could hear people talking, but loud enough that it kept him steady. He was diagnosed with high functioning blah blah. He didn't care.

But when Foxie was around, his brain was still, peacefully.

If a woman was ever trouble with a capital T, it was Kara Fox.

And he'd kill for her, with no need to know why.

He'd leave work in the middle of a job, to ride for hours, because she called and asked for help.

Kara was a lot of things to different people.

A daughter they'd never had to his parents.

A friend to many.

The hardest working assistant to the MC.

To Levi, she was the oxygen in his blood and the reason his psyche didn't go ballistic.

She held on for hours. Never complained that she needed to stop. Levi headed toward Utah, their home. And he connected a call to his best friend, the sociopath, to his psycho.

"Where the fuck did you go to, asshole?" Atlas said as a greeting. Such an ego on that one. Who did he think he was, the Prez? Ah, yeah, he would be soon.

"Listen, I've got Foxie with me."

"Oh, shit. Enough said. What do you need?"

"We're twenty miles away. Get me cover for a few days."

"Got it. Is she okay?"

"She's alive."

Atlas chuckled. "Will she stay that way?"

Of course. Levi wouldn't hurt a ginger hair on her head, and she knew it.

She knew how to use her devious tricks to wrap Levi around her skinny finger.

For years, they'd played the same forbidden dance.

He decided it stopped today.

He'd help her out of this final mess, and then he was out.

The state of his sanity was hinged on it being done between them.

He had to leave Kara the fuck alone so he could get on with his own life without his foster sister controlling every breath he took.

<u>Coming up is Diamond's story.</u>

Renegade Souls MC Series:
Dirty Salvation
Preacher Man
Tracking Luxe
Hades Novella
Filthy Love
Finally Winter
Mistletoe and Outlaws Novella
Resurfaced Passion
Intimately Faithful Novella
Indecent Lies
Law Maker Novella
Savage Outlaw
Renegade Souls MC Collection Boxset 1-3
Prince Charming
Forever Zara Novella
Veiled Amor
Renegade Souls MC Collection Boxset 4-6
Blazing Hope
Darling Psycho

Taboo Love Duet:
It Was Love
It Was Always Love
Taboo Love Collection

Forever Love Companion

From Manhattan Series:
Manhattan Sugar
Manhattan Bet
Manhattan Storm
Manhattan Secret
Manhattan Heart
Manhattan Target
Manhattan Tormentor
Manhattan Muse
Manhattan Protector
Manhattan Memory

Naughty Irish Series:
Naughty Irish Liar

Diablo Disciples MC:

Chains

Reno

Axel

Ruin

Tomb

Website: www.VTheiaBooks.com
Author Facebook: www.facebook.com/VTheia
Readers Group: Vs Biker Babes

Be the first to know when V. Theia's next book is available. Follow her on Bookbub to get an alert whenever she has a new release.

Made in United States
Cleveland, OH
11 March 2025

15071554R00187